Wildflower Bay

Rachael Lucas comes from the Highlands of
Scotland. She now lives by the sea in the
North West of England with her partner, four
children, and an assortment of animals.

For more, visit her website at
rachaellucas.com

You can find daily pictures on Instagram
@rachaellucas and chat at Facebook.com/
RachaelLucasWriter

Rachael Lucas

Wildflower Bay

PAN BOOKS

First published in the UK 2016 by Pan Books
an imprint of Pan Macmillan
20 New Wharf Road, London N1 9RR
Associated companies throughout the world
www.panmacmillan.com

ISBN 978-1-4472-6575-7

1 3 5 7 9 8 6 4 2

A CIP catalogue record for this book is available from the British Library.

Typeset by Ellipsis Digital Limited, Glasgow
Printed and bound by CPI Group (UK) Ltd, Croydon, CR0 4YY

Visit **www.panmacmillan.com** to read more about all our books
and to buy them. You will also find features, author interviews and
news of any author events, and you can sign up for e-newsletters
so that you're always first to hear about our new releases.

To Zoe, my brave, brilliant, beautiful sister.

Part One

Chapter One

The keys felt reassuringly expensive. Jingling them in her palm, Isla clipped down the stairs, pausing for a moment, as had become habit, to look out at the streets of Edinburgh stretching out below her, the golden sandstone buildings glowing gently in the pale early sunlight. This was what she worked for. This was what made the hours of slogging, day after day, fighting her way to the top of her game, worth it. She peered down to the road below where her pride and joy stood, its scarlet paint glossy as a pillar box. Isla Brown allowed herself a small smile of satisfaction.

Slinging her Mulberry bag over her shoulder, she circled down the stone staircase, the sound of her heels echoing in the silence of the morning. With a *plip*, the driver's-side door unlocked and she slid into the seat, inhaling the delicious scent of new car.

This was Isla's favourite time of day in the city. Nobody around but delivery men and end-of-shift security guards; streets empty but for seagulls and pigeons swooping down on the remnants of a night's revelling in the capital, helping themselves to discarded chips and half-eaten burgers. They'd be gone soon, the slate wiped clean every morning by council workers who swept up the detritus and restored the city to her stately glory.

Isla stopped at a traffic light, fingernails tapping impatiently on the steering wheel, feeling the smug purr of the engine. Flipping down her sun visor as she waited, she checked her make-up. Her face was an immaculate mask of primer and foundation, with a slash of red lipstick that matched her gorgeous new convertible perfectly. Isla brushed a speck of mascara from her cheek, pushed the visor back up and roared away from the stop light, sending a group of nearby pigeons flapping into the air in surprise.

Later on, the street outside would be nose-to-tail with traffic, on-street parking impossible, the pavement choked with office workers heading up to spend their lunch hour in the sunshine of Princes Street Gardens – but arriving at this time of day meant Isla was able to pull up right outside work and park. That way, she could spend all day looking out the window at the manifestation of her years of hard work. She locked the car, casually clicking the keys as she stepped through the gleaming glass doors of Kat Black Hair.

With a few taps she'd deactivated the alarm system and – as she'd done every day for two years, since taking over as head stylist – headed through to the little staff room. She liked her mornings to be routine. Breakfast was always alone in the flat; never a problem, as Hattie, her housemate, rarely surfaced before eleven. A quiet journey to work (until she'd bought the Mazda it had been on foot, with Isla changing out of trainers and into work shoes before anyone caught her looking anything other than immaculate) and then this – her daily ritual. Switching the kettle on, Isla set to work making sure that everything she needed was in place. Her trolley was neatly stacked, each little compartment filled with precise piles of everything she might need, from rollers to kirby grips, combs to clippers. 'The secret to a good cut is an organized stylist,' she would intone to the juniors, firmly.

'The secret to a good cut,' the parrot-haired Chantelle, who was second in command and snapping at her heels, would respond, archly, 'is a stylist who isn't afraid to take risks.'

Isla frowned, imagining Chantelle's cocky tone. Unfortunately Kat, who owned the chain of salons, had a soft spot for Chantelle, and for some reason didn't seem to recognize the merits of Isla's precise, methodical ways. It wasn't fair. She gave an experimental snip with her favourite scissors, imagining as she did so how it would feel to chop the irritating Chantelle's rainbow-tipped mohawk off 'by accident'. She wouldn't be so pleased with herself then, would she?

Taking one china and one paper cup of coffee through to the reception desk, Isla sipped as she waited for the computer booking system to kick into life.

There was a clatter as the salon door was shoved

open. A tangled head of hair, which hadn't seen shampoo in some time, topped a weather-beaten face.

'All right, Isla, hen?'

Isla looked up from the screen of the Mac. 'You're late today, Tam. Busy night?'

'Aye.' Tam gave her a wink. 'Had to see a man about a dog.'

He hitched up the shoulder of his oversized greatcoat. Isla pushed back her chair, picking up the coffee she'd made him.

'Thanks, darlin'. See you the morn'.'

Isla smiled at the routine of it. 'Not if I see you first.'

Tam raised his coffee cup in acknowledgement and headed back down the steps, where a brindled bull terrier sat waiting patiently. Isla turned back to the computer screen.

Another packed day – just how she liked it, and some of her favourite clients. And a note from Kat to say she wanted a cut and colour done on her own hair after closing tonight at six. That was good – the perfect time to remind Kat just why she was top stylist, and hopefully drop in a few hints about the benefits of moving Chantelle to the salon up in Morningside. She could suggest it as a career-enhancing move, after all . . .

'It's definitely blue.'

Isla looked in the mirror at Kat's thunderous expression and frowned slightly, shaking her head. This had never happened before, and there was no way – absolutely no way – that it could have occurred.

'It can't be.'

She never did anything without double-checking. Closing her eyes for a moment, she visualized herself standing in the back room of the salon, mixing the toner with the correct shade – no.324. She could see the figures on the box, could remember pulling it down from the shelf. At the time, two more boxes had fallen down from a nearby stack and Mel, the shyest, most junior of all the trainees, had darted to pick them up for her, stepping back deferentially without a word.

Kathleen Black glared at Isla. As owner of a chain of exclusive salons (patronized by a select clientele, famed for their discretion, known for their glossy-maned team of award-winning stylists), she expected the very best. And Isla – prize-winning perfectionist head stylist, super-focused ice queen – was the best.

Kat lifted a damp, most definitely blue-tinged tendril from her forehead. Lips pursed and eyes narrowed, she glared at Isla's reflection as she spoke, each word crystal-sharp and clearly enunciated.

'Chantelle? Here. Now.'

Isla caught a glimpse of herself in the mirror. Her carefully applied blusher now looked clownish against her blanched cheeks. She stood frozen to the spot. She didn't make mistakes.

'Kat,' Isla began, carefully. 'I know I didn't get the

shade wrong. The box is out the back. Let me show—'

Kat's pale blue eyes narrowed further. Her chin lifted slightly.

'I'd rather you didn't show me *anything*. If I were you –' her voice was dangerously quiet now, and Isla could feel the long-suppressed, yet all-too-familiar sensation of panic surging like a wave – 'I'd get out of my sight. I'll ring you when Chantelle has fixed this – mess.' She dropped the strands of hair, which flopped against her cheek. 'Life's too short for mistakes, Isla, you know that.'

Isla felt her hackles rising but she bit back a response, aware that if she spoke out of turn now she'd be on the receiving end of Kat's notorious temper. She'd gritted her teeth through a thousand shitstorms, covered Kat's back when she'd messed up at competitions, and watched countless junior stylists come and go, unable to hack the competition and the pace of being part of Kat's team. Isla had held on like a limpet, not taking her eyes off her goal for one second. And now, on schedule, she'd made it.

'Kat, did you call me?'

Chantelle, ears pricked at all times, appeared from the stockroom, head cocked slightly to one side, managing to direct the smirk playing at the corners of her lips towards Isla whilst still appearing assiduously sweet and helpful to her boss. Isla's nostrils flared as she held in her distaste. Chantelle was going to love this.

'I thought you were going for Raspberry Sorbet?' Chantelle's voice was innocent. As if examining a lab experiment, she picked up an offending lock of hair, looking at Isla, head to one side.

'I put the colour in myself.' Isla was clutching at straws, and she knew it. 'I checked the box. Followed the usual procedures.'

'Well, you can't have, can you?' Chantelle looked triumphant. 'Don't worry, Kat, sweetie.' Kat sat back with a satisfied expression. 'I'll have this sorted for you in no time.'

'I could—' Isla began, fruitlessly.

'You've said it yourself many times, Isla. There's no room for mistakes in this game.' Kat looked down at her phone, jabbing at the screen with glossy cerise nails.

'Right. I'll clear up.' Isla made to wheel her trolley back into the staff room.

'Leave it.' Kat's tone was final.

'Mel?' Chantelle called to the junior. Mel looked up from the pile of hair she'd been sweeping back and forth for the last five minutes whilst earwigging in to the whole conversation. 'Get rid of this stuff. Isla's just leaving.'

Isla opened her mouth to speak, but Kat's warning glance was enough to stop her in her tracks. Mel wheeled her trolley, equipment lying uncleaned and disorganized, into the staff room. Kat gave Isla another look, one that said quite clearly: 'Are you STILL here?'

Isla picked up her bag and slipped out of the door, fuming silently.

Chapter Two

The rush-hour fug of diesel fumes and traffic noise hit Isla in the face as the salon door closed behind her. Out of habit, she turned right and started heading down towards home, fighting her way against a sea of besuited office workers making their way towards Waverley Station. She'd made it as far as Hanover Street and was standing at the pedestrian crossing, foot tapping impatiently, when she looked down and realized she was still in work shoes and not the trainers she'd always walked in. It took her another second to remember the reason why.

With a sigh of irritation at her own incompetence, she turned and marched back up Hanover Street to where her car stood outside the shop, waiting. It was wedged so tightly between Kat's BMW and a side-on parked motorbike that it took her about five attempts to squeeze her way out, each one watched by a smugly judging Chantelle, who stood behind Kat's chair, repairing the damage. Isla shot her a look of hatred. She was almost certain she'd had a hand in what had happened.

She drove home in a haze of frustration and anger. Bloody Chantelle had been after her for ages. She climbed out of the car, slamming the door with more force than she intended. It was her pride and joy. No point destroying it in a fit of temper. She trudged upstairs, picking up the post for Mrs Jones in the middle flat, and popping it through her letterbox as she passed. The house, when she opened the door, was silent. No sign of Hattie. The huge sitting room was bathed in late-evening sunlight that shone in through the vast sash windows. The rug was rucked up and lopsided. Copies of *Vogue* and *Tatler* were scattered on the floor. The television was paused on an episode of *Gilmore Girls* and the gigantic, squashy sofa was strewn with wet towels. On the coffee table there was a disgusting stack of nail-varnish-remover-soaked cotton-wool pads and a bottle of Chanel varnish with the top off. Isla made a sharp noise of exasperation and kicked off her work shoes.

Hattie was lovely, but had literally no idea about real life. The daughter of an ex-Cabinet minister, she was loaded beyond belief. Rather than subject her to the dubious delights of student digs, Mummy and Daddy had bought her an Edinburgh pad when she came up here to study anthropology at university years ago. Easily bored, she had dropped out after a couple of years (just when the work got hard, she admitted, with a giggle, over a gin and tonic one night) and had befriended Isla when, on a whim, she took a year-long course in aromatherapy. Back then, Isla had still been living at home, saving every penny she could and taking the long, winding bus journey to and from the city from the outskirts of town, where her dad lived. They'd formed an unlikely friendship – and Isla had been flattered to be offered a room in Hattie's flat for 'your share of the bills only, darling – honestly, this place is some kind of tax dodge, they won't care a hoot if you're in here.'

Four years later, they were still rubbing along together – Hattie strewing chaos behind her, apparently oblivious, and Isla picking up the mess, out of a sense of duty and vague guilt that she was living rent-free in one of the nicest streets in Edinburgh's sought-after New Town, surrounded by the sort of expensively dressed people whose hair she cut daily. Hattie, meanwhile, worked (in the loosest sense of the word) for her cousin Jack's dress agency in a little shop in Stockbridge, the quaintest, prettiest corner of the city, where she spent most of the day flicking through her phone. She was so well connected, though, that she brought in a never-ending stream of well-to-do customers – and so charmingly ditzy and posh that nobody seemed to notice that she only turned up at lunchtime, and not at all if she'd been out on a Thursday night ('Fridays are basically the weekend, darling').

Throwing the wet towels into the basket in the utility room, Isla noticed a Post-it note stuck to the stripped-pine kitchen door.

Can't find phone so no point texting me. Off to Milly's house for weekend. H x

Isla furrowed her brow for a second trying to remember which of the glossy-locked, shiny-toothed identikit girls was Milly. The one with the bloody enormous country estate in Dalkeith – that was it. Squaring her shoulders, Isla checked her phone.

No messages – unsurprisingly. Realistically, the only person likely to text her was Hattie – or her dad, who was flat out at the moment with a music festival going on. She put the phone down on the coffee table and switched off the television. Later, she'd have a look at Facebook and see what was happening. There wasn't much point in stressing about what Kat was going to say in the morning.

Isla slipped out of her clothes and folded them neatly on the chair in the bathroom. Turning on the shower, she stepped into the huge walk-in cubicle, allowing the rainwater-style cascade to pour over her head before stepping back and carefully scooping out a handful of luxurious sugar scrub. She massaged the fragrant mixture in methodically before stepping back under the shower and rinsing herself thoroughly. Closing her eyes, she stood under the water and shampooed her hair before applying a moisturizing mask to smooth down the cuticles. No matter what had happened at work today, she wasn't going to let her standards slip.

Cocooned in an immaculate white waffle dressing gown, Isla curled up on the sofa with a pot of Earl Grey tea. She picked up her phone, tapping on the Facebook icon.

They'd updated the header. Beside the words 'Melville High School Reunion' was a new – old – photograph. Isla winced as she expanded the image. There she was, fifteen years old, scruffy and friendless, perched on the end of the front bench with the other nerds nobody would speak to. And – she scrutinized the photo – standing behind her, making a face, was Jamie Duncan, with a cheeky hand on the knee of Adele Downie from across the road. Adele's lipsticked smirk gave Isla another wave of the same feeling she'd experienced earlier: panic and fear, fear and panic. She swallowed it back with a too-hot mouthful of tea.

'We're turning 30 this year!' shouted the header. 'Join us to celebrate – sign up below.'

Isla looked at the list of names of people who would be attending. It had grown by ten since yesterday. Underneath there were long gossipy threads, people catching up after over a decade apart. Photos of babies and weddings, sad tales of motorbike accidents and silly reminiscences. She scrolled down and down, drinking her tea, drinking it all in. She hadn't clicked the button to say she was attending. But Isla had a plan, and she'd been working on it since the day she'd walked out of Melville High School for the very last time.

'Morning, Isla.'

Somehow it wasn't quite a surprise that Kat was sitting behind the reception desk when Isla stepped into the salon the next morning at half past seven. Kat was all too aware that her top stylist liked to get in early in the morning and stamp her authority on the place. And this morning she'd decided to get in first.

'Kat.' Isla lifted her chin slightly, readying herself for conflict.

Kat, with her newly raspberry-shaded hair tucked under a Greek fisherman's hat, pushed herself backwards in the sleek black designer chair, crossing one slender leg over the other. Almost casually, she leaned forward, adjusting the cuff of her butter-soft leather over-the-knee boots. She looked up through heavily mascaraed lashes.

'You screwed up.'

Isla gave one nod. Without the chance to check out what had happened, she had no way of proving that Chantelle had somehow sabotaged her – even though she was almost certain that was what had happened. There was no way she could have made a mistake. She'd been working her backside off, and she'd been a bit stressed of late, but she didn't make mistakes.

'I'm not in the habit of giving second chances.'

'Yes, I know, but—'

'I don't do *but*, either. You know the deal, Isla. You've worked here long enough.'

Isla stood stock still, unblinking. She knew what was coming, but couldn't quite believe it was happening to her. She'd seen it so many times over the last five years of working in Kat's salon.

'To be honest – and I'm being kind, here . . .' Kat

looked at her with a thin smile. Isla realized that she was trying her best to be generous – something that didn't come easily to Kat, who'd fought her way from a Saturday job washing hair at a tiny salon in Leith to a chain of award-winning salons across Edinburgh. 'If it was anyone else, they'd get the chop.' She smiled again, amused at her own joke. 'But you've worked hard for me, Isla, and I appreciate a grafter. You've gone as far as you can here. Chantelle has been bleeding off your clients over the last few weeks, and I'm promoting her to senior stylist.'

Isla stepped back, reeling. 'You want me to work alongside Chantelle?'

Kat inclined her head. 'You'd have a problem with that?'

'You can't do that.' Isla swallowed, trying to keep herself calm. There was no way she'd worked up to this point to have it all taken away. She had the reunion coming up, and this was all part of her master plan. Kat couldn't take this away.

'I can,' said Kat with a small, cat-like smile, 'Or you can go quietly. Two months' gardening leave, full pay. I don't want you taking any of my customers elsewhere. And I'll give you a good reference, naturally.'

'I should bloody well think so,' exploded Isla. 'I've worked my arse off for you for the last five years.'

Kat inclined her head again slightly, this time in acknowledgement. 'And it's dog-eat-dog in this world, darling. Get out, have a break. Go and have a bit of a life.'

She looked at Isla levelly, raising her eyebrows. 'God knows, you need one. And then you can find something else in town. I hear Daniel Pardoe's main girl is off on maternity leave soon. Well,' Kat gave a humourless laugh, 'either that, or she's been making one too many visits to Greggs the Bakers at lunchtime.'

Isla looked around the salon. Her stunned expression was reflected back at her from every shining mirror. Beside her, Kat sat, long legs extended confidently, examining her fingernails.

'I need to sort my kit. I haven't even had a chance to clean it after last night.'

'Fine.' Kat's tone was airily dismissive. 'The juniors will be in shortly. Best if you're gone before the others arrive, don't you think?'

She stood up, motioning towards the door with a sweep of her arm. Isla, nonplussed, found herself walking, robot-like, towards the exit.

And then she was standing at the foot of the steps on a chilly, deserted Edinburgh street. A discarded chip paper ruffled up in a gust of wind, lifting into the air before being plastered to her leg. Isla bent down to peel it off. The number 6 bus pulled up, depositing the first of a never-ending stream of office workers, laptop bags swinging from their shoulders, pouring into the coffee shop next door to Kat's salon, ordering the jolt of espresso they needed to start their morning. She stood, dazed, in the middle of the pavement. The swarm of commuters scurried round her, ant-like, heads down, not focusing.

'All right, Isla, darlin'.'

She looked up into a familiar face. Tam was standing in front of her, his dog panting obediently by his side. One ear was plugged into a headphone wire that snaked below the heavy overcoat. Of course – he was heading up for his morning coffee. Not much chance that Kat or Chantelle would sort him out with a drink, or sneak out a handful of chocolate biscuits every morning.

'Cheer up, hen. It might never happen.'

'It just did.'

Chapter Three

Getting pissed in the afternoon wasn't on Isla's to-do list. In fact, she thought as she swayed gently towards the impossibly chic Harriott's Bar on George Street, dressed immaculately, she didn't even have a to-do list. She didn't have anything to do.

Sacked, she'd gone home and dropped the car off, made her way upstairs, dropping off the post to a surprised Mrs Jones from downstairs ('Forgotten something, my dear? You're normally out first thing') and then headed into the flat, where she'd stress-cleaned the entire place from top to bottom because – well, what else was she supposed to do? What *did* people do, when their perfectly executed plans went tits up?

Five hours and seven bin bags of decluttering later, with the kitchen cupboards turned out and sparkling, not a speck of dust to be found even in the darkest of corners, and two of her nails having been administered emergency first aid in the shape of professional nail glue, Isla realized the answer as she slithered out from underneath the spare-room bed with the hoover hose in hand, sneezing from the dust.

People don't hoover when the shit hits the fan, thought Isla. *And I haven't come this far not to be in control.* After coiling the hoover wire neatly around the handle, folding the dishcloth into precise quarters and hanging it symmetrically on the mixer tap, she folded her arms in a childish gesture of defiance that would have made her dad smile, and decided that what she needed to do now was exactly what people in films would do at this point.

She showered, scrubbed, buffed, moisturized. She trimmed and shaved, plucked, varnished, blow-dried and tweezed. Foundationed and blushered to within an inch of her life, then and only then – dressed 'in the skinniest of skinny black jeans and the sharpest of scarlet stilettos, with her tiniest black vest top and a designer jacket that had cost a month's pay packet but which she'd allowed herself as reward for winning Stylist of the Year in the regional heats – she opened a bottle of champagne.

With the first glass she composed a text to Chantelle, telling her exactly what she thought of her snide behaviour and her back-stabbing – not to mention her shitty, uneven haircutting, and the time she missed a whole chunk of a colour job and Isla had to repair it the next day. It was deeply therapeutic. With the second, she booked a taxi into town for half an hour's time. The third and fourth glasses slipped down quite agreeably as she stalked Facebook, catching up on everyone's gossip on the school reunion page and deciding that even if she was temporarily unemployed (and they didn't need to know that), she had still done a pretty good job of making the best of herself, and she was bloody well going to show *them*.

Fuck it, thought Isla, who never swore. She got into a taxi, four glasses of champagne down on an empty stomach. *Fuck it. I'm going to allow myself one night to feel sorry for myself. I'm going to let myself have that. And then tomorrow I'm going to pick myself up and get back in control.*

Isla opened her eyes cautiously. Her tongue was glued to the top of her mouth and she pulled it away, wincing. Light was streaming in through the window of the sitting room. She must've fallen asleep on the sofa. Except – she realized, heart thudding – this sofa smelt of stale beer, and something she couldn't place that was vaguely herbal. And there weren't any curtains at the window of this room. And she was lying wrapped in the arms of a –

'OHMYGOD.' Propelled by a bolt of adrenalin that cut through the hangover fug, she jumped sideways off the sofa, sliding in the process on what looked like an ancient sateen bedspread from the 1960s, and nearly landing in a discarded pizza box with one slice of pepperoni curled up in the corner. She looked at the sofa where she'd slept. Lying in a pair of boxer shorts, fast asleep and with his arm still describing an Isla-shaped arc where she had been dead to the world just a moment ago, was a total stranger. Quite a handsome one, some part of her brain registered, not very helpfully – but a stranger nonetheless.

The stranger opened one eye at a time, grimacing. Underneath his thatch of glossy dark-brown hair were two soulful, chocolate-drop eyes. He looked up at her through his fringe, and a lazy smile spread across his face.

'Morning, gorgeous.' He reached out, finding the slice of pizza, and sat up, crossing his legs. His boxers gaped alarmingly. Isla averted her eyes.

'Want a bit?'

'No. No, no. No, I'm fine. More than fine.' Unable to look directly at him for fear of his accidental exposure, Isla peered out of the window. She had a vague idea that she was in Bruntsfield, or Morningside – all the streets in student Edinburgh looked the same.

'Right. Well, I'm going to –' She looked down at her phone. It was dead, completely out of battery. Her tiny going-out bag hadn't had room for the back-up battery pack that she carried as a matter of course. Where *was* her tiny going-out bag? Was this what champagne felt like? Isla, who had never drunk more than two glasses before the previous night, had a vague recollection of ordering bottles in a noisy bar in what seemed to be an underground vault of some kind. She caught a glimpse of her bag hanging from the corner of a broken wooden chair, and stepped over another sleeping body – which lay with its head beside an ashtray, half covered with a sleeping bag – to retrieve it. It came away dripping with what she hoped was stale beer. The alternative was too gruesome to contemplate.

'That was a belter of a night. When you got up and sang Dolly Parton in the Taverners . . .' Her sofa companion gave her an appreciative thumbs up.

Isla looked at him, recoiling in horror. 'I don't sing. And I definitely don't sing karaoke.'

'So you said. In fact, you told me about forty-eight times on the way home. And you told everyone in the pizza shop on the Meadows, too. D'you not remember?'

Isla felt a wave of nausea. Her skin was somehow alternating between ice-cold and clammily warm. Her head felt like someone had put it in a vice. She needed to be at home, in the cool embrace of her perfect white sheets – *now*.

'Oh, yes,' she lied. 'Yes, I remember all of it. Ha ha, the pizza shop. That was fun, wasn't it?'

'You're no' rushing off, are you?' Brown Eyes leaned back against the sofa, pulling the stained satin bedcover over his legs. He beckoned in what he clearly thought was an enticing manner. 'Get a bit more sleep. Tam over there does a killer bacon roll. He'll be up in a couple of hours.' He motioned to the sleeping lump beside the table.

Isla shook her head politely. 'Thanks, but I really need to get going.' She pulled the first excuse she could think of out of the hat. 'I've got to get to work.' Never mind that it was Saturday and she was off all weekend.

'Work?' Brown Eyes snorted with laughter. 'That

champagne was stronger than it looked. You spent all night telling us you'd got the sack, and how some bitch called Chantelle had stabbed you in the back.'

Isla closed her eyes. She'd forgotten, momentarily. Right, even more reason to get out of this hellhole and back to normality. A quick shower and a half-hour's sleep, and everything would be back to normal.

'Oh yes,' she said, adopting the breeziest tone she could, given the clanging in her skull. 'Forgot that bit. Ah, well, places to go. Thanks for a lovely evening. Would you mind just . . .' She paused for a moment, wondering how best to word the question. 'Where exactly *are* we?'

The taxi driver smirked as she climbed into the back of the black cab.

'Walk of shame, eh, doll? We've all been there.' He winked at her in the rear-view mirror.

Isla didn't reply. She sat in silence, damp bag by her side, her designer jacket crushed and stinking of cigarette smoke, as they wound their way down through the narrow streets of the Old Town, along Princes Street, which was already packed with tourists, and up Hanover Street. She looked the other way as the taxi idled in a traffic queue outside Kat Black Hair, not even allowing herself a glance inside. The thought of Chantelle catching sight of her in this state was appalling.

At her building, too mortified to ask for change, she

handed the taxi driver a huge tip and waved him away as he made for his bag of coins.

'Two paracetamol, a bottle of Irn Bru and a bacon sandwich,' he offered as a hangover tip, unsolicited, in exchange, 'and you'll be right as rain, hen.'

Giving him a thin smile, Isla clambered laboriously up the stairs to the flat. When she made it inside, slipping off her shoes and pairing them neatly by the front door, she paused only to plug her phone in to the charger by the sofa before heading for the bathroom cabinet, painkillers, and a mercifully hot shower.

Isla stood by the sofa, not knowing where to begin. She'd slept for hours, waking only to drain a pint of water and two more headache pills before falling into another unmoving, dreamless slumber. When she'd eventually surfaced, clambering bleary-eyed out of bed at five o'clock in the evening, it was to a phone screen plastered with notifications.

Dad: 20 missed calls

Dad: text

Dad: text

Dad: text

Dad: text

Kat Black: text

Chantelle: text

This must be what it's like to be popular, she thought.

And then it all came flooding back. She'd heard the girls in the salon of a morning, groaning with recognition as their wine-fuelled exploits from the night before came back to them piece by piece. But Isla wasn't a drinker. She liked life ordered and organized. She had a plan. She didn't lose focus. So it was with an unfamiliar sinking sensation that she sat down on the edge of the sofa and remembered how last night had unfolded. She opened up her messages, scrolling backwards.

Text Message to: Chantelle

I can't prove it but I'm certain you swapped the bottles over in the stock room. You're a poisonous bitch and you and Kat deserve each other. I won't forget this.

Text Message from: Chantelle

R U some kind of psycho? UR going 2 regret sending this.

Text Message from: Kat Black

Isla I would appreciate it if you could refrain from threatening my staff. I have to confess I wondered if I had been a bit severe. Your obsessive behaviour over the last few months has been increasingly erratic. You need a break. Get some help before it's too late.

Text Message to: Dad

Hiya Dad, if you're around tomorrow thought I might pop round, tidy up a bit. Got a bit of time off work. Love you.

Text Message to: Dad

Actually there's something I need to talk to you about, the thing is I ve don

Text Message to: Dad

Ops sorry, didn't mean to send the last one. Mistake

Text Message to: Dad

Oh god dad I messed up and,I don't know what to do. I've lost my job and I can't even get a job here for 2 months because am banned from working for any other salon in case I poach any clients not that I'd have any to poach Because my reputa-tion is probably shot but anyway

Text Message to: Dad

Sorry hit send by msistake I blame autocooret anyway don't worry have met lovely friends in pub who has said they can find me job working at the chicken factory will be nice and relaxing also free chiken ehich is nice

Text Message from: Dad

sounds good – all ok? Flat out here, haven't stopped all day

Text Message from: Dad

don't worry darling – we will sort this x

Text Message from: Dad

where r u now? Am worried you are not ok

Text Message from: Dad

sweetheart I'm worried about you. Don't worry about the job, something will come up. Let me know when you're home safe.

Text Message from: Dad

BTW – is your phone keyboard broken?

Isla swallowed back a sickening wave of hangover mixed with terror. What the hell had she done? With trepidation, she pressed the keypad, activating her voice-mail inbox.

'Hiya Isla, it's your dad here. Just checking you're OK.'

'Isla, darling, give us a call when you get this. Just wanted to say a wee hello.'

'It's Dad. This isn't like you, sweetheart. I'm a wee bit worried about . . .'

Isla hit the button, stopping her father's message in mid-flow. There was no point putting it off any longer. She hit the dial button and waited.

'Dad, it's me.'

'Isla! You're no' dead then?' He laughed.

'Not quite, no. I'm sorry about last night. It was a bit of a . . .' She paused, trying to think of a suitable word for the horrors that were coming back to her, bit by bit. Disaster? Nightmare? Total meltdown?

'Ach, darling, you need to let your hair down once in a while. Anyhow, I've taken the evening off. You about?'

'About' was one way of putting it, thought Isla, looking around the immaculate sitting room. Completely devoid of anything to do, with no friends and no job, was another way. She suppressed a sigh. 'Yes, I'm free.'

'Give me half an hour.'

Isla pulled out her leather overnight bag from underneath the bed and laid it carefully on the table. She removed a creaseless pair of white cotton pyjamas from the drawer and stacked with them a pair of pale skinny jeans, a beige cardigan, and one of her standard-issue white vest tops in the case. Her weekend outfits were always the same – summer was vest tops, winter was crisp white shirts and chic scarves. Streamlining her wardrobe meant she didn't have to think about what to wear, and she always looked immaculate. Her travel toiletries were, as ever, ready to go – the thought that she never went anywhere except to visit her dad crossed her mind as she zipped them into the side compartment, but she chased it away, closing the case. Everything was sorted. The flat was spotless – for now, at least. When Hattie returned tomorrow evening it would be about ten minutes before the place was in a state of devastation.

The beep outside alerted her to her dad's arrival. He waved up at the window, grinning. She gave him the thumbs up and ran down the stairs into his waiting arms.

'Shove that in the back, darling.' Her dad opened the door of the black cab, and Isla slid her case into the footwell before climbing into the passenger seat and strapping herself in.

'Can you take me to Gilmerton, please?'

Her dad sucked his teeth, shaking his head in dismay. 'All the way to Gilmerton? That'll cost you.'

'It's fine. My dad'll pay at the other end.'

She couldn't help smiling despite everything.

'Sounds like you've got a good dad there.'

Isla turned to look at him with a smile. 'The best.' He'd make everything better.

Her dad switched off the For Hire sign and, with a growl of the diesel engine, they set off through the cobbled streets to home.

The Georgian terraces of the New Town gave way eventually to the crazily stacked buildings that made up the ancient Old Town. The early evening streets were still packed, shoppers with armfuls of bags standing waiting at the bus stops, trams sliding silently past. Her dad always took her home by what he called the scenic route, past all the old sights, up the hill past the Meadows where students lay in lazy Saturday-afternoon piles. She averted her eyes as they drove past the late-night pizza shop where she'd stood the night before. There was no way on earth she was ever drinking again. How people chose to do that every weekend was completely beyond her.

The genteel streets of Morningside passed by – delicatessens and cafes, old ladies with baskets of shopping returning to their pretty garden flats, mums pushing expensive prams along the pavement whilst toddlers wheeled along on tiny wooden balance bikes. Down the hill, and out of town – the houses getting newer now, 1930s villas squatting in square gardens dotted precisely with neat mounds of ubiquitous purple aubretia. And then they were turning left and over the flyover, down the hill and into the estate. A gang of kids were playing kerby on the pavement as they slowed up, bouncing the ball from one side of the road to the other. A toddler pottered around on the edge of the pavement, wisps of hair flying loose from a plastic hairband, her face sticky with the biscuit she held in one pudgy hand. She toppled forwards and in a flash a bigger girl, skinny legs in brightly coloured leggings, leaped to her rescue, scooping her up and twirling her away to safety.

'These kids.' Her dad, already driving at almost walking pace, slowed down even further. 'I tell you, someone's going to get hurt one of these days. No' everyone drives at my speed. You get the hooligans coming through here in their souped-up motors . . .' He shook his head.

They drove up the hill, through stacked blocks of identical white-rendered houses, each with a tiny patch of garden outside. Isla felt the familiar combination of security and revulsion. It was so good to be here with Dad, but this place – she shuddered slightly.

'Here we are,' said her dad, as he pulled the taxi to a halt. 'That'll be eighteen pounds, please.'

'Eighteen?' Isla shook her head. 'That's daylight robbery.'

'Lucky your dad's paying, eh?' He reached across, giving her knee a squeeze, pulled the keys out of the ignition and fetched her bag from the back.

'Come on then, darling. You look like you need a cup of tea.'

And then she was in the hall and she was ten years old again, hands running along the bumps of the woodchip paper as she stood with her too-big schoolbag waiting for a lift to school in the morning. Being dropped off early every day in a taxi made her stand out amongst the other kids, who walked to school in a noisy, squabbling, teasing bunch along the canal path and across the field where the two grey ponies stood, incongruously surrounded by barbed-wire fencing with a stable made from a disused lorry container, their hay nets tied up with frazzled orange baling string. Isla used to escape there on the weekends when her dad was working, on the days when she was sent to play with Aunty Theresa (who wasn't even her aunt) across the road. Aunty Theresa didn't have any children – and didn't want any, either, as she told a disconsolate Isla regularly, shoving a plate of toast across the teak folding table before getting back to her knitting and watching a never-ending cycle of quiz shows on the television set that dominated her tiny sitting room. It was stuffed full of grey velvet furniture and a malevolent ginger cat that glared at ten-year-old Isla with distaste.

It was tacitly agreed that nobody would mention to Isla's dad that she sneaked off every Saturday and Sunday, spending the days in the library or down by the canal, kicking her legs as she sat on a disused barrel watching the barges pass by, or lurking in the corner of the horses' field, daydreaming about the kind of life she could have had. Over time, she grew to love the horses – and they seemed to quite like her, whickering their affection as she climbed over the stile, mooching across to graze close by when she sat down with a packet of Polos and a stack of library books in a quiet corner under the hedgerow, where nobody noticed her. At least, most of the time. She'd hear the kids from the estate before she saw them, the loud shouts of Jamie and Allison, ring-leaders, King and Queen of Muirton, and she'd gather up her books in an armful and scuttle off, heart thumping, stomach a knot of panic. If she didn't make it in time, she'd know all about it.

'Eh, look who's here!'

'Got your nose in a book again, Isla? Swotting up to make sure you're top of the class again?' Jamie would beam at her, blond hair ruffling in the wind, blue eyes sparking with mischief. He'd stand, hands on hips, legs akimbo, completely aware of his place. He took up the space – and made the noise – of two people.

'Can you smell that?'

Allison Graves was ginger-haired and freckly, tall and athletic, the fastest girl in school, the most popular, clever, cheeky, and loved by the teachers. Nobody would dare tease her for being a ginger. She flaunted her wiry halo of red fuzz like a crown. The one thing Isla could do that she couldn't was come top of the class for English – and Allison had it in for her as a result.

The other kids swarmed behind them, an amorphous moving blur of scruffy hair and too-short trousers, hand-me-down jackets and beaten-up trainers. Isla would sidle away, blushing so hard her cheeks stung, books under her arm, climbing over the barbed wire, avoiding the stile because *they* were there, trying not to rip her jeans because her dad had only just bought them from the market and she knew he didn't have much money.

It never made sense to Isla. She had the same trainers as Allison Graves. She'd studied them carefully when they were getting changed after PE, making sure she directed her dad to the exact same ones when they went down the High Street. She'd carried them home in a box, heart full of hope, desperate that these grey and pink Dunlops might be the answer. She'd rubbed a palmful of mud in them out the back when her Dad was making dinner, trying to make them look worn in, desperate not to look like a try-hard. But no: she sat at the dining table at school, and nobody commented admiringly on them. She was all ready with her response. 'These? Oh, yeah, had them for ages. I've got two pairs, actually. My new ones are at home.' But nobody asked. She sat at the lunch table with Amira and Costas and Helen as usual, and nobody noticed. Amira and Costas and Helen didn't care. They were too busy eating their lunches with the same haunted expression, looking up between mouthfuls, waiting to see which of them would be butt of the lunchtime jokes today, which one would get the piss taken out of them for their crappy packed lunches or their free school meals. It didn't seem to matter that half the school was on free lunches back then. Somehow, their table was the lowest of the low.

'You all right, hen?'

Her dad, who'd gone ahead into the kitchen, peered back out into the hall where Isla was standing. She shook her head.

'Sorry, I was just daydreaming.'

He gave her a fond smile. 'Aye, you used to do a lot of that as a lassie. Anything nice?'

'Just thinking about school.'

'Best days of your life, and all that?' He gave her a rueful look. He'd comforted a crying Isla in the night until she fell asleep often enough to know that there wasn't much about her school days she'd want to remember.

Isla watched as he sat back, releasing his stomach from the constraints of the top button with a sigh. He ran a hand through his hair so it stood on end in thin wisps, a halo around his ever-expanding bald patch. He desperately needed a trim, and his eyebrows were taking on a life of their own. His good looks – because he'd been a handsome man, and the photos Isla had seen were proof of that – were still lurking beneath the surface, the indentations of good cheekbones still almost evident despite the weight he'd gained over the years.

'Best days – yeah, something like that.' Isla shook her head, with an ironic twist to her mouth.

'Right then.' Alan settled down at the little table in the kitchen. Radio Scotland was playing quietly on the same tiny transistor radio that had stood in the corner, covered in a layer of frying-pan grease and dust, for as long as Isla could remember.

Isla was silent. She poured the tea from the aluminium pot, which dribbled, as ever, onto the table. She handed a mug to her dad, who added three sugars before stirring vigorously.

'You said you were going to cut down.' She looked across at her dad, whose bulk spread out across the chair, legs wide apart, allowing the heft of his stomach to sit comfortably on his knees. He wasn't getting any thinner, despite the GP telling him his blood pressure was through the roof.

He tutted, reaching into an old metal biscuit tin. She couldn't remember when they'd ever had a huge square tin of Crawford's biscuits, but the tin had always sat on the kitchen table, there whenever she needed one – not that she ever did. She shook her head as he waggled the tin in her direction, custard creams shoogling around in a sea of leftover crumbs.

'I'll just have the one, then. How's that?'

'Better.' She smiled across at him fondly, watching as he sipped his tea, big hands wrapped around his favourite mug.

She'd bought it for him when she was eleven – she remembered picking it up at the school fete and carrying it home with excitement. 'World's Best Dad', it said. And he was. He'd brought her up from the age of seven when her mum had died of a cancer that had come on so suddenly, and brought her to her knees so quickly, that nobody had had time to realize what was happening. It always seemed to Isla that one day her mum had been standing at the kitchen window peeling potatoes, the radio playing, frilly apron tied round her waist, the house full of the smell of Mr Sheen and drop scones, Scotch broth bubbling on the stove, her dad coming in between shifts to sneak a kiss and slip his arm around her mum's waist, ruffle Isla's hair and sing a silly song to make her laugh . . . and the next moment, her mum was a tiny little birdlike shape in a hospital bed, smiling weakly and telling her to be a good girl for her daddy.

Isla had tried her hardest. She'd been a good girl for her daddy and worked hard at school, and she'd bitten back her disappointment when he'd found her a job working as a trainee in his sister's friend's hairdresser's round the corner, when she dreamed of going to Edinburgh University and studying to become an English teacher. She saw all the gorgeous, glamorous, exotic-looking students as they passed every day with their long floaty cardigans and their folders under their arms, laughing over pints of cider in the beer garden of the Pear Tree pub and chatting about books in confident little cliques as they lay on their backs on the Meadows. Isla used to sit there with a book on her days off, hoping someone might mistake her for a student.

She'd made the best of it. She'd worked up from sweeping up hair to learning the ropes, studied her hardest on her day release course at college, and passed with honours and a special distinction as top of her class. Isla had a plan. If she was going to be a hairdresser, she was going to be the best hairdresser in Edinburgh. And she was going to save every penny she had until she could afford to buy her own place, and then she was going to employ the best staff and sit back and let them do their jobs. Then she'd head to university as a mature student, and study for the English degree she'd dreamed of all this time.

And then – oh, and then – Isla had one other plan. She was going to turn up to the Melville High School reunion, whenever it happened, and she was going to walk in there and prove to Jamie Duncan and Allison Graves and every single one of their cronies that she was worth something. That they'd underestimated her. That she was worth ten of them, with their nasty little jibes and their vicious little teases. Isla had carried this grievance for years, nurturing it, visualizing as she worked her way up how she'd march in, dressed from head to toe in designer clothes, and everyone's head would turn. How they'd marvel at how perfectly turned out she was. How they'd turn to each other and say 'Is that –? No, it can't be,' and, like a character in the old John Hughes films she loved to watch, she'd walk over, pick up a glass of champagne, take one mouthful, turn around, and smile.

And then – oh, and then – Jamie Duncan would look at her and realize. Because the thing that Isla never admitted to a soul, the thing that Isla didn't even admit to herself for so, so long, was that Isla's heart belonged to Jamie Duncan. Sometimes, when she met him on his own, he could be sweet and kind and funny. There had been a couple of weeks during the summer they turned fifteen when Allison Graves had gone camping in Newquay, and the rest of the gang had somehow melted away, and suddenly he'd shone every bit of that charm and charisma in her direction, and she'd basked in it. They'd messed around at the park, cadged money for ice lollies from her dad, wandered up to the woods to walk and chat about nothing for hours and hours. And then – Isla closed her eyes, remembering – he'd grabbed her hand quite suddenly one afternoon as they sat, legs swinging, in the bus shelter, the drizzle gathering on his hair like dew, and his long dark eyelashes starfished with rain, and he'd leaned forward and kissed her.

'You're all right, Isla Brown.'

There was another side to him that nobody else saw. And Isla knew – just *knew* – that if Jamie Duncan could only see her for what she really was, he'd fall utterly, irrevocably, totally in love with her. And she'd love him right back. And he'd fall at her feet, devastated with horror at the nasty childhood things he'd said, and he'd apologize and he'd take her hand and he'd tell her he was going to make it up to her and they'd live happily ever after, just like a film.

But Isla never said this aloud to anyone, because Isla didn't share her thoughts with anyone. Isla worked hard. Isla got to the salon first, and left last. Isla turned down the chance of a night out with the girls so many times that in the end, they stopped asking. And if Isla ever felt lonely, she remembered that she had a mission, and that one day all this hard work would be worth it, and she'd be with Jamie Duncan, and then her life would begin.

'Penny for your thoughts, darling?'

Her dad's voice broke through her reverie. She looked up at him, startled. Coming back here always brought a whole raft of memories, ones she'd rather keep locked away. That was why she'd moved out, in the end – it was easier to keep her mind away from the past at Hattie's flat, easier to spend her days working and her nights reading, keeping herself busy clearing up the place. And if she ever felt like Hattie took her domesticity for granted – well, she reminded herself that she was living in a dream house in the perfect part of town, and snapped on her Marigolds. Cleaning kept her mind off everything.

'I was wondering what the doctor said the other day,' she lied.

'Ach, the usual. Cut down on saturated fat, get some exercise, no more pints in the Arrow after work, no pork pies. As far as I can see his suggestion is, take everything nice in the world and stop doing it. That's no life.' He pulled the biscuit tin closer, tapping a tune on the lid with his fingers before opening it up, studiously ignoring Isla's look of disapproval.

'What's the alternative?' Isla shook her head, frustrated. She'd had this conversation with her dad a thousand times over the years, watching as he grew from stout to slightly rotund, from tubby to obese. He was a big man, and he carried it well. But he was a good six stone overweight, and Isla worried. 'I don't want you to –' she stopped. She couldn't say it. Her gaze lifted above her dad's head to the photo frame on the kitchen wall where her mum smiled down on them, her mouse-brown hair neatly blow-dried, the silver pendant that Isla now wore hanging around her neck.

Her dad looked up for a second at his late wife. 'No, fair enough. No. I promise you I will try, sweetheart.' He put the lid on the biscuit tin and pushed it away, towards Isla. 'No more biscuits. Well, maybe one a day with my tea.'

'And maybe a bit of a walk?'

He nodded, begrudgingly, emitting an unwilling sigh. 'Right enough.'

'How about now?'

'You want to go today?' Her dad looked startled. 'Maybe we could go for a Sunday stroll instead? Take a wander down the canal path?'

'Now.' Isla finished the last of her tea and put the mug down, decisively. Her head was still banging, and a bit of fresh air might help to clear it. She stood up, rinsing out her mug in the battered stainless-steel sink before leaving it upside down on the draining board. She fixed her dad with a steely glare. 'Half an hour. No more. And then I'll come back and give this place a tidy up.'

'But I wanted to have a word about last night. You gave me a bit of a fright, you know, darling.'

Isla stepped back, shaking her head. 'We can talk as we walk.' Frankly she didn't want to discuss it with her dad, and was planning to sweep it under the carpet. With her bridges burnt with Kat Black, she knew that finding a job was going to be tricky. There was nothing in her contract about gardening leave, but she was going to find it impossible to walk into another salon without addressing their falling-out – the hairdressing world had the fastest and most efficient jungle drums around. By now, *everyone* would know they'd had an argument, and Chantelle would be delightedly telling the story to anyone who'd listen. Isla realized, watching her dad push himself up from the table and shuffle his keys and wallet around, that her clients would get wind of it pretty soon, too. At that point, nobody in town would touch her with a bargepole. The best thing she could do was take a bit of time off, and let it all blow over.

'So, about your little night out last night, Isla.' Her dad was ambling along like an amiable bear beside her. It mightn't be power walking, but it was a damn sight better than sitting in front of the television, can of beer in hand, watching the football results as they ticked along the bottom of the screen.

'It was a one-off.' Her voice was firm.

'I'm sure it was. But you've no job, hen.'

'I'm going to take some time off. Have a hiatus. A breather. Whatever it is people call it.'

'That'll no' look good on your CV. You cannae just stop working.' Isla's dad was old fashioned, and had no truck with gap years. You left school, you got a job, you worked hard, then you retired. It was simple.

'I'm not stopping,' Isla began, 'I'm just – having a break.'

He made a scoffing noise. 'That sounds like a nonsense. You need to get on to the other salons in town, hen. Let them know you're on the lookout for something.'

'It's not that simple, Dad. I didn't just lose my job . . .'

She hadn't expected him to laugh at her predicament.

'You're more like your mother than you realize, young Isla. She'd a temper like a firecracker too. I tell you, I steered clear when she was in one of her moods. I mind her giving my sister Jessie whit for after she'd messed up a booking for a caravan holiday to Wales. They never got on after that, y'know.'

Isla smiled. It wasn't often they talked about her mum. 'Anyway, no matter. Something will turn up. It always does.'

'Aye, sure enough it will. And you've been working far too hard for long enough now. The world isn't going to end when you hit thirty, you know.'

Isla halted in her tracks for a second, looking at her dad as he carried on walking.

'You OK, sweetie?' He turned back, concerned.

'Yeah, fine.' She slipped her hand in his arm, and they moved along the canal bank together.

The world wasn't going to end when she hit thirty – but for her mum, it had done just that. Somehow, Isla realized, she'd hung everything she had on getting as far up the ladder as she could, determined that if she could just make it there, the rest of her life would sort itself out somehow.

They returned to the house.

'That's Jock on the phone, asking if I'll take Margaret up to the shopping centre.'

Isla shook her head, smiling. He was supposed to be off duty, but she knew he wasn't going to say no to a mate. She had half an hour or so to get the place sorted whilst her dad did one last run for the night as a favour to Jock. Filling the sink with soapy water, she snapped on a pair of rubber gloves she'd brought round last time she'd visited.

She whizzed round with a duster first, wiping down the surfaces and spraying them with polish. The house hadn't changed in forever. She plumped up the sagging sofa cushions, shook out the rug and left it by the front step whilst she ran the hoover around the sitting room.

She gave her mum a quick shine, thinking as she did so how young she looked in the picture, something she'd never noticed before. She was probably only about twenty-four there – five years younger than Isla was now, and with only another six years left.

Isla took the picture down for a moment, studying it

afresh. She'd focused for so long on hitting what everyone at work called *the big 3-0*, and everything she wanted to achieve by then – it hadn't occurred to her that there was a reason behind it. Now the reason was smiling back out at her, hazel eyes shining in the sunlight, hair clipped back from the side of her face with a gold clasp.

'Don't worry.' Isla spoke aloud. 'It'll all work out in the end. That's what Dad says.'

Her mum smiled back at her, silently. Isla liked to imagine she was giving out love.

'That's me done, Isla.'

She heard the front door slam shut and her dad's heavy, solid footsteps in the hall.

When she came back down the stairs, bottle of bleach in hand, her dad was on the phone.

'That's a stroke of luck, then, isn't it?' she heard him saying. 'Well, no, not for Pamela, obviously, but – well, they say the Lord moves in mysterious ways, do they not?'

Isla paused on the last step, listening. What on earth was going on?

'Aye, she'll love that, I'll tell her the now. She can come over this week. No, she's got nothing else on. I can't see it being a problem. Aye, right up her street. Eight weeks.'

'Dad?'

She walked into the sitting room as he replaced the old-fashioned receiver with a beaming smile on his face.

'I tell you what, you wouldn't believe this.'

'Try me.' Isla felt a lurch of panic in her stomach. There was something in his tone that made her quite sure he hadn't just won the lottery.

'That was Jessie on the phone.' Formidable Aunty Jessie, who'd had a run-in with Isla's mum. She was a tiny, no-nonsense woman who lived on an island off the West Coast, not far from Glasgow.

Isla stood and waited for her dad to continue.

'Well, luckily for you, your cousin Pamela's broken her arm.'

Pamela. A solid lump of West Coast lassie who'd always had a packet of sweeties in one hand, and a finger up her nose. She'd had four children by the time she was twenty-four. Isla hadn't seen her in years, and didn't regret it one bit.

'Lucky for me?'

'Aye. She needs to go and look after her. Pamela's just had another bairn – that's six now she's got. Anyway. Jessie's needing someone to look after her shop, and I've said to her you'd be perfect for the job. Eight weeks, she said. That's your time off sorted out. Get away from it all.'

'A shop?'

'Aye, a hairdresser's shop.'

Isla blanched, but didn't say a word. Her brain started working quickly. There was no way she could do this. A million and one reasons why not.

'When I told her what had happened,' her dad began – Isla swallowed back a gasp of horror, looking at him wide-eyed – 'well, no, I didn't mention you'd got hammered on champagne and given your ex-boss what for on the telephone, obviously. I just said you were taking a break, and looking for something to do to keep your hand in.'

It got worse. Isla visualized the kind of hairdresser's 'shop' that her sturdy, no-nonsense Aunty Jessie would own. She hadn't even known Jessie was a qualified hairdresser, let alone that she owned a salon.

'What kind of –' Isla thought for a moment, choosing her words cautiously – 'what kind of shop is it, exactly?'

'Well, you'll remember they always had a summer place across the water when you were a wee girl? Do you no' remember visiting there in the summer?'

Isla remembered perfectly well. When everyone else in her class was off on the bus to Blackpool for a summer break of sunshine and funfair rides, ice cream and flirting on the pier – or flying off from the airport to the Costa del Sol for two weeks in a hotel, coming home with boastful tales of kissing Spanish boys at midnight on the deserted beaches – she had spent most of her summer holidays in a caravan in the Highlands. One exotic summer, the year she turned fifteen, she and her dad had spent a thoroughly miserable wet week on the island of Auchenmor, where there was nothing to do but feed twopence pieces disconsolately into a rigged slot machine and eat ice cream in a shabby seafront cafe. It had been hideous, she'd run out of books to read, and she'd sworn she was never setting foot in the place again.

'I can remember it a bit, yes,' Isla fibbed. 'But I honestly don't think—'

'Your Aunty Jessie was so pleased, you know. She's always felt bad that you and she don't have a closer relationship. I think she feels bad that she'd fallen out with your mum when she got sick. I shouldn't have let that get in the way. She could have helped out more when you were growing up, maybe had you stay over there for the summer holidays when I was working.'

Thank God you didn't, thought Isla, trying to keep her expression neutral. The thought of an extended stay in the world's most boring holiday resort was appalling.

'Anyway, you'd be doing her a favour, and I think it'd do you the world of good. Get a bit of colour in your cheeks, a bit of sea air . . . What's the matter?'

'Nothing.' Isla shook her head, stalling. 'But really, I don't think I can just up sticks and go off for eight weeks to the middle of nowhere.'

Her dad's face fell.

'It was just an idea,' he said, covering his tracks. 'I'm sure we can sort something out with Jessie. She'll have someone else who could take over. I'll just ring her and—' He made to reach for the phone.

'Dad, no.' Isla put a hand out to stop him. 'Just – it's just a surprise, that's all. I tell you what, I've used all that furniture polish sorting out the hall and stairs. I'll nip out to the corner shop and get some more, shall I?'

'Give yourself time to think of an excuse, more like,' her dad replied, half-teasing. But his expression wasn't hard to read. She'd disappointed him, and if there was one thing she didn't want, it was to make her lovely dad feel bad. He was the only thing that actually mattered to her. And after all – Isla slipped through the back door, along the narrow garden path, and out the gate – he wasn't asking for much. He was trying to *help*.

The path between the two rows of gardens was narrow, the houses divided by the same thickly slatted wooden fences that had been there since she was a young girl. She ran a hand along the roughly hewn wood, inhaling the scent of creosote that lingered, always, in the passageway. And then she was out, stepping underneath the strange bridge bedroom that always looked so exotic, joining one white-harling covered house to another. She'd always wondered how those bedrooms stayed upright.

'All right, hen?'

Mrs Glennison had owned the corner shop since time immemorial. She stood, queen of all she surveyed, chief gossip, judge and jury. If a child was caught nicking sweeties, she didn't bother sorting it with the parents. She gave the offender a skelp round the lugs and sent them on their way. Being banned from the sweetie shop was the most effective punishment there could be – and after a suitable sentence, being allowed back in was heaven on earth. Isla watched as two scruffy boys left, hands already dipping into paper bags full of gummy snakes and bubble gum. Back when Isla was a little girl, they'd cost twenty pence for a mixture. Nowadays, she noticed, it was 50p.

'Hiya.' She could be ten years old again. It didn't matter that the badly cut brown hair was now a sleek chestnut bob, and that the ill-fitting, badly washed clothes had been replaced with expensive designer outfits. Mrs Glennison had watched Isla growing up a motherless bairn, and that's what she would always be.

'I hear there's one of they school reunions going on for your year soon. Will you be going?'

'Me?' Isla feigned disinterest. 'Not sure. I doubt I'll be here.'

The old lady crossed fat, freckled arms across her blue overall, a knowing expression on her face. 'That's a shame. I think the rest of your gang will all be going. I saw Allison Graves the other day when she was back visiting her mum. She's got two bairns now – a wee lassie and a baby boy. No plans yourself?'

Isla shook her head. 'No.'

'Aye, well, people seem to be leaving it later these days, right enough. You'll need to be keeping an eye out. You don't want to leave it past thirty-five, mind. My niece Sandra left it too late; she had an awful time trying to catch pregnant.'

'Sorry, can I just squeeze past?' said a voice. Isla looked up briefly from the magazine shelf where she was studying the front covers, trying to decide which to buy.

'Sorry, of course.'

There was something vaguely familiar about the

woman who handed over a ten-pound note, shoving the contents of her shopping basket into a fabric bag before she slipped through the door, hair knotted up in a loose ponytail, a faded T-shirt over leggings that had seen better days. Isla busied herself with trying to find the furniture polish.

'Isla?'

She looked up as the woman came back in and pulled the shop door closed behind her.

'I thought it was you.' The woman smiled at her shyly, and Isla was thrown back in time to the school dinner hall.

'Helen?'

Helen smiled back at her, suddenly familiar. 'You're braving the school reunion then? I saw you signed up on the Facebook page last night. I wasn't sure about it, but . . .' she looked down at her scruffy leggings and baggy T-shirt.

Isla felt another wave of the night before washing over her. Oh God, of course. She'd signed up for the reunion in a fit of bravery – or madness. Now there was no going back.

'Well, how bad can it be?' Isla tried to brazen it out.

Helen looked dubious. 'Pretty awful, if school was anything to go by.'

'Are you coming?' Isla tried to look casual. But God, if someone she knew was there, at least she wouldn't have to stand on her own for the whole night.

'You're definitely going to be there?'

'Yeah.' Isla's mouth formed the word, to her surprise. 'Oh, come, it'll be OK if we're together. Plus, maybe time will have mellowed everyone.'

Helen took a deep breath. 'Or they'll be even more vicious, and we'll be balancing our buffet food on our knees whilst they take the piss out of us for having the wrong clothes and looking like shit.'

Isla looked down at her dusty jeans and the old shirt of her dad's that she'd put on whilst she was doing the housework. She looked as scruffy and shapeless as she'd ever been. Thank God it was Helen she'd bumped into, and not one of the others.

'We can stick together. Safety in numbers, and all that stuff. I'd better get back, my dad's going to be wondering where I've got to. See you there?'

'That would be lovely.' Helen gave another shy smile.

Oh God. So now there was no getting out of the reunion. And what the hell was she going to say to her dad? There was no way she could go and spend eight weeks – what about Hattie? The flat? What would she do for money? She supposed maybe she'd get paid for looking after Jessie's place, but – eight weeks doing shampoo and sets for old ladies, and making polite conversation whilst trimming old men's ear hair? She shuddered at the thought. No, there was no way she could put herself through it.

'Is that you, hen?'

'Hi, Dad.' Isla pulled the back door closed behind her. It stuck, as always, and took two hands to wrench it shut.

'That was your Aunty Jessie on the phone again. She's – och, no. Don't worry.'

'She's what?' Isla could feel the weight of inevitability settling on her shoulders like a thick, suffocating blanket.

'Well,' her dad began, carefully. 'She's so relieved you've offered to step in.'

Isla's eyebrows shot up to her hairline.

'Well, not so much offered, maybe – anyway, she's over the moon. Apparently the girl she had helping her isn't much use, so she was loath to leave her in charge. I've told her you know your stuff, and she's delighted to have you take the reins.'

Isla closed her eyes.

'Eight weeks. Maybe seven, if your cousin Pamela gets the cast off early. But it's a bad break, I think, and she needs the help. Imagine trying to look after all those weans with one arm.'

This was unbearable. Her dad had given up all attempts at subtlety now, and was layering on the guilt in spades. She heaved a heavy sigh. 'Fine.'

His face was one huge, beaming smile. He jumped out of his armchair faster than Isla had seen him move in years, throwing his arms around her.

'Darling, I'm so glad. I have a feeling this is just what you need. A break from all this pressure. Get a bit of sunshine, enjoy a different pace of life.'

'For eight weeks,' Isla reminded him. 'And then I'm coming back here and getting on with it.'

Eight weeks. By then the reunion would have taken place. She felt her stomach contract with fear. What if Kat Black wasn't going to give her a decent reference? No, she'd have to give her something – employment law saw to that, surely? And Isla was certain she'd be able to find something else. Maybe in Glasgow, where the rumour mill wouldn't be quite so active. In fact, she could keep an eye out whilst she was working over on the West Coast. Maybe make a few exploratory visits, scout the place out a bit. That was it. She sighed.

'When does she want me?'

'An *actual* island?' Hattie's face was wreathed in smiles. Life was so uncomplicated for her. She just blithely floated through, expecting everything to go well – and invariably it did. 'Oh what *fun*, darling, you'll have an absolute ball – just imagine all those gorgeous handsome islanders with their woolly sweaters, chopping logs. Dreamy . . .'

Isla looked at her blankly. Hattie had breezed in from her weekend in the country with bags overflowing with mountains of washing, hair knotted loosely in a ponytail, her striped Joules shirt half-untucked from a pair of battered old Jack Wills tracksuit bottoms. She slid down over the back of the huge sofa and swung her legs down, sprawling in a heap, her beautiful face looking up at Isla. Despite two very late nights ('up all night, darling, you know what it's like, Milly made us play hide and seek at midnight and then sardines of all things – her place is vast – and then her ma made everyone crumpets for breakfast . . .') her smooth tanned face was untroubled by black shadows or lines. Hattie was living proof that a life without worries created a perfect complexion. She slept the sleep of the just each night, and positively glowed with health. Isla, in comparison, had realized that morning that she was looking seriously grey and in need of a facial. With no time to spare, she'd have to sort something out when she got over to Aunt Jessie's place.

'But what about the –' Isla cast a glance over her shoulder at her bedroom. The huge cast-iron bedstead stood on a bleached, stripped wooden floor. Stacks of white cushions lay atop a White Company waffle bedspread. A fragrant aromatherapy candle glowed on the bedside table, emitting delicious and soothing scents of lavender and jasmine. It was her sanctuary. Neutral, immaculate, perfect. And if she left, how would Hattie cope with living alone? When Isla had arrived, the place hadn't looked quite like this . . .

'Eight weeks?' Hattie reached into her bag, pulling out a Mars bar. Through a mouthful of chocolate, she continued thickly, 'I won't even have time to notice you're gone, sweetie. And – between you and me – I'm rather hoping that Marcus might spend a bit more time over here.'

Isla wrinkled her forehead, trying to remember which one was Marcus. Hattie was generally followed by an adoring string of admirers who were pretty much interchangeable. Despite the fact that they were universally well brought up, polite and charming, Isla regarded them all as vague irritations who got in the way of her relaxation and tended to leave a trail of wet towels and shaving cream in the bathroom when she'd just cleared it up.

'Anyway, you can always come back at the weekends, it's not like you're emigrating to Australia or anything like that.' Hattie still hadn't noticed – after all this time – that hairdressers don't get weekends off. Friday and Saturday were Isla's busiest days, the salon always packed with people desperate for a last-minute appointment.

Hattie crumpled up the Mars wrapper, throwing it at the coffee table. It missed, landing on the floor. Hattie stretched her arms above her head, flicking on the television. 'Excellent, *Real Housewives of LA*.'

Isla had to resist the temptation to pick up the wrapper and put it in the bin. It was Hattie's house, after all, and she'd have to face facts – eight weeks away from here would mean it was going to be in a state of devastation on her return. She'd leave some Marigolds and cleaning stuff out on the kitchen worktop when she left. Maybe Hattie would take the hint.

It was hard-going fitting everything into her little car, which wasn't exactly designed with practicality in mind, but Isla wanted to be prepared for every eventuality. Who knew what island life was going to be like? She was being installed in the little flat above her aunt's salon, which had been used for years as a holiday let. It had lain empty for the last two summers, used only as a storage space for the shop equipment. Jessie had assured her dad that it was 'a bonny wee place, lovely views over the sea, and nice and close to town for Isla – she'll be able to do a bit of exploring when she's not working.'

Isla, who had absolutely no intention of exploring whatsoever, shoved the box of books she'd brought along to keep her going onto the back seat. That was everything. She didn't have much faith in the library having anything from this century. She didn't have much faith in *anything* on the island being from this century, to be truthful. She closed the back door of the little car, and locked it with care. One last trip upstairs to gather everything she needed for now, and she'd be gone.

She took a last look around the flat, straightening the sofa cushions and neatening the edges of the rug by the fireplace. She didn't have anyone to wave her off; after spending the last couple of days with her dad she'd said a final goodbye to him the night before, and he was on a long day shift today, though he'd promised to give her a ring at Jessie's house that evening. It was hard to believe that only a week ago she'd gone to work as usual, on top of the world. Now a new week stretched in front of her – and an entirely different life.

Isla set her chin determinedly, and closed the door on Edinburgh for the next eight weeks.

Chapter Four

'That's a braw motor you've got there, hen.'

Calum was Aunt Jessie's second husband, and the human embodiment of an ageing Popeye. His thick, tattooed arms were squeezed into a white T-shirt. In the corner of his mouth was a smouldering cigarette, rather than a pipe. He ran an appreciative hand along the bonnet of her car.

Picking up her suitcase without waiting to be asked, he hefted it into their whitewashed house, which sat over the hill, looking down into the little valley where the town of Kilmannan stood.

'What've you got in here – a dead body?' Calum joked, swinging it down onto the spotless carpet in the hall.

Isla felt herself blushing. 'Nothing much, running kit and things.'

'I know what you young lassies are like. Jessie's Pamela comes away from here with a ton weight of stuff from SemiChem every time she's back home. It'll be all thae bargain shampoos and the like, am I right?'

Isla shook her head. After the early years, where she'd worked with hands red raw from the strong chemical products she'd used, she'd sworn never to go anywhere near anything like that again. She wasn't taking any chances on what Jessie would have in her salon, so she'd stocked up in advance – not just for her own personal use, but enough to keep the salon going until she could order in supplies. And Calum was trying to heft the whole lot into the sitting room, only to have to bring it back out again. He puffed his way back to the car and pushed the door closed.

'I've made a brew for us, hen. Now are you absolutely sure you don't want to stay here tonight? I've got a spare room made up.' Aunt Jessie, who was almost as square and solid as her brother, stood in the doorway to her kitchen, hands on hips. She had an apron tied around an ample waist and her dark hair set neatly in curls that framed her handsome face. The house smelt of a combination of bacon sandwiches and air freshener.

'No, honestly,' Isla felt a wave of panic. 'I'd rather just get in and get myself settled. And you must be desperate to get off to Pamela and the children.'

'Aye, well, her William has to get back to work, right enough. If you're sure, hen?'

'Absolutely certain.'

Isla sat down on the pink velour sofa and waited for her drink to arrive. The television was on in the corner, playing a radio station through huge speakers that were wired to each corner of the room. Everything else, though, was just how she remembered it.

'I'm sure you're self-sufficient enough, being Ellen's lassie, so I'll let you find your way round the shop in the morning, seeing as you're the expert in the family.' Jessie bustled in, handing Isla a mug with a cartoon Highland cow on the side, and offering her an opened packet of chocolate digestives.

Unthinking, she took two. The unexpected mention of her mum's name had thrown her slightly. At home with her dad it seemed to have become an unspoken rule that she wasn't mentioned. She smiled down on them from the wall, but when Isla had been younger she hadn't been able to find the words to ask her dad about her. Once she was old enough, the time seemed to have passed and Isla had found herself skirting the subject awkwardly.

'Aye, your mum was an independent woman.' Jessie gave a knowledgeable nod, settling herself down into the cushions, holding her hand out for the mug of tea, which was passed to her, wordlessly, by Calum, who appeared to be very well trained. 'It's a shame your dad was always so busy once she passed away. I'd have liked to have seen a bit more of the two of you.'

Isla smiled politely and sipped her tea. Jessie, apparently oblivious to her silence, continued, filling in the gaps where Isla should have responded.

'Aye, she was a nice enough lassie, your mum. It's a

shame our Pamela is no' well, she'd have loved to have seen you.'

'Mmm,' smiled Isla. The summer holiday she'd spent over here on the island had been painfully dull – Pamela, who apparently was keen to catch up and reminisce about old times, clearly didn't remember the hideous night they'd all spent at the Winter Gardens disco, where Isla had had to keep watch whilst a game of Spin the Bottle took place, fuelled by bottles of illicitly acquired cider. By some silent agreement, Pamela and her friends had judged that Isla wasn't eligible to join in – not, Isla remembered, that she'd wanted to. A gaggle of gawky-looking boys who'd clattered up and down the promenade on skateboards hadn't held any interest for her at all. The feeling had been mutual. They'd jostled their way past Isla, standing in her post by a rhododendron hedge, and knocked the book she was reading out of her hands.

'Anyway, maybe now you're spending some time here you'll fall in love wi' the place, see why we all enjoy it so much.'

I think that is extremely unlikely, thought Isla, swallowing the last of her tea in a burning-hot gulp to get it over and done with. 'Well, I've got eight weeks.' *And counting*, she added silently.

'Aye, I'm very grateful to you for it, as well.' Jessie stood up. 'Right, if you're absolutely sure you'll no' stay, let's get you along the road. Just remember Calum's here if you need anything, and I'm on the end of the phone, and the girls will keep you right until you find your way about, and . . .'

The flat was directly above the salon, tucked down a little side street that led down to the seafront promenade (or, as Isla noted grimly, the pavement beside the harbour, as it could also be known). Next door was a boarded-up shop with a worn-out sign that read 'JIM'S F SH' in plastic letters. The letter *I* had been picked up and placed on the stone windowsill, where it sat accompanied by a left-over takeaway coffee cup and a fish-and-chip wrapper. Auchenmor had that much in common with Edinburgh, at least.

'Here we are.'

Jessie opened the door to the flat. There was a narrow staircase with a utilitarian blue carpet, and the whole hallway smelt very strongly of some kind of artificial flower scent.

'Lavender and geranium.' Jessie noticed Isla sniffing the air. 'I love those plug-in air fresheners, don't you? This place smells beautiful now. I've bought a load to take over for Pamela, hide the smell of the bairn's nappies.'

Isla refrained from responding that she thought she'd prefer the smell of dirty nappies to the chemical pong of whatever-it-was, and followed her aunt up the stairs.

'It's no' been used for a good while, but I've given it a quick sort out. It needs a good clean, mind you, but if you're OK with that . . .' Isla's Aunty Jessie stood back, arm open in a gesture of welcome, as Isla stepped forward into the flat that would be her home for the next eight weeks. It was hideous. The floor was covered in a nauseating green swirling carpet, and a stained wooden fireplace surround framed a dubious-looking old-fashioned gas fire. Brown floral nylon curtains hung at a window that looked onto the tiny castle, and down the street to the tired-looking amusement arcade Isla remembered from her youth.

'A bit of fresh air and a bunch of carnations to cheer it up a bit, and you'll have it looking like home in no time.' Jessie beamed at her niece before leading her through to the bedroom. Isla closed her eyes. It was only two months. And maybe Pamela might turn out to have developed Wolverine qualities, and her bones would repair overnight. *Please*, thought Isla.

'The view is amazing, isn't it?' The side of the bay window looked down a narrow lane and beyond to the sea. She could see the ferry sailing away, and with it any chance of escape for another two hours. Isla turned away, feeling despondent.

'And this is the kitchen,' Jessie called from across the hall. 'Isla, are you there?'

'Coming.' She shook her head in despair and headed towards what should have been the heart of the home. Trying not to think of the sleek, metallic beauty of the kitchen in Hattie's place, she stepped into a room that had been the height of fashion in 1984. Pale brown

61

cupboards trimmed with fake wood handles, a brown sink (a brown sink? Isla didn't even realize such horrors existed) and an under-counter fridge that hummed and rattled alarmingly.

'I've made up the bed for you, and there's a pint of milk and a packet of tea in the cupboard here.' Jessie opened the cupboard where a tiny packet of PG Tips sat beside a packet of chocolate biscuits, some alarmingly orange pasta sauce, and a box of Cup-a-Soups.

'Now, I'm away on the next boat to Pamela's place. I'm going to give you the keys to the salon downstairs so you can open the doors for the girls, but if you want to have a wee nosey around and make yourself at home before tomorrow morning, that's fine by me. We're open until Saturday lunchtime, closed Sunday and Monday, and we do a half day on Wednesday.'

'So many days closed? Is that normal?' She was going to be climbing the walls with boredom.

'Well, we've only got our regulars and they know the days they want to come in. There's a lassie who does mobile hairdressing for the people who can't get out and about so easily, and the young ones all seem to want to go off the island to have their hair cut for some reason.' Jessie sniffed disapprovingly. 'And of course nothing is open here on a Wednesday afternoon. Half-day closing,' she explained, as if it was the most natural thing in the world.

Which it was, Isla reflected, in 1975, which is where this godforsaken hole seemed to be stuck. She shooed her aunt out with words of reassurance, grabbed the keys and headed at speed towards the Spar round the corner. There was only one thing for it – she was going to have to gut the place and scrub it from top to bottom before she unpacked a single thing. God only knew how long it had been since the place had seen a duster, never mind a bottle of bleach.

By the time she'd finished later that afternoon, Isla had used the best part of a bottle of Mr Sheen, three dusters and six J-cloths. It had been absolutely no surprise to her to discover that the bathroom was also nauseatingly green in colour, nor that the tiles were ingrained with several decades' worth of holidaymakers' fingerprints and grime. She scrubbed the last of the walls with a final flourish.

The bedding she'd been left with was clean, but spark-inducingly nylon and covered with bobbles. It'd do for a night, she decided, but then she'd have to make another trip back off the island to Glasgow to get something decent to sleep on – that, or order something online. That was a thought – she hadn't actually found out whether the place had broadband. Somehow, it seemed unlikely.

She searched the sitting room for a phone socket. Lying under a curtain was a yellowing plastic dial phone from the mid-seventies that was plugged into the wall. It had a dialling tone, at least. Maybe she could ask Jessie to sort it out. In the meantime there was always the library, or an internet cafe, or – well, someone somewhere must be online, surely? The salon must have some kind of internet connection. She opened the door that led downstairs to investigate. She'd been determined not to look until she'd finished cleaning the flat – there was only so much grimness that one person could take.

It was everything she had expected – and more. So much more. The chairs hadn't been replaced since the dark ages, and there were old-fashioned helmet hair-dryers, 1950s-style, in the corner of the room. On wheels. The sinks sat in a neat row (at least they looked clean, and the taps sparkled) with a line of shampoo behind them – not the luxury aromatherapy stuff that she was used to, but the cheapest, most chemical-saturated products available from the wholesaler. Isla shuddered. That stuff was on a par with washing-up liquid. It would strip everything from your hair – and worse. She'd have to order in some stuff from the supplier, get it couriered up before Tuesday. The juniors' hands would be red raw, washing hair in that stuff all day long – and she wasn't going to subject anyone to that.

She withdrew from the salon and climbed the stairs back up to the flat above. There was no need to sort everything out in one go, and she was suddenly absolutely ravenous.

She looked at herself in the mirror. Pulling out her hairbrush and her powder compact, she tidied herself up. It might be the middle of nowhere, but she wasn't going to let her standards slip. She applied a slash of

Chanel red to her lips, swept a top-up layer of mascara onto her lashes, and patted some powder on her nose. With a final sweep of the brush ensuring her glossy bob had not a hair out of place, she headed down Kilmannan's main street.

It was every bit as grim as she'd remembered. There was a charity shop, a tired-looking newsagent's, a bakery with the shutters already drawn closed (Isla checked the time on her phone: half past five. The supermarket was probably shut already) and the Spar on the corner. She pushed the door open. Stacked in the corner in a bargain bin were a pile of calendars, reduced to 20p. Who on earth would want a calendar in June? Isla had a sudden thought, picking one up and popping it into her shopping basket. The choices for dinner were pretty depressing fare. She picked the least wilted-looking packet of pre-packed salad, a vegetarian lasagne, and a pot of yoghurt from the fridge, adding them to her basket. She wasn't going to drop her standards and start eating crap. If the food selection was going to be this awful she'd take the car back on the ferry to Glasgow and pop to M&S once a week. It was unbelievable that people actually lived like this

Back at the flat – Isla realized with a grimace that she wasn't going to allow herself to call it home, in the hope it would make it more bearable – she hung the calendar from a hook in the wall. Then she got a marker pen out of her handbag, circled every single day that led up to the end of eight weeks, and scored through the first one.

Chapter Five

'I'm sorry, the reception is terrible – you're breaking up.'

Finn MacArthur headed out of the front door, and took the narrow stone steps two at a time. He crossed to the other side of the road, which overlooked the little harbour. The signal was far better there than it was in his little Victorian flat, where the thick stone walls kept everything out.

'Give me two seconds – you want *how many* wooden *what*?'

'Phallic totems.' The voice was slightly husky, with clipped public-school vowels. 'Penis sculptures. I was told you were the man for that sort of thing in these parts.'

'And you want six?' Finn wrinkled his brow in confusion.

'Yes, please. Quite urgently, actually.'

An elderly couple were walking towards him. He didn't dare move, though, and risk losing reception – and a lucrative commission – at the same time. He lowered his voice.

'You have an urgent need for six carved wooden phallic symbols?'

'I'm sorry, what was that?' said the woman on the end of the line.

'I said, YOU HAVE AN URGENT NEED FOR SIX WOODEN PHALLIC –' He stopped mid-sentence, realizing that the old man was looking at him with some distaste. His wife, however, looked frankly fascinated, and was slowing down her already sedate pace.

'And would you like these phalluses to be, er, erect, or . . . ?'

'Come on.' The old man tugged at his wife's elbow. She had stopped now, and was taking a remarkably long time to empty the contents of her coat pockets into the nearby rubbish bin.

'Oh, yes, very much so,' said the breezy voice. 'Quite big.'

'Right, so definitely erect.' Finn gave a nod to nobody in particular. The old woman gave him the ghost of a wink. 'And are we talking with, um, testicles, or without?'

'That's a very good question, really, isn't it?' There was a moment's pause to consider before the voice continued. 'They might be helpful from a handling point of view, I suppose, but – well, they're not very aesthetically pleasing, are they?'

'Testicles?'

'It's such an ugly word, don't you think?'

'I have to be honest, it's not one I'm in the habit of using that often.'

The elderly gentleman coughed discreetly.

'Anyway, it would be wonderful if you could perhaps start with just one and we can check it handles properly. It's vital it has the right *feel*.'

The whole conversation was insane. Finn was beginning to wonder if he'd accidentally taken some kind of hallucinogenic drug with his cornflakes that morning. He looked around – everything on the island looked as it should. Fishing boats bobbed out on the water. Little rowing boats were moored by the edge of the tiny harbour. On the beach a couple walked their dog, and a gang of children stood by the water's edge skimming stones.

The old couple were still hovering close by.

'Right. Do you think it might be useful to send over a photo of the sort of thing you're looking for?'

As soon as the words were out of his mouth, Finn realized just what he had said. The old lady hooted with laughter, her husband looking on with undisguised disapproval. She was towed away reluctantly, still laughing.

'Yes, of course,' the woman replied. In contrast, she didn't find the situation amusing at all. 'I'd be more than happy to send you over some images. Better still, perhaps we could meet? Do you have some sort of gallery, or a studio?'

Finn did indeed. He'd cut down his hours recently, no longer working five days a week as head of forestry for the Duntarvie Estate. Having handed over control to

Dave, his friend, who was grateful for the promotion with another baby on the way, he was working on a project that saw timber from the island used to create custom-made, sustainable wooden garden furniture, and as much as he could, he focused on his sculpture. Normally this meant a bit of pottering, doing anything he fancied, music blaring in the workshop, pleasing himself. It suited him perfectly. No ties, no commitments. Friday evenings now and again he'd do a spot of DJing in the Winter Gardens or the local hotels if they had something on, and he picked up a bit of work playing bagpipes at weddings and funerals; but only when he felt like it. Once in a while, he'd pick up a commission – often from one of the visitors to Duntarvie House, where his best friend Roderick lived as Laird. Over there at the far end of the little island, in a turreted, Scottish Baronial castle buried deep in the countryside, Roderick was host to beautiful and exclusive weddings, and the guests were often taken with the wooden carvings dotted around the public rooms. Kate, Roderick's wife, was used to people departing with one or two carefully wrapped carvings lying on the back seats of their cars.

Later that afternoon, with the workshop radio blasting out an ancient Oasis song and the whine of the wood plane in his ears, Finn couldn't hear a thing. He silenced both at the sight of a pair of extremely slim legs clad in cropped white leggings.

'You wanted some photographs?'

Finn turned off the drill, securing the safety lock out of habit before placing it carefully on the workbench beside him.

'Hello, I'm Scarlett,' said the husky, breathy voice of earlier.

He looked up into a pair of navy-blue eyes in a smooth, tanned face, framed with loosely waved, streaky blonde hair. She had a smattering of freckles on her tip-tilted nose. He'd always liked freckles on a – no, this was a work commission. He cleared his throat, brushing saw-dust from his hands onto his jeans before reaching out to shake her hand.

'Finn MacArthur.'

She cocked her chin upwards slightly, stepping back. He watched as she licked her lips unthinkingly, tugging at the neckline of her floaty chiffon tunic. She played with the crystal pendant that hung low between her breasts.

'So,' he said, grinning. 'You're here to talk phallic symbols?'

He was amused to see a slight blush stain her cheeks. She really was very pretty. 'We call them totems, actually. For a retreat my boss is running.'

'Men getting in touch with their inner caveman, that sort of thing?'

Finn had recently read something about a course like that in the Sunday paper. He'd been having a pint with a mate before heading back home for a Sunday lunch with Roo. He'd laughed when his friend down the pub had suggested it was the last thing he needed. 'I'm not that sort of bloke, actually . . . appearances can be deceptive.'

'Yeah,' his mate had snorted with laughter. 'Renaissance man, that's you.'

Scarlett smiled slightly. 'No, it's a retreat for women. I'm not quite sure what they're for –' she broke off here, pulling a face. 'Anyway. Here you are.' She held out a sheaf of priapic images clipped from magazines and tourist guides. 'There's a bit of a variety . . .'

Finn looked down. There was everything from minuscule men with huge erect cocks five times the size of their heads, to solid-looking wooden implements that looked like they could inflict serious injury. A vision of a newspaper headline, MAN FELLED BY HUGE PHALLIC TOTEM, popped into his head, making him laugh aloud.

'It's very important this is created in the right spirit,' said Scarlett earnestly. She moved a little closer to him.

'Oh yes, yes, definitely.' Finn nodded solemnly. He leafed through the pictures. Bloody hell, some of them were downright terrifying. 'Did you have a – er, a size in mind?'

'Well, as I said earlier, quite big.' Scarlett allowed herself a flirtatious smile, looking up at him through lowered lashes. 'Needs to be something you can hold on to, don't you think?'

Finn returned the smile, with interest. Two could play at that game.

'So are you new to Auchenmor?'

'God, no, I'm not *living* here.' She looked alarmed.

'I'm only here for a month, helping Lily – she'll be running it – set up the retreat centre.'

'So what d'you do, then?'

'I work for an investor. He has a string of holistic retreats across the country – they're big money at the moment, now everyone's into finding themselves. He heard about this place, and thought it was perfect. Near enough to the mainland for people to get here easily, remote enough that they feel like they're getting away from it all. And tied in with the weddings up here at Duntarvie House, he'll be hoping we're going to rake it in.'

'I'm sure you will. Doesn't sound very spiritual, mind you.'

She raised a sceptical eyebrow. 'There's nothing unspiritual about wanting to live abundantly.'

Finn, who'd learned the art of non-confrontation, backed out of the corner, changing the subject. It didn't really matter what he thought, and at the end of the day, any financial investment in the island had to be a good thing. With most of the young people who were brought up here leaving as soon as they could, anything that brought in visitors and money was good. And if these holistic-retreat people were planning on working alongside Roddy and Kate, that meant more job security for him.

'Shall we have a look at these carvings?' He motioned to the wooden shapes waiting on the workbench. 'Which one d'you reckon is up to the job?'

It wasn't exactly planned that Finn would end up in town that evening, taking Scarlett for a welcome-to-Kilmannan drink at the newly refurbished Anchor Bar. Nor, when the late spring evening stretched on into darkness and the purple fingers of night reached across the sky, did he expect to take her on a slightly tipsy stroll along the beach where they sat, flirting and chatting, watching the stars come out. And neither of them could possibly have predicted that they'd end up back at his place, music playing and candles lit, not quite making it to the bed, falling asleep, limbs tangled, surrounded by their discarded clothes on the sofa in his sitting room . . .

The phone woke Finn with a start. Eyes half open, he reached back behind his head, groping for the source of the bleeping.

Coffee's waiting. This is your morning call.

He looked at the message blearily for a moment before it sunk in. Shit, it was half nine. It was half nine and there was an extremely pretty girl lying beside him, draped in one of the blankets that usually covered the back of the sofa where his cat, Alfred, had scratched several holes as a kitten, years ago.

She covered her mouth as she yawned, opening her eyes as she did so. 'Morning.'

'Hi.' He'd done this a million times. There were several directions this conversation could take. He inhaled deeply, preparing himself.

'That was a good night.' With a graceful movement

she sprung off the sofa and hooked her black cotton knickers from the leaves of a geranium that stood on the windowsill. She climbed into them, apparently unconcerned by her nakedness, and strolled around the room collecting the rest of her clothes. 'Anyway,' she looked up at the clock, which hung on the wall above the sitting-room door, 'I must love you and leave you. Got the ten-thirty ferry to catch. I'm out of here for the weekend.'

As she spoke she pulled on her white leggings and slipped her top over her head.

'Thanks for dinner. Maybe see you around!'

She scooped up her bag from where she'd discarded it last night by the front door (they'd come in, Finn remembered, kissing, and he'd pushed the door shut with a foot as his hands had been wrapped around her waist, pulling her close) and gave him a wink – the second he'd received in twenty-four hours.

And with that, she was gone.

On my way now.

Near enough, thought Finn, as he hit send on the text and stepped into the shower. Scalding hot water cascaded down his face, dripping from his chin as he stood directly under the blast, eyes closed, contemplating what had just happened. Was he losing his touch? He squirted a handful of shower gel, soaping the muscles of his stomach, running his hand through his hair as he rinsed it. It wasn't the first time a woman had legged it in the morning before he'd had a chance to open his mouth, and he'd done it countless times himself. But this morning, for some reason, it left him feeling a bit dissatisfied. The sex had been good, that wasn't the problem. But it might've been nice to share a coffee and a chat before parting ways. Scarlett hadn't even stayed around long enough for the kettle to boil.

He stepped out of the shower and towelled himself dry, found some clothes and pocketed his wallet. He was already late, and he really needed a coffee.

As he slid into the booth at Bruno's cafe, Finn noticed a knowing look exchanged between Roddy and Kate.

'What've you been up to?' Roddy sat back, arms folded, teasing.

'Don't you mean *who*?' Laughing, Kate tucked a stray curl of dark hair behind her ear, then elbowed Finn in the ribs.

Finn shook his head. 'Just slept in, that's all.' He didn't know why, but for some reason he wasn't in the mood for his friends' gentle piss-taking today.

'Morning, handsome.' Bruno called from across the Formica counter. 'The usual?'

He nodded. The bustle of the cafe filled his ears and he listened to Roddy and Kate talk about their latest wedding, which had taken place at the big house – a low-key celebrity event that had been stalked, unexpectedly, by a helicopter funded by one of the big gossip magazines. Neither of them noticed he wasn't quite his usual ebullient self; their loving, jokey chatter filled in the spaces where he'd normally have been teasing them back.

'One black Americano. Three slices of millionaire's shortbread. Anything else, you lot? I've got paying customers over there waiting.'

Bruno, who had known Finn and Roddy since they were children, and who lived with Kate's mother Liz in a little cottage on the outskirts of Auchenmor, wouldn't ever take a penny in payment for anything they had in the cafe. Roddy made up for it by supplying him with logs for the wood-burning stove that warmed the cosy, book-lined sitting room of the cottage, while Finn was always happy to lend a hand with any repairs that needed to be done in the cafe – not that there were many. Bruno kept the place immaculate; and if it was a bit dated, and the Formica fading – well, it was much loved amongst the residents of Kilmannan, and beloved by the tourists, who were charmed by its 1950s decor.

Sitting back with his coffee, Finn looked across at Roddy and Kate. They exchanged a smile, and Roddy reached across, putting his hand on his wife's knee.

'We wanted you to know,' Roddy began, pushing his dark hair out of his eyes, a habit familiar to Finn since childhood.

'The thing is –' Kate continued. She looked at him, eyes sparkling. Life on the island suited her enormously. She'd settled into her role as mistress of Duntarvie House

and was a popular, much-loved addition to the community.

'We're – well, Kate is – we're having a baby.' The smile
that burst across Roddy's face was ridiculously wide.
Finn looked at his friend, watching as he turned to Kate
with an expression of such love that the whole room
seemed to disappear for both of them, leaving them
wrapped in a bubble. Kate beamed back at her husband,
placing a hand across her stomach – which showed no
sign of looking any different than normal, Finn noticed.

'That's – I'm so happy for you both.' Roddy beamed
back at him. Kate stood up and he reached across the
table, hugging her closely for a split second before pulling back. 'Shit, I haven't squeezed you too hard have I?'

Kate laughed. 'No. I'm pregnant, not made of china.
And there's another six months to go. I fully intend to
carry on with life as normal.'

'Not completely normal,' Roddy shot her a vaguely
worried glance. 'I mean, you're not going off riding with
Morag or anything like that, right?'

Kate rolled her eyes. 'No, I'm not planning on taking
part in any show-jumping competitions, but there's no
harm in a potter round the estate on one of the Highland
ponies, is there?'

'Kate, seriously. I think you need to watch it. Imagine
if you fell off, or—'

Finn cleared his throat ostentatiously. The two of
them seemed even more madly in love after two years
of marriage, but the other thing that hadn't changed was

the good-hearted bickering that characterized their relationship.

'Sorry.' Kate pulled a mock-chastened face. 'Anyway, the thing is, that's not the point of this conversation. We were thinking we'd love you to be godfather. And I know you're supposed to wait until they're born before you ask that bit, but – well, we were so excited, and . . .'

Finn felt a stab of something he didn't quite recognize. Pride, perhaps. He reached a hand out, squeezing Kate's fingers then giving Roddy a blokey pat on the arm. 'I'd love it. I'd be honoured.'

The conversation carried on then, Kate full of excitement and plans for the future, Roddy showing him the photographs from the twelve-week scan they'd had the day before. Finn nodded appreciatively, but honestly wasn't quite sure which end was which when they passed the blurry black and white print across the table.

A couple of hours later, they headed for home. Finn changed quickly and grabbed his mountain bike, deciding the best way to clear his head was to take it up to the woods and blast round the dirt tracks as fast as possible. He was feeling something, but he honestly couldn't put a finger on it. Whatever it was, it was making him uneasy. Pushing hard, heart pounding in his ears, chest tight with exertion, he reached the highest point on the island and pulled over onto the grassy patch that held the stone triangulation point. He let his bike fall and collapsed, every muscle screaming, on the bench, lying back for a moment. The feeling was still there.

Kate and Roddy were going to be a family now. Life would be all baby carriers and *Postman Pat*. There wouldn't be any more drunken evenings hanging out round the fire, or late nights hitching a lift back to Duntarvie House after a lock-in at the Farmers' Arms. Everything was going to change, and – he realized with a jolt of surprise – he wasn't resentful. He was envious.

Chapter Six

'Who are you?'

The girl coming into the salon looked at Isla, her chin jutting out aggressively. Isla, who'd been in the back room trying to make order of the motley collection of towels and equipment, felt herself tense, hackles rising.

'I'm Isla Brown. Jessie's niece. And you are?'

'I'm Shannon. I work here. For Jessie.'

Isla didn't miss the emphasis on her aunt's name.

'Right.' She gave a single nod. Shannon didn't seem impressed.

Shannon stood in the doorway, one hand on her hip, the other on the reception desk. She was chewing gum and sizing Isla up. Isla grew a little taller, and stepped forward.

'Well, if you work for Jessie,' she said calmly, having learned while training many junior stylists over the years that it was easier to come in super-strict than to give any indication of weakness, 'then for the next eight weeks you'll be working for me.'

Shannon raised one eyebrow, and carried on chewing.

She was a riot of colour – rainbow-coloured hair and arms covered with brightly inked tattoos.

'First things first. I'm not sure when our first client is in, because the book isn't up to date and I can't get the computer to turn on. Secondly, whilst you're working for me I'm afraid I have a no-chewing-gum policy.'

Shannon simply looked at her, and chewed a bit harder.

'And I'm going to need you to clear out and bleach the shelves in the back room. The corners are full of dust. This place needs a major clear-out, if you ask me.'

Shannon raised the other eyebrow, cocking her head sideways in a challenging gesture. 'Nobody did ask you, though, did they?'

'I think you'll find Jessie did.' Isla bristled. This girl was impossible. If all the staff behaved like this, it was going to be a long eight weeks.

'Aye, and Jessie employed me. And she disnae mind me chewing gum. Better that than breathing bad breath all over the customers.' She looked at Isla as if *she* was somehow a halitosis-ridden culprit. Nettled, Isla ran a tongue across her teeth, double-checking they felt clean. All those years of being picked on at school had never quite left her. Yes, she'd brushed and flossed and rinsed with mouthwash that morning, as always.

Crossly, angry that she'd allowed Shannon to hit a nerve, Isla moved sideways, motioning with an arm towards the back room. Her voice was clipped. 'Anyway. If you can get on. Thanks.'

Shannon skulked across the salon, making her way to the back room, where she proceeded to spray and wipe in a desultory fashion.

'When are we expecting the junior?' Isla looked up from the computer, which she still hadn't managed to coax into life. Without it, she had no idea how she was going to operate the EFTPOS payment system that stood on the countertop.

'Jinny?' Shannon strolled out of the back room. 'She's always late in. Got to get her wee brother to nursery first.'

Isla tutted. This place was the most inefficient salon she'd ever experienced. There was no way of saying as much to her aunty Jessie, mind you; and her uncle Calum, who was following his wife over to the mainland a few days later, didn't seem to have a clue what was going on. She tried his number again. Still no reply.

'Who you calling?' Shannon asked, nosily.

'I'm trying to get hold of Calum, so I can ask him how the computer works.'

'The computer? It's not exactly rocket science.' Shannon rolled her eyes and slouched over, still, Isla noticed, chewing like a cow in cud. She pressed two buttons simultaneously, and the system kicked into life.

'Is it online?'

Shannon indicated the broadband router on the shelf behind, hidden by a dusty stack of out-of-date hair magazines.

'Do we need these?' said Isla, more to herself than

anyone else. Not waiting for an answer, she hefted them down and carried them outside onto the pavement, where she shoved them into the bin.

'They're recyclable, you know.' A low voice behind her made her jump. She turned round to see a sandy-haired stranger on a mountain bike regarding her with interest.

'You're not Jessie.'

'Very observant,' said Isla, briskly.

'Because Jessie's good at recycling,' he said, with a tease in his voice.

'And life's too short,' Isla retorted. 'This place needs a good clear-out. In fact, I'd say the whole town could do with one.' She waved a hand to indicate the tattered state of the streets.

'That's a load of bollocks,' said the stranger, reaching into the bin. He pulled out the magazines, slotting them under his arm. 'I'll sort it out. You get back to your de-cluttering, or whatever it is you're doing. What have you done with Jessie? Have you decided she's surplus to requirements?' He made to check the bin, clearly amused at his own joke.

'She's gone away.' Isla had no idea who this man was, and she wasn't about to start sharing family secrets with a random stranger.

'Aye. I can see that.' He laughed. 'There's no flies on you, are there?' He eyed her confidently, with a level gaze. 'Well, it's been lovely chatting, but I must get off.

Recycling to do, people to see, that sort of thing. Plus I'm not hanging around here to be decluttered.'

Isla, realizing with a start that she'd been dismissed, watched him as he wheeled the bicycle down the street, stopping at the paper recycling bin on the corner of the harbour road. He turned back as he dropped the pile of magazines in, giving her a wink.

How did he know she was even watching? *Arrogant sod*, she thought, turning back to the salon. Whoever he was, he clearly thought pretty highly of himself. Isla turned and made her way into the salon.

A tiny, elfin-faced, very pretty girl burst in through the door. 'Sorry I'm late, Mikey wouldn't go into nursery. He was having a complete meltdown about the weather. Said he wanted to wear welly boots. I told him it was far too warm but he wouldn't listen. Anyway I gave up in the end and took him back to the house because I couldn't face the fight. Then he got there and started crying because he didn't have his sandals on like Sara so I had to go all the way home again and – oh. You must be Jessie's niece Isla. I swear I remember you coming to visit years back. Your dad's a taxi driver, right?'

Isla, taken aback, hadn't even begun to form a sentence before the girl – Jinny, presumably – continued.

'Anyway I said to Jessie I was sure I remembered you from the arcades one summer because I never forget a face, except you don't really look the same at all – she was really scruffy-looking and you are super glam – I mean you don't look like I expected at all. I suppose people change, mind you, don't they.' She drew breath before continuing. 'I mean I haven't, I'm exactly the same as I was the first time you met me but you don't remember meeting me – but then actually I was six, so . . .'

'I'm Isla.' Isla extended a hand. 'Lovely to meet you.'

'And you've met Shannon, then?' Jinny asked. Shannon had the decency to look a bit guilty.

'So you knew I was coming?' Isla raised her eyebrows.

Shannon fidgeted. 'Yeah, but I had a feeling you were going to be a stuck-up cow, so I thought I'd take you down a peg or two. And I was right. But to be honest, I haven't got the energy for it. Cup of tea?'

Isla looked at her in amazement. This island clearly sent people slowly insane. *Just keep counting the days down*, she thought, gritting her teeth.

'Yes, please.'

Shannon climbed over the stack of towels she'd placed on the floor (Isla winced, thinking of the hygiene rules) and headed for the tap, filling the kettle from one of the hair-washing sinks.

'You can't do that, it's completely against the rules!' How on earth was this place still running?

'I just did.' Shannon snapped her gum and raised a cocky eyebrow at Isla.

'Well, it's the last time for eight weeks.'

Shannon shot a glance at Jinny. Isla, who'd clawed her way up from behind a broom at the tiniest two-chair shampoo-and-set shop in Dalkeith to the gleaming perfection of Kat Black's designer salon, fixed Shannon with a steely gaze. She had attitude. It would be nice if it turned out she had talent, too. Isla had seen plenty of girls like Shannon over the years she'd worked in the salons, watched them grow under her tutelage until they were ready to spread their wings and head out – the teaching was her favourite part, these days, more than the styling work, not that she'd ever have admitted that to Kat. But these girls – well, Jinny was young enough – not even twenty, by the look of her – and Shannon . . . she had plenty of time to get her under control. Turning on her heel, she returned to the computer.

'How many clients do we get on an average day?'

Jinny counted on her fingers. 'Well, we always get the wifeys coming in for their shampoo and set on a Tuesday morning, and again on a Saturday – that's . . . five. Jessie always does them.'

'I do the younger ones,' said Shannon with a challenging look. 'I'm young enough to know what they like.' She scanned Isla's outfit with distaste, smoothing down the sequin-covered T-shirt that clung to her chest, barely skimming the top of her jeans.

'I think I'll be the judge of that,' said Isla, shortly.

Leaving a sullen-faced Shannon in charge of clearing out the back room, Isla sipped coffee and checked through the order book. She'd worked in enough small salons to know that this one was so set in its ways, it would take a miracle to get anyone to do anything differently. In which case, Isla decided, she wasn't even going to bother trying. She'd keep it ticking over and then hand it back with a sigh of relief. The part-time hours would give her more than enough time to focus on getting herself ready for the reunion. And thank God she had the car, and she could escape back to Edinburgh for the weekend and spend some time hanging out with Hattie.

'Well, hello. Who's this then?'

The bell above the door announced the arrival of the first client of the day, a sweet-faced old lady. Her hair floated in grey wisps around a face with cheekbones that suggested she must have been a striking beauty fifty years ago.

'Mrs Mac, in you come. Cup of tea?'

Mrs Mac nodded and sat down gratefully in the chair in front of the mirror, placing her handbag by her feet. Then she looked up with a smile. 'How's you, Jinny?'

'Oh, waiting for the word from college.'

'Can't be long now.'

'No, well, we'll see. I'm no' sure Mum can spare me, to be honest.' Isla watched Jinny's heart-shaped face drop for a second before she gathered herself. 'I'll maybe do a day release or something. Anyway. Sit yourself down.'

'Kettle's just boiled.' Shannon hopped down from the worktop in the back room, where she'd been sitting (to disapproving looks from Isla) folding up the towels and placing them back on the newly cleaned shelves. Moments later, Isla watched as Mrs Mac folded her gnarled fingers around a steaming cup and looked up at Shannon's reflection in the mirror.

'And how was the big date?'

Shannon hooked a strand of yellow hair behind her ear and sat down on the stylist's stool, wheeling herself in close. She leaned forward, confidentially.

'He's asked me out for a drink on Wednesday.'

The elderly woman's rose-pink lipsticked mouth formed a perfect O of delight. 'And you'll be going?'

'I said no.' Shannon looked pleased with herself.

'You did not?' Mrs Mac, enjoying the scandal, shook her head.

'Just for long enough to keep him on his toes.' Shannon's face was a picture of mischief. 'It says in *The Rules* you mustn't make yourself too available. I got it out of the library.'

Jinny propped herself up on the sweeping brush. 'Aye, but that maybe makes more sense when you're livin' in New York or London or somewhere like that. Rab knows you're no' busy, because he lives two houses down from you. And you can't fart in this place without everyone knowing about it.'

Shannon gave a snort of irritation.

'Ahh,' Mrs Mac closed her eyes with the first sip. 'You girls.' She gave a cackling laugh. 'I'm not worried about my hair. I only come in for the tea and the gossip.'

'Aye, we know,' Shannon said, a tease in her voice.

'So, is anyone going to do the introductions?' Isla's voice rang out clearly in the little room. Shannon swung round in her chair, including her for the first time in the conversation.

'Mrs Mac, this is Jessie's niece Isla. She's the hotshot stylist from Edinburgh. Isla – this is Mrs MacArthur.'

Isla flushed uncomfortably at the tone of this introduction. Shannon looked at her, registering her unease and marking up ten points for herself on an imaginary score chart. Isla pulled herself up taller in her five-inch heels.

'I'm in charge for the next couple of months whilst Jessie is away looking after my cousin. Now, Shannon, I think perhaps you should get back on with sorting out the mess that back room's been left in.'

Isla stepped forward, staking her claim with prize position at the back of Mrs Mac's chair. She pulled a comb out from her apron. Shannon stepped back, her expression flat. Isla felt a pang of regret at taking over from Shannon and throwing her weight around – but if she didn't stamp her authority now, the next eight weeks would be impossible.

'Now then.' Back in control, fingers running expertly through the pale candy-floss of Mrs Mac's hair, Isla felt herself settling in. 'So what would you like today? Maybe a light colour rinse to warm it up a bit?'

Mrs Mac's reflection registered alarm. 'Ooh, no, no. None of that. I'd like a shampoo and set, like I have every week. Shannon knows what I want'

Isla looked across at the back room, where Shannon was spraying cleaning fluid into a cloth with a hard-done-by expression.

'Don't worry, Mrs Mac, I'm sure Isla will do a *lovely* job with your hair.' It was clear from Shannon's face that she thought no such thing, and the old lady looked at Isla through hooded green eyes, sizing her up.

'Och, I'm sure Isla here has done her fair share of shampoo and sets, would I be right?'

Isla felt her rigid cheeks breaking into a small smile. She'd spent years in the salon in Dalkeith, combing through the perfumed setting lotion, rolling fine grey hair onto narrow rollers, parking elderly ladies side by side under the hood dryers with cups of tea and copies of *My Weekly*. She'd show Shannon. She'd earned her place. Much as she'd loathed the aching feet and the raw skin on her fingers, the scent of setting lotion that had stayed lodged in her nostrils long after she'd got home, she'd loved working with the older women, listening to their stories. She'd enjoyed their company far more than that of the brittle, glamorous women who'd made up the majority of her clients at high-class salons as her career took off. The older clients had such humour and kindness, and they made her feel at home. Mrs Mac gave her the same feeling. She was smiling up at Isla now, crinkles forming at the corners of her eyes.

'I've done a few.'

Isla's uncharacteristically modest response seemed to please Mrs Mac. She sipped her tea and gave an approving nod. Shannon slunk out of sight, muttering something to Jinny. Isla cast about, looking for the trolley that held her equipment. It had moved since she'd placed it by the window earlier. Hooking it with a foot, she drew it closer, casting a quick eye over the rollers, making sure she had everything to hand.

'Jinny, can you please shampoo Mrs Mac, whilst I get organized?'

There was an ominous silence.

'Jinny?'

Isla peered across the salon to where Shannon stood, a picture of industry, folding towels. Her face was completely blank.

'Shannon, can you ask Jinny to come out here and wash Mrs Mac's hair for me, please?'

There was a small, triumphant snap of gum. 'She can't.' Shannon tipped her jaw up, a tiny smile forming at one corner of her mouth. 'She's away to get the milk. We were almost running out.'

Isla narrowed her eyes slightly, pinning Shannon with a gaze that she hoped said everything. She'd deal with this later. She'd brought a new bottle of milk down to the little salon fridge just that morning, and there was no way that three mugs of tea had used it up. It was pretty clear that Shannon and Jinny were in cahoots, determined to reassert their positions in the pecking order.

Isla picked up a gown and towel and helped Mrs Mac up from her seat. Three could play at that game. Isla had spent years learning from the masters. She went for the surprise tactic. Shannon, who was waiting with an excuse, stood watching, trying to disguise the expression of surprise on her face as Isla sat her client down at the sink, and – using one of the bottles of aromatherapy shampoo she'd brought from home – proceeded to carefully massage the lather through her hair, explaining as she did that with the application of conditioner she'd perform a relaxing head massage.

'That was very nice.' Mrs Mac, eyes closed in blissful relaxation, sat forward as Isla carefully wrapped the towel around her head.

Isla hadn't washed a client's hair in years. Standing by the sinks, it was almost impossible to remember that just a couple of weeks ago she'd been queen bee at the best salon in Edinburgh, her appointment books full for weeks in advance.

For a moment, standing there, the warm water cascading down, it had felt like she'd stepped back in time. She was back at the salon in Dalkeith, nervously washing the hair of her first clients, watching and learning from the girls who could casually gossip amongst themselves whilst styling their clients' hair. Isla seemed to spend months biting her lip in concentration, brow furrowed as she made sure she did everything right. Back then, she'd gone home every night with a headache from the effort of concentrating so hard.

'Right, let's get you over and sorted out.' Isla, looking at Shannon – who busied herself stacking the towels neatly, corner to corner – decided that she wasn't even going to give her the satisfaction. She extended a hand to help Mrs Mac out of the shampooing chair.

'Sit yourself down here,' Isla gave her a smile. 'That tea's gone cold. Do you want me to get you another?'

Shannon had the decency to look a bit surprised, Isla noticed, as she bustled around the back room, preparing another china teacup for Mrs Mac, who was now reading a copy of *Woman's Own*.

'Here you are,' Isla placed it down carefully in front of her. 'You relax, and I'll just comb your hair through and neaten the ends before we get it set.'

It was like working on autopilot. Isla combed the setting lotion through, parting the hair deftly with the handle of the pintail comb, picking up one roller after another and twisting Mrs Mac's soft grey hair up, clipping it in place. The old lady sat peacefully, sipping her tea. Isla looked up from her work eventually, realizing that she was being studied in the mirror.

'So, you're Jessie's niece.'

Isla nodded. 'I am.'

'And you're a big-shot hairdresser in the city.' Mrs Mac looked at her, pink-painted lips pursed in thought.

Isla made a non-committal sound of agreement. It sounded a bit egotistical to agree, even if she'd worked her backside off to get to that position. Somehow, in this tiny little salon, she felt a bit awkward about flaunting the awards and competition prizes she'd won over the years.

'Well, I was head stylist for a salon in the city centre.' She downplayed it, realizing as she spoke that Shannon had drifted a little closer, sensing there might be gossip, and was now spraying cleaning fluid onto the shelves behind the sinks, wiping down the surfaces, her cloth moving slowly as she flapped in on the conversation.

'It's kind of you to help Jessie out like this.'

Isla could have sworn Mrs Mac cocked an eyebrow at her, but in the second it took to look closely at her expression in the mirror, it was gone.

'Well, I'm between jobs at the moment – I can't start my next one for two months.' Isla snapped the end on another roller, completing a neat row. 'Gardening leave.'

Mrs Mac nodded, saying nothing.

'I've never been a fan of gardening myself,' piped up Jinny, who'd reappeared and was standing, propped against the reception desk, a Spar bag of milk in her hand. 'Too much mess, and all those worms and beasties and God knows what else in the dirt. It's no' natural.' She waggled her pale, skinny fingers in explanation.

'Och, I'm not that much of a fan myself,' smiled Mrs Mac. 'I do like my nice window boxes, mind. But I've a gardening friend who does them for me, fortunately.'

'That's nice,' said Isla, absently.

'She works up at the estate, too.'

'I didn't realize there was a housing estate on the island. It doesn't seem big enough.'

'Not a *housing* estate,' chuckled Mrs Mac. 'Duntarvie Estate – the Maxwells' place.'

Jinny was flicking through a magazine from the rack, forehead creased in a frown, muttering to herself. She stopped, opening up a double-page spread, and thrust it at Shannon. 'Here. You must've seen this? Debbie Anderson married Jack Starr there the other week? It was in *Hello!*'

Isla had spent most of her working life watching her clients sitting, designer clothes protected by a gown, flicking through celebrity-filled glossy magazines. She didn't pay the magazines much attention, only skimming through on a lunch break if she was stuck for something to read – she was generally nose-deep in her latest novel, her childhood reading habit having lasted into adult life. Shannon, roused from her blasé attitude, pressed the open magazine into Isla's hands with an expression of pride. 'Look at that. I bet your hotshot Edinburgh salon never made it into *Hello!* magazine, did it?'

Isla murmured a vague acknowledgement as she looked at the pages, seeing a huge and expensive-looking castle in the background and two fake-tanned, perfectly dressed soap stars beaming out from the photograph. The place wasn't familiar, but the faces were. And, Isla noticed, the hair was expertly styled – they must have brought their own stylist up with them for the event. There was no way that had been done by anyone here in Jessie's place. Unless there was some other salon hidden away – and she definitely hadn't seen any sign of one during her brief exploratory tour of Kilmannan.

'That's Duntarvie House in the photos, look.' The pride in Jinny's voice was unmistakable. 'Imagine our island in *Hello!* magazine. Bruno from the cafe says he had half the cast of *Hormel Heights* in there the next day, picking up bacon rolls before they got the ferry back home. Those of them that didn't get taken off the island in a helicopter, that is.' Her eyes misted over, and she ran a fond finger across the page. 'One day I'm going to live that jet-set life. Get myself a posh salon in Edinburgh. Maybe when you've finished working here, Isla, you could give me a wee job working in your place? I'm a hard worker.'

Isla, who'd so far watched Jinny turn up twenty minutes late, slope off to the shop for chocolate biscuits, and now daydream over *Hello!* magazine, raised an eyebrow in the mirror at Mrs Mac.

'Thanks very much, dear,' Mrs Mac opened her purse, pulling out a ten-pound note. 'Keep the change, get yourself something nice.'

Isla dutifully slotted the money into the till, withdrawing a two-pound coin. It had been a long time since she'd received a tip like that. At Kat Black's salon it was more likely to be tickets to a theatre show, or a day in a spa, or a discreet fifty-pound note handed over with a smile as her client left, delighted with their latest high-fashion style.

The bell jingled as the door slid closed.

'Well, I'm surprised to see you slumming it.' Shannon sat back against the counter, her arms bare, ornately patterned tattoos curling down her toned bicep. 'I didn't think you'd lower yourself to a shampoo and set.'

Isla looked at her with surprise. Shannon appeared to have some pretty entrenched ideas about what she was like, given that she'd only just walked in the door. 'What did you expect?' Her tone was sharp. 'Some of us are here to work.'

Shannon gave a begrudging nod. 'Aye, and I'm glad to see you're more than happy to pull your weight. Making tea and all.'

'That's what I'm here for.'

By the end of the day Isla had done four more shampoo and sets, trimmed three shaggy-ponytailed little girls' fringes, and dealt with the unexpectedly long comb-over of a gnarled old farmer who parked his tractor on the road opposite, lumbered in in work overalls, and demanded 'his usual'.

'I don't know what your usual is,' Isla had explained, trying to be diplomatic.

'Damned if I know,' he'd replied, waving an arm around his head as if he was expecting the answer to suddenly materialize. Shannon and Jinny had been hiding, sniggering, in the corner.

'Let's just give it a bit of a trim all over,' Isla had said, sitting him down in the chair. He'd left quite satisfied, the long strands of hair still balanced across his bald head, and beamed with delight as he paid, explaining as he did so that it was the Young Farmers' ball that evening and he was helping out on the door, so it was a good job he looked sharp.

It had been a long day. Isla, accustomed to long hours on her feet, was surprised by just how tired she was. It was the newness of everything, she told herself – not to mention the incessant questioning of every client, who wanted to know all about her and how she'd ended up here, and how was Pamela's arm doing, and how long would Jessie be away?

'Fancy a quick drink down the Belmont?'

Isla had been wiping over the counter of the reception desk when Jinny's clear voice broke through her thoughts. She carried on, assuming Shannon was going to respond.

'Isla?'

She looked up, surprised. Jinny's expression was kind, and she was talking to her. 'We're going for a quick cider. It's a tradition on a Tuesday. Well, on most days, if I'm honest. If I go home I end up having to help Mum out with dinnertime, and that lot are hard enough work as it is, so it's worth staying out of the way until they've eaten. Anyway, we always need something to look forward to, and Shannon's hoping Rab will be behind the bar, aren't you Shan?'

Shannon looked up, indignant. 'I am not.' She flushed pink, belying her words. 'I told him I wasn't going out, remember?'

'I'll get the drinks. You can hide behind the snooker table. Isla?'

'Thanks, but no, I'm fine.' Isla had made it a rule that she didn't mix work and social life. She'd watched the girls and boys from Kat Black's salon follow the old adage of working hard and playing hard, but she didn't want to appear unprofessional, and she certainly didn't want to give them anything on her. And, God, if her one drunken champagne experience was anything to go by, that had been a sensible decision.

An hour later, she happened to be looking out as Jinny and Shannon emerged from the pub opposite. Sharing a hug and a last joke that set them off giggling, they left for home in opposite directions. Isla, who'd cleaned the kitchen and put a vegetarian lasagne for one in the oven, looked on silently from the window of her borrowed flat. It was best to stick to her no-socializing rule. No matter that it meant she'd only ever gone out once in a blue moon, when Hattie happened to be around to offer her the scraps of friendship she had left over after her packed weekends. Clichéd as it might sound, Isla knew that if she could just reach all her goals, get her life sorted, *then* she'd sort out the social-life side of things.

The school reunion was going to be the start of it. Helen had been messaging her via Facebook, asking what Isla was planning to wear and worrying that she couldn't fit her post-baby tummy into the dress she'd chosen. It was quite nice to have someone to chat with – and it made the idea of the reunion a tiny bit less terrifying. She was going to show everyone what she'd made of her life – 'smelly Isla, Isla-no-clue, Isla-no-mates'. Only then could she prove she'd made it; and then, with that point made, she'd get on with sorting out the rest of her life. It would all fall into place then, she was certain of that. She didn't need Shannon's copy of *The Rules* to work this stuff out.

Part Two

Chapter Seven

Ruth MacArthur might have been eighty, but she wasn't too old to appreciate the new fashion for beards – although, thankfully, they weren't those hairy, scruffy ones that had been around in the sixties and seventies, when everyone looked like they needed a good wash. No, these beards were well trimmed, and looked lovely. And there was no getting away from it: Doctor Lewis was a good-looking man. The mischief-maker in her was tempted to ask the young doctor if she could give his beard a wee pat, just to feel the springy sensation beneath her hands. He wouldn't take it well, though. He'd probably think it was a sign she was losing the plot. Mind you, if she was thirty years younger, she'd . . . Ruth paused for a moment in the doorway of the surgery, rubbing in a squirt of the newly installed antibacterial hand gel. She counted the years in her head. Forty years younger, maybe, she supposed.

It was a bit unfair that the body aged at a completely different rate to the mind. Nobody ever told you that part. They talked about the arthritis, and getting forgetful, and all that nonsense. When she was a wee girl, she'd imagined herself growing up into a tiny, contented little old lady, but it hadn't seemed to work out that way. Just the other day she'd been walking past the window of the pet shop and had caught a glimpse of the reflection of an elderly woman hunched in a raincoat, shopping bag over one arm, head bowed against the spring rain. It had been a moment before she'd realized that the image she was looking at was her own. The change from spry young woman – she'd had a lot of looks in the old days, turning heads at the Winter Gardens dances – to this creaky old shell had apparently happened, somehow, when she wasn't paying attention. It didn't make much sense. She'd walked down to the cottage along the old familiar streets, head full of memories. That afternoon, in her head, she was seventeen and full of energy, slim and bright-eyed, up to mischief. She still didn't feel like a proper grown-up inside.

Back home, Ruth hung up her raincoat on the peg by the front door and slipped off her shoes, easing her feet into slippers with a sigh of comfort. It was good to be home, and a cup of tea was just what she needed.

Waiting for the kettle to boil, she pottered around the sitting room of the cottage, turning on the television in time for the lunchtime news, straightening the neat row of cushions that sat on their points against the back of the sofa. She never sat there, preferring the upright armchair that her grandson had bought for her and carted back over from the specialist shop in Glasgow. She'd protested at the time that she was fine as she was, but she had to admit to herself (if not to him) that it made a huge difference. Getting up and down out of that low sofa had been increasingly difficult, but she could sit quite comfortably in her chair, with Hamish the cat curled up on a cushion on her knee, and watch the world go by outside the window. One of the nicest things about getting old was the absolute delight she now took in a nice sit-down and a cup of tea.

Hearing the kettle click off, she turned back, knocking a picture from the mantelpiece as she did so. Dusting the top of it with the sleeve of her cardigan, she placed it back alongside the collection of others, which jostled for space. A blond toddler grinned out at her, sitting beside a pretty young woman, her hair cut in a punky 1980s style reminiscent of Shannon's newest look. She had an arm slung round the little boy's shoulder and they were holding a melting ice-cream cone each, squinting into the late summer sunshine, sitting on the wall by the river up in Inverness, the castle in the background, the Highland sky a cloudless blue. Ruth closed her eyes for a moment and could hear the gulls circling overhead, the excited chatter of children as they poured off the boat for their holidays, the jangle of the little merry-go-round that was parked beside the bowling green by the promenade. That had been one of their good days. One of the last good days.

The truth was – not that she'd admit as much to any doctor, no matter how charming and attentive he might be, or how handsomely trimmed his beard – her bones complained when she stood up too long, and she often found herself getting breathless and tired, which was immensely frustrating. Of late she'd taken to sitting down, watching more than her fair share of afternoon quiz shows. Her eyes had grown frustratingly misty, making reading – always her first love – difficult, even with the bold large-print books that were available at Kilmannan Library. The idea of having someone poking around doing a cataract operation made her feel queasy. She'd put the appointment off again and again, until they'd stopped writing and calling. Then they'd tried to interest her in audiobooks, but inevitably those lulled her to sleep. She'd wake up hours later, neck stiff from drooping like a sleeping daisy in the armchair by the fireplace, Hamish circling her feet, prowling for dinner. Getting old was – quite literally – a pain in the neck.

Only once she was sitting down in her armchair with Hamish slinking around her legs, his tail a question mark, did Ruth – reluctantly – open her bag and take a look at the information leaflet Doctor Lewis had given her.

'It's just a spot of water retention, isn't it?' It hadn't really been a question, more of a statement.

Doctor Lewis had rubbed his dark beard, twisting round in his chair to look Ruth straight in the eye. She had noticed the dark shadows under his eyes. The surgery hours were long, and they were under pressure to perform in difficult conditions, the target-driven structure not fitting well with an island still set in the ways of its past. The islanders were used to the personal care of an old-fashioned GP and a village hospital, and the current government structures didn't leave much room for flexibility.

'I'm afraid it's not that straightforward, Mrs Mac-Arthur.'

Ruth took a breath in, straightening her shoulders, preparing herself.

'The blood tests we took show elevated levels of something called BNP in your blood.'

'I don't think so,' she snorted. 'I'm a card-carrying member of the Labour party.'

Doctor Lewis smiled, a smile that suggested it wasn't the first time he'd heard that particular joke. He gave a slight nod of acknowledgement, but pressed on. Ruth felt her shoulders sag slightly.

'Politics notwithstanding, these levels, together with the other symptoms you've been showing, suggest that we are looking at a bit of a problem with your heart.'

She was eighty years old. She'd kept an eye on her figure all her life, walked everywhere she could, switched from butter to margarine when they said that was the thing to do, and back to butter again when they changed their minds. She'd eaten home-cooked meals and didn't drink (well, besides a wee glass of cream sherry once in a while, and at her age she deserved a treat with *Coronation Street*). She hadn't so much as touched a cigarette in her life. It was a ridiculous notion to suggest there was anything wrong with her besides a bit of—

'There's medication you can take that will help a bit, and it's a matter of re-education. Take things a bit more slowly, don't overstretch yourself, that sort of thing.'

'You'll be telling me I'm to give up all the foods that are worth eating next.' She could hear the asperity in her voice.

'No, everything in moderation, that's the key.' He smiled at her reassuringly, pulling a sheaf of papers from a drawer in his desk. 'I'd like you in tomorrow morning for a quick test called an echocardiogram, just to confirm that my suspicions are correct.'

'You're not covering me with electrodes and wiring me up to some machine.'

'Just for five minutes or so. It won't hurt.'

Ruth tutted. 'I'm helping with the teas at the community centre tomorrow morning.'

'Five minutes.' His voice was firm. 'Let's get this sorted out, and we can work out what we're going to do from here. There's a support group that meets once a week in the library, I could give you the—'

'A group of old people grumbling about their ailments? I don't think so.'

She could just imagine it. No, she wasn't having any of that nonsense. She had a wee bit of swelling round her ankles, and she'd been a bit tired and achy of late. But who wasn't, after eighty years of walking around?

'I'll give you the details tomorrow, in any case.'

Turning back to the desk, he quickly tapped some information into his computer. Without looking up, he added, 'And for the record, it might be an idea for you to stop helping out with the teas, and start sitting down and enjoying one yourself.'

'Pfft.' Ruth gave a snort of disapproval. 'I'm not headed for the knackers' yard yet.'

He looked up, giving her a brief smile.

'Right, well, if that's us, I'll be away then.'

'And you'll be back in the morning.' His tone was warning. He scrolled down the screen, pointing to a calendar page. 'There. I've put you in myself, for half past nine. No excuses.'

'What if I decide I'd rather get my hair done?' She was teasing him now.

'I'll be at the salon in person to pull you straight up here. Don't make me come down there, you hear me?'

'As if I would.' Chuckling to herself, Ruth had headed out of the consulting room.

Chapter Eight

Isla had always thought being woken by silence was something that only happened in books. But as she lay in bed there was nothing – absolutely nothing – outside. The absence of cars and buses thundering past, the hum of people and noise and clattering and chatter that wove together to make the fabric of city life – none of it was there. The silence was huge. It was unnerving.

She climbed out from under the duvet and pushed open the window, still waiting for the familiar sounds to fill the room. She'd always loved early-morning Edinburgh, before anyone else was up, but the city streets were never silent. Right now, back in the New Town, the road sweeper would be chugging by, the air brakes of early morning buses hissing in the emptiness.

But here, there was nothing. Over a plate-glass sea a haze of low cloud – or was it mist? – rose to a pale blue sky smudged with thin wisps of cloud. The sunrise was beautiful, Isla admitted to herself. As she stood watching, she realized that where her ears would have been filled with the sounds of the city coming to life, here morning was announced with birdsong. It started with one melody that Isla had to strain to pick up; then there was another. Somewhere in the distance – it sounded like miles away – she could hear a dog bark. And there was the familiar call of the gulls, too, just like home. Before long the noise was deafening, the air filled with birdsong.

And then the boat came into view. The hum of the engine came to her on the wind as she watched it slide across the water towards the mainland. Isla checked her watch – six o'clock. It must be going over to collect the first passengers. The first ferry over wasn't scheduled until 6.45 a.m. – she'd checked last night when, filled with dread, she'd seen the harbour gate locked down for the evening and the ticket office closed.

Isla sat, chin on her hands, watching the boat as it slipped across the water until it curved around the headland and out of sight. If she'd been on holiday here, she admitted to herself grudgingly, she might have quite liked the peace and quiet.

Later on, another day at the salon negotiated without disaster – apart from Jinny turning up late again, explaining that her brother Mikey had refused to walk to school and lain down on the pavement, where he'd waited for ten minutes before getting up and trotting off quite cheerfully – Isla tucked her house key into her armband and set off running, down the narrow lane that led towards the ferry landing. Turning left, she glanced down at her watch. Six-thirty in the evening, and the sky was still bright blue, cloudless, seagulls whirling overhead. She ran on along the seafront road, past storm-weathered Victorian hotels and boarded-up shops. This place had nothing going for it, as far as she could see. Casting a dismissive glance over her shoulder as she turned right down the fork in the road towards the little village of Port Strachan, she pushed herself harder, the sound of her breath thrumming in her ears as she ran on. The rocky outcrops jutting out from the shoreline glowed in the evening sunlight. The road curved round, revealing the colourful houses of the little fishing village three miles from the main town. Port Strachan actually looked quite nice. Nice in a holiday postcard sort of way, Isla thought, but living here full-time must be the most mind-numbing thing on earth. She was still smarting from the thought that following her run there was no chance of popping into Yo! Sushi for something quick for dinner.

Solid grey houses sat back from the roadside, secure behind sturdy stone walls. The gardens were neatly kept, many of them with hoardings outside advertising themselves as 'B&B' or 'Guesthouse (rooms to let)'. Isla kept on running as the road curved round and the metal railings alongside the pavement stopped, until she was running beside the beach, which was strewn with seaweed-covered rocks freckled with limpets and tiny barnacles. She'd settled into a rhythm now, and her arms and legs were pumping along in time to the insistent beat of the music blasting in her ears. She couldn't hear the sea, or the gulls that swooped overhead. The music was loud enough to block out everything.

Isla didn't want to think about the fact that the disturbing sensation she'd felt, watching the girls from the salon as they joked and teased their way out of the door at the end of the day, was loneliness. It wasn't something she allowed herself to feel. Years of training at school, where the only way to survive was to create an impenetrable shell, had been the answer.

It was going to have to hold her together here, too. There was something strange about this place. Everywhere she went, there was a feeling that everyone was talking about her behind her back, that the whole island knew exactly who she was and why she was there. It was unnerving, and she didn't like it one bit. She'd gone into the bakery that morning, thinking she'd have a coffee and a sandwich as an early lunch break. The lunch itself had been surprisingly nice, but the feeling of sitting, awkwardly, eating her lunch whilst pretending to read her magazine as the girl behind the counter looked at her, had been uncomfortable. A man had come in then and sat down at the table across from her, spreading himself into the space, filling the whole room. Legs akimbo, sitting back against the wall, he'd sat waiting for his coffee, checking his phone.

'A'right James?'

'Aye.'

A younger man had come in, hooking his dog to the post outside. He'd picked up a pre-ordered roll for his lunch and stepped back outside, tapping his forehead with a finger in a salute: 'James, how you doing?'

'No' bad, herself?'

This had gone on and on. Everyone who walked in through the door knew this mythical James, or knew his wife, or – it was suffocating.

She upped her speed, pushing herself harder, faster. She could feel her calf muscles aching as she pounded forwards, making a split-second decision to fork left, up a narrow single-track road. The incline was punishingly steep but she forced herself to maintain the pace, heart thudding against her ribcage. When she reached the top, she'd stop.

There was no space to think about anything. Everything was white with effort and pain, and then with a gasp, slowing down gradually as she crested the hill, she began to catch her breath, bending double, hands on hips, breathing through the stitch that had been niggling her the whole way.

'*Shit!*'

There was a screech of cycle brakes, and a crash. Isla threw herself sideways on instinct and therefore missed being taken out completely by a lunatic cyclist, who had lurched off his bike and now lay flat on his back, hands gingerly checking his ribs for breakages. His bike lay across the middle of the road, the front wheel spinning. The back wheel, however, was a different matter.

'My bloody wheel. Bollocks.' Pushing his helmet off

his nose, the cyclist looked up at Isla from his prone position. He gave a broad, slightly dazed smile.

'Are you – OK?' She wondered if he might be concussed, or something. It wasn't normal to be grinning like that when you'd just gone flying through the air on a bike.

'Yep.' He pushed himself up with his hands. 'Yeah – *ow.*' He gasped, before continuing, 'Fine.'

Isla recoiled slightly, feeling awkward. She reached out a cautious hand, hoping that he wouldn't take it. His hands were filthy, his face spattered with mud. He took her hand with another smile and hoisted himself up with his own weight. Isla let go and stepped backwards.

The cyclist wiped a sleeve across his face, revealing a deep, outdoorsy tan (which, Isla couldn't help thinking, looked like he hadn't set eyes on anything with a sun protection factor for at least a decade) and blue eyes beneath fair, extremely muddy brows.

'I know you, don't I?' He narrowed his eyes for a moment, frowning.

'I doubt it.' Isla shook her head.

He cocked his head to one side, looking thoughtful. 'Yes, I do. I do. You're Recycling Girl.'

Isla raised her eyebrows. 'I think you're confusing me with someone else.'

'Nope. I never forget a face. Well, only if I've had a few, but let's face it, we're all guilty of that, aren't we?'

He gave her a rueful smile, one that clearly expected something in return. This guy was well aware of his good looks. He had a cockiness that Isla recognized. Hours of people-watching at work had taught her the art of reading people – not just through their words, but through their manner. And this one was sizing her up, working out his next line. Even covered from head to toe in mud, she had to grudgingly admit he was pretty handsome in a slightly pleased-with-himself, Ewan-McGregor, rugged sort of way. And he knew it. He smiled at her, and went on, 'You're looking after Jessie Main's place whilst her daughter is sick, aren't you?'

Isla made a vague noise of acknowledgement, shifting from foot to foot in her running shoes. She was starting to get cold, standing here like this after running up the hill so fast, and if he was OK, she was just going to . . .

'Yeah . . . you're the recycling criminal. Didn't recognize you for a second, without your six-inch heels on. We take that stuff very seriously around here, y'know.' His teasing tone belied his words. He gave a groan, rubbing his side. 'Ow. I think I might've bust a rib.'

Isla looked at the bike. It was unrideable, even if he had been up to cycling home.

'Do you want me to call a –' She began untangling her phone from the armband and headphone wires.

'No reception this part of the island. Well, at a push you might get one bar with a following wind.' He moved in slightly closer, looking down at the screen. 'Nope, as I thought.'

Isla tried to disguise the irritation in her voice. 'Would

you like me to push the bike back for you? Can you walk?'

He shook one muddy leg, then the other. He was obviously pretty fit – beneath a down of fair hair, muscles stood out tautly. 'Yeah, they're both working well enough. If you wouldn't mind, I'd really appreciate it.'

'It's fine.'

He gave a half-smile. 'You do a pretty good impression of not fine, for someone who's OK with it.' He reached out his hand again. 'Finn MacArthur.'

'Hello,' said Isla, unnecessarily. She shook his hand awkwardly and reached for the bicycle, pulling it into an upright position. At least it was still capable of being wheeled, even if it was a bit wonky. 'You ready?'

Finn nodded, and together, slowly, they headed down the hill.

'So, Jessie's place.'

Finn was holding his arm across his torso now, clearly in some discomfort. Chatting would at least take his mind off it for now.

'Yes.' Isla could make polite conversation with anyone who walked through the door of a salon. As soon as she stepped over the doorstep and into the room, she was on duty. It was a perfect performance. Elderly women were charmed by her interest in their pets, young girls by her impressive knowledge of the latest music and YouTube videos. But outside, she wasn't ready for conversation. She fished around, trying to think of something to say. There was something about the way this Finn looked at her, his blue eyes penetrating, that was slightly unnerving. 'It's a bit – different to my last salon.'

'That doesn't come as a huge surprise.' Finn laughed. 'Jessie's lovely, but that place is like something from 1967. Mind you, you'll have noticed half this place is preserved in aspic. Have you seen the shop with the yellow plastic in the windows?'

Isla laughed. 'I think that place was here when I last visited fourteen years ago.'

'It's been there since I was at school, and I'm pushing thirty-five.'

He looked sideways at Isla again as they walked. 'So, you can't be planning on hanging around here for long?'

'Six weeks and three days.' Isla said aloud the words she'd been chanting in her head all day.

'Not that you're counting.' Finn was amused.

'Well, this place isn't really my sort of thing. I'm not exactly an island person. Too much countryside, not enough – well, not enough anything.'

Finn gave a scoffing noise, laughing. 'Not enough anything?'

'I was at the little corner shop after I finished work this evening and two American tourists came in, asking where the nearest shopping mall was. I felt as sorry for myself as for them when the woman behind the counter said "one hour and a boat ride" in response.'

'Oh come on,' Finn looked at her, disbelieving. 'You're not serious.'

Isla raised an eyebrow. 'Deadly.'

He shook his head, laughing again. 'Well, I reckon we're going to have to do a bit of work to persuade you this place isn't all bad, then, eh?'

Isla snorted. 'You'll have a hard job. I like to be within striking distance of a Pret a Manger at all times. The nearest thing I've found to that is a bacon roll from the bakery.'

They were passing through the little fishing village Isla had run through earlier. The journey back seemed much further when walking slowly with a squeaking bike.

'Give it a chance. It's not for everyone, but I reckon it might grow on you.'

'Mmm.' Isla nodded non-committally.

'This is me, here.' Finn lifted an arm to point, wincing again as he did so.

On the opposite side of the road, looking out across the water to the distant hills of the peninsula that reached out from the mainland, was a stone-built villa with a neatly kept garden outside, the gate flanked by two pots full of pansies.

'You're a bit of a gardener?'

Finn followed her gaze, realizing with a laugh what she was seeing. 'God, no, that's Ethel, my downstairs neighbour. I live in the flat upstairs. I can't keep weeds alive.'

Isla checked both ways (thinking, as she did so, that she hadn't seen a single car pass by in the whole time she'd been out running) and wheeled the bike across the road.

'Just stick it in the close there, I'll give it a look tomorrow when I'm feeling better.'

Isla looked at him dubiously. If his rib was broken, he'd be in no state to fix anything for a good long while, and definitely not tomorrow.

'I'll wheel it round out of sight, shall I? You don't want it getting stolen.'

'Round here?' Finn called after her as she propped it against the side wall of a wooden shed in the garden. 'Who'd nick a bike? They wouldn't get it off the boat, and if they started riding it round the place, word would be back to me in five minutes flat. This place is like that.'

'Fair enough.' Isla, who'd spent the morning listening to her customers gossiping over the latest goings-on 'up at the big house', could believe it.

'Thanks for helping me back with it.' Finn gave her another smile, looking directly into her eyes. His looked tight with pain, she noticed, but he hadn't lost his manners.

'You're welcome.' Isla turned to leave.

'One thing.'

She spun round, looking at him standing on the path, filthy.

'You didn't tell me your name.'

'I thought you island people knew everything about everyone.' Surprising herself, Isla turned on her heel and walked away. Once she was out of sight, she found herself grinning at her comeback.

Chapter Nine

Ruth had woken – as seemed to be routine, these days – at half past four in the morning. She'd shrugged her cosy pink quilted dressing gown around her shoulders, slipped her feet into furry slippers, and made herself a cup of tea. Hamish, after a quick pop outside, was more than happy to make his way back inside and join her in bed, where she'd sat listening to the early-morning radio.

Sitting, propped up by pillows, she thought back to her appointment with Doctor Lewis yesterday morning.

'Now, Ruth, you can't argue with technology.' He'd turned the screen around, showing her what he could see.

It wasn't anything she didn't already suspect. Sometimes, doctors just took the mystery out of life. She sighed.

'Right, well, we can have a chat about lifestyle adjustments, and what we can do to make things easier. There's medication, and –' he paused.

Ruth leaned forward, placing a hand carefully on his

desk as if for emphasis. Everything on there seemed to be sponsored by some drug manufacturer or another. No wonder they were so keen to shove as many pills down your throat as they could.

'I'm not rattling around with a pillbox like some hypochondriac.'

Doctor Lewis shook his head slowly. 'Nobody is suggesting you should.'

'Right, well, that's a start.' Ruth gave a nod of satisfaction. She inhaled slowly, taking a moment to think. This place smelt like hospitals and cleaning fluid and plastic and – she didn't want to end up stuck in a bed in some geriatric ward.

'I don't want you saying a *word* to anyone about this.' A finger lifted in warning.

'Of course not.' Doctor Lewis widened his eyes. 'I can't discuss your condition with anyone unless you give me explicit permission.' He paused for a moment, raising his glance skyward, rubbing his temples. 'However, it might help if we could perhaps share the care plan with a family member, let them know what medication you're supposed to be taking, that sort of thing. We find it often helps if you're—'

Ruth pursed her lips, and fixed him with the same steely glare that her late husband had always referred to as her no-messing-about look.

'It's my heart that's failing, not my mind,' she'd said, crisply. Taking her walking stick and the prescription slip he'd printed, she'd made her way out of the consulting room with her head held high.

Later that afternoon, Ruth balanced her new iPad on the mantelpiece, wedging it in place with the doorstop in case it fell off. She'd been given it as a present, but it was still a bit of a mystery to her. She could watch the news on television, and she far preferred to read from a newspaper than from an ever-scrolling, lights flashing, high-tech thing, no matter what the rest of the world thought. There was something quite comforting in deciding that she was too old for this nonsense.

But it was lovely to be able to chat to Shona, and see her face. She still couldn't understand how video calls worked, but it was such a change from the years when calling her daughter in Melbourne had meant sky-high phone bills and conversations peppered with delays. Instead she just arranged a time (she was fairly impressed with herself for getting the hang of this Skype messaging lark, proving there was life in the old dog yet) and waited for the familiar ringing tone to begin – and there would be the face she loved, and hadn't seen in real life for just over ten years.

'Mum. How are you?'

Och. The only trouble with this Skype business was seeing her own wrinkly old face looking back at her from the screen.

'Hang on a wee second, my dear.' Ruth pulled her chair a bit closer to the mantelpiece, then took a left-over birthday card and stuck it in front of the corner of the screen where the little box with her face in it sat.

'That's better. I can't concentrate on talking to you when I can see my own face rabbiting away nonsense in one corner.'

'Fair enough,' Shona laughed, eyes crinkling up at the sides in suntanned, well-worn laughter lines. It was hard to believe her little girl was fifty-three this year – but the evidence stood before her. Shona had a fair few wrinkles of her own, but she was just as beautiful as ever, her high cheekbones and fair hair highlighted by the morning winter sun that shone in through the kitchen of her suburban house.

'How are you keeping, Mum? Taking those supplements I ordered you?' There was a distinct Aussie twang to Shona's accent now, not that she'd admit it.

'Och, yes,' lied Ruth. Shona, a health-food nut, had made an online order for some kind of wheatgrass and vitamin concoction that Ruth was supposed to take twice a day. The supplements arrived in the post, the size of horse tablets and probably far less palatable.

'Great. And you're getting out and about? I see you've been to the hairdresser?'

'Aye. In fact I had it done by a top stylist, nonetheless.' She gave her hair a pat. 'Jessie Main's daughter broke her arm, and her niece is watching the place whilst she's away looking after the bairns.'

'She's done a good job. You're looking gorgeous.'

'It was very swish. I got a head massage, too. She's a

lovely girl – quiet, nothing like her Aunty Jessie – not that you'll know her, do you? Anyway, you'll need to give her a try if she's still here when you come over.'

Shona's face was wreathed in smiles. 'I can't wait. I can't wait to give you a great big cuddle and soak up the island and –' she paused for a second, her expression clouding – 'and – how's the boy?'

Ruth gave a slow nod. 'He's doing fine. Looking forward to seeing you when you come over.'

If Shona knew Ruth was lying, Ruth reflected later, she did a good job of hiding it. They'd chatted about Shona's plans to fly over to Scotland that summer, about the Australian grandchildren who were off out playing tennis and riding their bikes, and who had no time to talk to a grandma who was not much more than a name on a birthday card and a half-remembered face on a Skype screen to them. They had an Aussie life – their own Aussie granny, who was there every weekend and looked after them whilst their mum worked hard running her business. And now, at last, after a tough time when the business she'd set up had gone under in the recession, and things had been hard, Shona had enough money to fly home and visit for the first time in years. Ruth couldn't wait to see her, hold her, and – she closed her eyes, thinking about it and sending out a silent wish – maybe, just maybe, mend some fences.

Chapter Ten

'Lucien, darling, could you get down from the window ledge, please?'

Isla could feel her shoulders seizing up more tightly with every passing second. After two days off work during which she'd found the tiny flat both lonely and claustrophobia-inducing, she was in desperate need of an aromatherapy massage, a hot bath, and some time alone with a book. The bad news was, she was only dealing with the first client of the day. Lily had arrived this morning in a whirl of expensive essential oil scent, drifting along in a pair of wide-legged, clearly extremely expensive linen trousers. Her toenails were painted aquamarine and she wore Birkenstock sandals. Jinny had wrapped her in a gown, protecting the long, gauzy white shirt that trailed almost to her knees.

'Cup of tea?' Shannon called from the back room, where she was waiting for the kettle – now filled from the recently repaired tap, and not from the hair-washing sink – to boil.

Isla shot her a warning glance. She'd tried – thinking

it was best to start as she meant to go on – to instil a sense of decorum in the salon, pointing out that it would be lovely if clients could feel that their visit was a little oasis of calm in their day. Shannon, pulling out her gum and tossing it in the bin (her concession to sophistication), had raised a sardonic eyebrow.

'Reckon if anyone's gasping for a cup of tea, they wouldn't care less whether I shout it from the back room, or hold up a sign with six-inch letters,' she'd replied. To give her her due, Isla thought, as she stood waiting for Jinny to finish shampooing, Shannon was trying to remember. And half the time she did. The rest of the time, though, the clients were jarred out of their relaxing head massage (Jinny, who was a real sponge for anything new, had loved learning how to do that, and had turned out to have a really good feel for it, which pleased Isla) by a fishwife screech over the sound of the bubbling kettle.

'I don't suppose you have peppermint?'

'Oh aye, we've got all kinds of fancy stuff now.' Shannon turned back to attend to the drinks, flashing a cheeky smile at Isla, who raised her eyebrows reprovingly in response. Shannon had beetled off to the supermarket to buy a range of herbal teas, and between waves of her natural cynicism, seemed to be embracing the salon's move into the twenty-first century. And it seemed they were bringing in some new clients: this one had wafted in without an appointment, a wicker shopping basket under one arm, long hair knotted back with a clasp.

'All right, Lily, if you could just come over here, we'll

get started.' Isla smiled at her, taking her elbow as Jinny stepped back, having wrapped the towel carefully around Lily's head, turban-style. In the waiting area Lily's small, sturdy-legged son had retreated from the windowsill and was drawing peacefully in a colouring book, a box of crayons in one hand.

'Lucien, sweetheart?' He carried on scribbling, completely ignoring his mother. 'Mummy is going to have a quick haircut now. And then we're going to go to Little Acorns for playtime.'

Lucien looked up briefly, catching Isla's eye. Was that a hint of a smirk at the corner of his mouth?

'I really just want the *tiniest* of trims. Just the ends off.'

Isla held back a sigh. In the last few days she'd done so many blue rinses, set so many 'this'll do me over the weekend' hairdos, trimmed countless fringes for grubby straight-out-of-school children, their harassed mothers juggling prams and baby carriers, piles of school book-bags lying on the floor creating a health and safety hazard that made Isla twitchy with discomfort. And now – another quick trim. At this rate she was going to forget everything she'd ever learned – or become a world expert in old-lady hair.

Isla had just begun combing through Lily's shoulder-length hair when she felt something hitting her leg. She turned round in surprise.

'*Hyahhhhh!*' yelled Lucien, thwacking her again with the cardboard tubing from the rack of hair products by the front door.

'Lucien, sweetheart,' said Lily, in a placatory tone. 'We don't hit. Weapons are destructive and damaging. You remember what Mummy told you this morning after we had our quiet time in the relaxation room?'

'Ow!' Isla's leg buckled as he hit her squarely behind the knee.

Shannon, who had finished making the tea at last, appeared, a cup and saucer on the tray with a small wrapped biscuit on the side.

'All right, wee man,' she said, grinning at Lucien. 'You want a biscuit?'

Lily whirled round in her chair so the strands of hair that Isla had just begun combing neatly into place, ready to trim, flew wetly around her shoulders.

'Yes,' said Lucien, reaching out with one pudgy hand, wiping a green blob of snot from nose to sleeve with the other.

'No,' said Lily, simultaneously. 'Lucien, sweetie, you know we don't have refined sugar. Just a moment.' She stood up, leaving Isla standing behind an empty chair, scissors in hand, and headed for her huge, expensive-looking handbag. She pulled out a brown paper bag and handed it to Lucien, who took it sullenly, still looking longingly at the plastic-wrapped biscuit in Shannon's hand.

'You sit over there and eat your rice cakes, and see if you can make a picture for Lizzy at nursery.'

Isla began combing through Lily's hair again. It was fine, and there were several knots – the sea wind had a habit of whipping hair up in the air and tangling it. She'd recommend a leave-in conditioner to Lily when the cut was completed.

'So are you on holiday here?' Isla realized as she asked that if the demon child was attending nursery, that was pretty unlikely.

'Me?' Lily laughed. 'No, I've lived here for a few months. We've taken over Meadowview House.'

Jinny, eavesdropping, sidled a little closer. '*You're* the one doing the meditation retreat thingy.' She stood coiling the flex of a pair of straighteners around her hand, looking thoughtful. 'You don't look like a hippy. I kind of thought you'd be dirtier.'

Isla flashed her a warning look. 'Jinny!'

'Soz.' Jinny gave a cheeky grin. 'Y'know what I mean though, eh?'

'I think it's possible to embrace a holistic lifestyle and still keep in touch with a modern style,' said Lily, unruffled and apparently completely devoid of any sense of irony.

'Aye, but I thought you were all naked dancing round trees, and that.'

Isla felt Lily shift slightly in her chair.

In an attempt to get her out of the way, Isla said, 'Jinny, could you just get me the spray-on conditioner, please?'

'There's some there.' Jinny, implacable, pointed to a bottle on the shelf, just out of Isla's reach. Was she being deliberately obtuse?

'A new one.' Isla gritted her teeth.

'Shannon only opened that one yesterday.'

Isla fixed Jinny with an unmistakable glare. Jinny uttered a little squeak of recognition and scuttled away, realizing she was being dismissed.

'I'm quite into all that spirituality stuff myself.' Shannon, who'd remained silent until now, ripped open the biscuit wrapper and ate it, sitting behind the counter of the reception desk. Opposite her in the little waiting area, feet up on the chair, Lucien looked at her with undisguised loathing, his currant eyes narrowed in his pale, round face. He bit into one of the rice cakes, chewed a mouthful, then spat it onto the floor.

''Gusting.'

'Ugh!' Jinny exclaimed.

'You're not in the mood for rice cakes, Lucien?' Lily turned back towards her son, whipping her hair out of the way once again. Isla inhaled quietly, gritting her teeth. The customer is always right, she reminded herself for the thousandth time in her career. She smiled tightly at Lily's reflection. Jinny giggled.

'Lucien is *very* mature for his age. He's got a very sensitive palate. *Loves* olives, don't you my darling?'

'Yuck.' Lucien poked at his teeth, pulling out another piece of rice cake, before smearing his wet finger onto the fabric of the chair. Isla watched Jinny mouthing *gross* at Shannon, unseen by his loving mother.

'So, are you offering residential retreats?' Isla worked carefully through another tangle.

'Yes. We're going to be offering everything from shamanistic drumming through to yoga meditation weeks, as well as primal femininity gatherings where we'll be making offerings for the red tent. We've got several residents already. They're on a longer-term stay basis, doing some wonderfully creative work with the trees.'

'Sounds wonderful.' Isla kept her expression neutral. She wasn't quite sure what a primal femininity gathering was, but if it was anything like the coven of witches who used to hang out in the school toilets at break time, she didn't want to know. Groups of women still made her uneasy. When she was back in Edinburgh, she'd always escape at lunchtime to the bookshop cafe round the corner from Kat's salon and sit there for an hour in blissful silence, uninterrupted by anyone. But the difference then, she now realized, was that she'd had familiar surroundings around her. The streets and the beautiful buildings of Edinburgh had been like kindly old friends, ones she'd known since childhood. With so much time alone in the holidays when she was growing up, she'd spent long hours riding around town on buses, exploring all the hidden delights of the city, sitting by the Water of Leith eating an ice pop and watching the river. Her dad would have gone spare if he'd known. But now she was here on the island, and the whole place was like a new and unfamiliar haircut. The streets didn't fit right, everyone seemed to know everyone else, and she felt horribly conspicuous.

There was a screech of metal on flooring as Lucien

somehow managed to slide between the two waiting chairs, plopping onto the ground with a squawk of surprise.

'I wonder if perhaps we could pop Lucien up here on the chair beside me?' Lily motioned to the empty seat beside her where Shannon's cutting kit sat in the trolley, waiting for her 11 a.m. client.

'Go for it,' said Shannon, pulling back the chair. 'On you go, wee man. I'm away to post that package for my mum, Isla, OK?'

Shannon grabbed her purse and ducked out of the door before Isla had time to respond.

Lucien skidded across the floor in his socks (Isla was almost certain he'd had shoes on when he came in) and leaped into the chair, which hurtled along the wall, crashing into the hair-colour display rack and knocking down a pile of boxes.

'Destruction Powers: Activate!' he roared at the top of his voice.

'He's in a very *physical* phase of his development,' Lily explained, smiling beatifically at Isla in the mirror. Lucien jumped down from the chair and began wheeling it back and forth across the floor, making motorbike noises. He scratched his head, then started removing Shannon's neatly stacked rollers from the trolley, loading them onto the chair and whirling it round so they flew off, centrifuge style, landing on the floor. Shannon was going to go mad. Jinny was scooping them up as quickly as he fired them across the salon.

'Would you like me to cut in some layers, Lily, or are you just looking for a blunt trim?' Isla kept her voice neutral. The sooner they got Lucifer the demon child out of the salon, the better.

'Just a blunt trim should be fine.'

Isla began combing again.

'I think I may have a bit of a problem with a sensitive scalp,' Lily said, as Isla used a Tangle Teezer brush to try and fight her way through a knot that was as tight as a dreadlock.

'Really?' Isla carried on brushing.

'*Terribly* itchy in the evenings.'

Isla felt her blood run cold. She slowed down her combing, looking down at Lily's hair for a moment, trying not to make her sudden suspicion apparent.

'Really?'

'God, yes. I've tried eucalyptus oil and bathing my hair in cider vinegar – I read in *Holistic Health* magazine that was supposed to help – but it's just getting worse. What do you think of this "no poo" idea, where you don't wash your hair at all?'

'Poo!' shouted Lucien, delightedly. 'Arse bum willy big fat POO.'

'That's not outside language, darling, now, is it?' said Lily, smiling benignly at her demon child, who was now wearing three of Shannon's crocodile clips as hair decorations.

'But *you* say fuckybloodybloody when you're angry.' Lucien looked at her challengingly.

The child was possessed. And what was worse, he was probably infested.

'I'm just going to –' Isla hurried into the back room, where she searched through Aunt Jessie's box of supplies. There was bound to be one in there, in the – *there* it was.

'Is that a special sort of hairdresser's brush?' Lucien looked at Isla with interest as she returned, holding the tiny fine-toothed metal comb tucked discreetly in her palm.

'Something like that,' said Jinny, who'd already worked out what was going on. Isla watched as Jinny sidestepped across to the front door, casually flipping over the 'WE ARE OPEN!' sign to 'SORRY! WE'RE CLOSED'.

Isla ran the comb through one lock of Lily's hair and flinched slightly.

'Lily, I'm *awfully* sorry –' her dad always said she got posh when she was embarrassed – 'but I'm afraid we're going to have to stop here for now.'

'Oh dear,' Lily's face fell. She lowered her voice. 'I know L-u-c-i-e—'

Isla interrupted her. 'No, it's not Lucien at all – he's absolutely fine.' Jinny's eyebrows shot into her hairline. OK, he was anything but fine. He was clearly left over from a remake of *The Exorcist* but, thank God, he wasn't her responsibility.

'But I'm afraid you've caught a little case of – your head's itchy because—'

There was a crash as Shannon shouldered her way in

through the door with a crate of cans of Irn Bru. 'Special offer in the Co-op. There wernae many left, so I thought I'd get one whilst I was passing the Post Office.'

Which is on the opposite side of town, thought Isla, inconsequentially.

'Why're we shut?' With a shift of her head, Shannon indicated the sign on the door. In the same moment she caught sight of the comb in Isla's hand, and of Lucien, who had a finger up one nostril and was now scratching at the crown of his head, furiously.

'Jesus. No' the nit invasion?'

Lily jumped up from her chair in horror. 'Head lice?' She pulled the towel and gown off, throwing them across the floor as if they were infectious. 'Oh God, no.'

'It's very easy to eliminate them,' said Isla, trying to regain control of the situation. 'If you just pop into the chemist, they'll have metal combs just like this one. Lots of conditioner, and comb through your hair daily, and you'll be fine in no time.'

Lily shuddered. *'Ugh.'*

'They're actually quite interesting, if you study them in detail,' began Jinny. 'Their life cycle is amazing. You know, it only takes three weeks for two head lice to make enough eggs to completely colonize your hair.'

Lily looked at Isla, an alarmed expression on her face.

'Don't worry,' continued Jinny, cheerfully. 'It's extremely unlikely you could die from a head lice infestation, because you'd have been so itchy first that you'd have discovered them, so you don't—'

'As I said,' Isla cut in, shooting Jinny a look, 'comb, conditioner, let's give it two weeks to be sure, and then you can pop back and we can sort you out.'

'Have I got mice in my head?' Lucien patted his thatch of dark hair.

'Not quite, my angel.' Lily picked up her bag. 'How much do I owe you?'

Isla shook her head. 'Nothing at all. Sorry for the inconvenience.'

She locked the door behind them as they left. 'Right, you two: you know the drill, I expect?'

Jinny gave a gusting sigh of exasperation. 'Oh, yes, we ken the drill.'

Shannon put the kettle on again.

'We don't need boiling water yet, Shannon – we need the disinfectant solution first. Let's get this stuff cleaned. We're going to have to do the entire contents of these trolleys and bleach the floor.'

'Aye, I know that.' Shannon reached into the cupboard, pulling out three fresh mugs. 'I'm no' doing anything until we've had a cup of coffee. After surviving the demon child we deserve it.'

Isla laughed, surprising herself. 'You've got a point. Don't suppose you picked up any biscuits at the shop?'

It was funny, Isla thought, that something like this, which would have utterly horrified Kat Black – who had a 'strictly no children' policy for just that reason – actually made work quite fun. The girls laughed and joked together as they cleaned up the salon, and somehow, Isla found herself drawn into it.

The date was emblazoned on the clock above the counter. *Not that long to go*, she chanted to herself again. She wasn't here to make friends with anyone, she was just here to do a job, get herself through the gardening leave, and meanwhile – she'd really better think about looking for something else. Maura, the one stylist she'd liked at Kat's place, had moved to run a beauty salon in Edinburgh's West End. They weren't the best of friends – Isla didn't really do best friends, after all – but it was worth a try. She'd give Maura a shout via Facebook when she got back to the flat.

She'd realized that no matter how hard she wished, an M&S wasn't going to pop up on the disused piece of land behind the hoardings by the dilapidated old church. And whilst the cafe – she grudgingly admitted – did a pretty good flat white and a goat's cheese panini that would put an Edinburgh cafe to shame (and for half the price), it still wasn't the same. But she could certainly handle another few weeks – unless, God forbid, Pamela fell over and broke her other wrist. Frankly, if she did, Jessie would be on her own. This place was manageable when the end was in sight, but eight full weeks was enough for any sane person to spend here.

Keeping her head down, eyes set firmly on the pavement to avoid getting into conversation with anyone, Isla slipped out of the side door beside the salon entrance and got into the car. The supermarket was walking distance away, really, but she was planning to take a drive round the island on the way back to charge up the car battery – it had been sitting all week outside the shop, flanked occasionally by small curious children who would edge up to it, stroke the glossy bonnet and hurtle off at speed when Isla gave them The Look. Years of growing up on the estate had perfected that look, and it worked every time.

'Morning, lassie.' An old man nodded to her as she pulled out a trolley. Isla smiled vaguely in reply. If she'd thought about it, she would have brought headphones – that way she could have kept herself a step removed. As it was, she focused hard on the products on the shelves, hoping not to draw attention to herself. But as she made her way through the shop she felt glaringly conspicuous – everyone seemed to know everyone wherever she went, and the whole place was so bloody claustrophobia-inducing. She kept picking up snippets of conversation as she shopped.

'And I said to him . . .'

'You know Jennie Morrison's been up to the school about what happened?'

'Morning, Jim.'

'Braw day.'

She closed her eyes in the dairy aisle, imagining for a second the blissful anonymity of the huge supermarket close to her dad's place where she could amble up and down, picking up whatever she needed, switching off her ears. This place was a permanent hive of gossip and activity. It was suffocating.

'Morning,' said the woman at the checkout. Isla managed a faint smile. 'I'm not that keen on the natural yoghurt myself,' the woman commented as she passed it over the scanner. 'Oh, apricots – now I love them . . .'

Just let me out of here, thought Isla, *and I will quietly escape back to the flat, close the door, and speak to nobody for a whole thirty-six hours. And then I'll be another two days closer to leaving.* She gritted her teeth and made the appropriate noises before heading out to the car.

She'd just loaded up the boot and was returning the trolley, when she heard a muffled crash.

'Och, for goodness' sake!'

It was Mrs Mac, the client who'd come into the salon for a shampoo and set the other day. She was standing on the pavement, the broken handle of a cloth shopping bag in one hand, the contents lying around her feet – which, Isla noticed, were quite swollen, her ankles puffed up thickly. She bent over stiffly, managing to scoop up a tin of beans that was rolling towards the edge of the pavement.

'Let me help you with that,' Isla offered instinctively. She couldn't leave her standing there, no matter how desperate her need for solitude.

Mrs Mac looked up at her gratefully, her eyes crinkling in a smile. 'This blooming bag. I had no idea it was on the way out.'

'Don't worry, I'll get you another.' Isla bent down, capturing three tangerines that were heading slowly towards the drain.

Ruth watched as Isla ran quickly up and into the supermarket, returning with a handful of plastic shopping bags. She couldn't help smiling at the girl's back as she scooped up the spilt groceries, and placed them back into two bags. Then she unfolded gracefully and handed the torn bag over.

'There you are.'

She clearly didn't want to help – it was written across her face – but the words 'Let me take them back to the house for you,' were out of her mouth before she could stop herself. *Well brought up*, thought Ruth. *She's a nice girl despite herself.*

'It's fine, I'll be all right from here.' Ruth reached across, trying to take hold of the two bulging bags.

'I insist.' Isla's voice was firm. 'In fact, I've got the car. I'll drive you home. Where do you live, Mrs Mac?'

'Oh, that would be lovely. But it's Ruth, please.'

Well, the girl seemed to be quite determined to give her a hand, thought Ruth, and the glossy red convertible was a far cry from her usual lift in a beaten-up, mud-covered Land Rover. Isla's little convertible was a lot harder to climb in and out of, mind you – but it was much more fun.

'This is a bit fancy, isn't it?' Ruth gave a little shimmy

of her shoulders against the expensively upholstered seat. 'I could get used to this.'

Isla turned to her with a smile, pausing at the junction to let a flock of schoolboys on bikes hurtle past.

'I always promised myself, by the time I was thirty I'd have a decent car. And we maybe don't get as many sunny days in Edinburgh as you'd want with a convertible like this – but when we do, it's lovely.'

'You'll get a fair few here on the island.'

It was funny how the weather went. Ruth's dad had always joked that living on Auchenmor meant you often got four seasons in one day. As far as Isla could see, the focus was fairly strongly on winter. Isla smiled politely.

'Where am I going?' Isla looked ahead at the road that ran parallel to the rocky beach.

'Just here.' Ruth motioned to a little stone cottage sitting back from the pavement, fronted with two neat squares of lawn and bordered with primly gathered geraniums.

'Oh, this is pretty,' smiled Isla. She was a good-looking girl in any case, but her pale, fine-featured face took on another level of beauty when it relaxed and softened. 'I'll just give you a hand in with this shopping, and I'll let you get on.'

'You'll stay and have a cup of tea?' Ruth, pulling herself out of the low seat of the car, looked up at Isla, who extended a hand in support. Doubt flashed across her face for a moment, her brows gathering together in thought before she smiled again.

'I'd like that.'

Isla lifted the shopping out of the boot of the car, and followed Ruth inside.

'Can I give you a hand?'

'No, sit yourself down.' Ruth motioned to the velvet-covered sofa. 'I'll just put the kettle on.'

Leaving Isla in the sitting room, she pottered about the kitchen, opening the packet of nice biscuits she'd just bought – luckily they'd survived, and weren't all crumbs.

She laid them on a plate, setting a tray with teapot, milk jug, and her favourite cups and saucers. Isla seemed like the sort of girl who'd appreciate good china, instead of the thick mugs Ruth brought out when her grandson popped by in the afternoons between forestry jobs.

'Here we are.' She laid a tray down on the sideboard. 'I always think tea tastes that bit nicer from a cup and saucer, don't you?'

Isla, who'd been looking at the photos on the mantelpiece, sat down with a guilty expression. 'Sorry, I wasn't being nosy, I just –'

'Don't worry. I always do just the same. Most of my family have flown far away now, though. I've got them all up here to keep me company.'

Isla glanced up at the picture of a tousle-haired toddler and a teenage girl that stood on the side, propped there after the other day when Ruth had knocked it down. Ruth motioned to the sugar bowl, milk jug in hand.

'Just milk, please.'

'So tell me how you're finding life on the island.' Ruth

sat back with her cup and saucer, and looked at Isla with interest. She was cut from a very different cloth to her Aunt Jessie: quiet and guarded, but she seemed to be making changes in the salon that were the talk of the town at the moment. Ruth had heard a couple of young ones in the supermarket saying they'd decided to give the salon a go instead of heading off island. That had to be a good thing, given the state of the island's economy.

Pausing to gather her thoughts, Isla picked up her tea, looking out of the window and across the water towards the distant mainland.

'I'm only here for a short time. I thought I'd be back to Edinburgh more often than I have been, but it's not quite so easy to get away, is it?'

'I wouldn't know,' Ruth found herself chuckling. 'I've been here almost all my life. I think this place gets under your skin.'

'It seems to,' said Isla, politely.

'I left for a few years, made my way to Inverness – but all roads lead to Kilmannan, we say. You can't get yourself away from the place.'

'My dad says the same about Edinburgh.' Isla smiled. 'I've managed to make it from the outskirts of Edinburgh to a flat in the New Town, and that's about it. I had plans to travel –' she shook her head as Ruth offered her a biscuit – 'but I haven't quite made it yet.'

'Plenty time yet. You're a young thing. Your whole life is in front of you.'

'I keep telling myself that.' Ruth picked up a cushion and held it on her lap.

'As long as you've got something to aim for, you'll be fine.'

'Oh, I do,' said Isla, suddenly animated. 'I have a school reunion coming up. I always wanted to be able to turn up there and have a decent job and prove that I've made something of myself.'

She was a nice girl. So earnest and determined.

'I wish my boy had some of your drive.' Ruth looked across at the photograph on the mantelpiece. 'He's got an amazing talent for art – he won all the prizes at art school – and I'm still waiting for him to make something of it.'

Finn had been full of ideas when he'd headed off to Glasgow, determined to make his mark. When he'd specialized in sculpture and woodcarving she'd loved watching him fill the house with all sorts of gorgeous, ornate work, beautifully tooled hand-made shelves, wooden picture frames he'd carved and the like. But over time his artwork had dwindled, and the furniture side had taken over. In latter years the forestry work with Roderick had taken up so much of his time that there had been long periods when he hadn't made anything creative at all, and Ruth mourned the loss of that side of him. When he was creating, it fuelled a drive in him that otherwise seemed to get lost in partying and hanging out until all hours, DJing at the local pub and messing about. She knew he'd developed a bit of a name for himself. Really, it was time he settled down.

'I'm sure he will in time,' said Isla, politely.

Ruth gave a vague nod of agreement. 'So tell me more about this reunion. Any old flames waiting in the wings?'

Ruth had read a lovely book a while back, before her eyes got weaker, all about a woman who'd headed back to her school reunion and met the love of her life.

Isla's pale cheeks flushed pink suddenly. She hid her face in her teacup.

Ah, thought Ruth, *I've hit on something here.*

'I always wonder what happened to my first love. He left the island when he was sixteen, and his family moved down to Essex. We didn't have things like Facebook and all that internet stuff in our day. No way of knowing what happened to people when we lost touch.'

'I'm not sure if it's a blessing or a curse,' began Isla, thoughtfully. 'Everyone seems to be getting so excited about this reunion, and all I can think about is how they used to pick on me when I was at school for having the wrong clothes, and the wrong hair, and—'

'You certainly look the part now, though,' said Ruth, reaching across and patting her on the arm. 'You'll be wowing them.'

'Do you think?' Isla's brow wrinkled with doubt.

'Och, yes, absolutely.' Ruth took a bit of a gamble. The joy of getting to this age was that you could say what you liked without beating about the bush. 'So, who's this old flame you're after?'

'Oh, he's nothing.' But Isla gave a smile. 'He used to tease me, call me names – I had a thing about him for years, but he really had no idea.'

'So you're going to march in there and show him what he's been missing?' Ruth chuckled at the prospect. Shame, really. She'd have made a good match for Finn.

Isla pulled an uncertain face. 'Well, that was the idea when I sent a message agreeing to go – but I had drunk quite a lot of champagne at the time.'

'Well, he's going to get a surprise. You're a bonny girl, Isla. And you've worked hard to get where you are.'

'Thank you.' The colour rose once again in Isla's cheeks.

'I don't give out compliments unless I mean them, so you're welcome.' Ruth took another biscuit. Never mind what Doctor Lewis had said about restraint, she could worry about that in the morning. 'Anyway, I'm glad you came in for a wee cup of tea. It's always nice to have a chat. And you must get a bit lonely, staying up there in the flat above the salon.'

'A bit,' said Isla, sounding surprised at herself.

'Well, I'm always here if you fancy a wee cup of tea and a chat.' Ruth smiled at Isla, and she returned a smile of her own.

'I'd like that.'

Back home, Isla unloaded her shopping. The cupboards – and the kitchen – were clean and serviceable now, but the place was completely soulless. It didn't help that it was in shade most of the time, the light catching the windows only in the middle of the day when she was at work. Maybe some flowers would help – back home she'd always filled her bedroom, and the sitting room, with huge, vibrant vases full of anything beautiful that was in season. Rescuing Ruth meant she'd missed the florist – maybe tomorrow she'd leave the girls in charge, pop out and have a look at what was on offer. In the meantime, though, she scrubbed out the two grubby-looking fake crystal vases she'd found in the cupboard under the kitchen sink, and filled them with the supermarket chrysanthemums that had been the only thing available. She placed one vase on the windowsill, and the other on the little coffee table. It gave the place an even more seventies feeling. All she needed now were some dodgy canapés and a kaftan.

With the shopping unpacked, she realized another evening of staring at the walls was going to send her mad. Even the thought of reading didn't appeal. Grabbing her cardigan and wrapping a thin scarf around her neck – the wind coming off the sea was strong, taking the warmth out of the evening sun – she set off for a wander around Kilmannan.

It was the strangest feeling to know that across the water right now – only an hour away – Glasgow was thronged with commuters, and the shops were still clamouring with people.

There was a little putting green next to the closed-up ice-cream stand. She'd gone there as a teenager with her dad – a sudden image of him, a sunhat on his head, face scarlet from unexpectedly hot sunshine, flashed into her mind. She'd give him a ring when she got back to the flat, make sure he was eating properly and getting out for a walk, doing all the stuff the doctor had ordered. He'd sent her a text that morning, telling her how proud he was of her for helping Jessie out. She wasn't about to admit to him that the place was hell on earth, and she was utterly alone and completely miserable in a way even she hadn't expected.

The one set of traffic lights in town turned to red. Isla smiled despite herself as an old man sat obediently at the empty crossing in his tiny brown Vauxhall. When the lights turned to green again, he drove off.

There was a rumble as the ferry engine started up, and she stood and watched as the final preparations were made and the boat got on its way. The sign at the harbour gates flashed up in bright letters:

Thank You For Sailing
NEXT BOAT DEPARTS 0645

Isla sighed. The words in front of her were an inescapable reminder. She was trapped here with no means of escape – well, save breaking a bone and being airlifted off in the air ambulance, which from what her Uncle Calum had said, was a pretty hairy way of making your way to the mainland.

Chapter Eleven

The salon was empty of customers. Isla looked up at an unexpected knocking on the glass of the door.

Shannon, too, glanced up briefly from the computer. She gave the impression of working diligently, but Isla had already clocked her shopping for package holidays on a separate web page, flipping the browser back to an ordering site for hairdressing supplies whenever anyone approached. *Not quickly enough*, Isla had thought. Years of working alongside some of the wiliest girls and boys in the business had taught her every trick in the book. Isla let it slide. Shannon had been making a real effort lately, taking in everything she was told. Both she and Jinny were keen to learn more, rather than spend their days doing the same shampoo and sets over and over again.

Standing behind the glass door, hair plaited into row upon row of tiny, neat braids, was Lily. And thankfully – Isla cast a glance over Lily's shoulder – no sign of Lucifer the demon offspring.

'Lily, hello.' Isla stepped out of the salon, where Lily

was standing, one foot twisted round the back of her other leg, her expression anxious.

'I absolutely don't want to come in,' she said, unnecessarily. 'But I just wanted to give you these –' she handed Isla a beautiful hand-tied posy of wildflowers and foliage – 'as an apology for bringing our little visitors to the salon.'

Isla, as ever, had to resist the urge to start scratching her head at the merest mention of head lice. 'Thanks. You really didn't have to. It's all part of the job.'

'Yes, but you were *so* lovely, and it was just wonderful to find somewhere where Lucien was able to express himself *freely*.'

Isla tried to make a sound expressing agreement, but it came out as a muffled snort. Lily appeared not to notice.

'Anyway, we've used the special comb, and I've treated both of us with tea tree oil and an infusion of lavender and lemon balm.' She indicated the flowers. 'These are rosemary and balsam for cleansing the room aura, and lavender, which is a natural disinfectant, and hawthorn has amazing powers, and I've blessed them with a healing spell for positivity and good vibes.'

'Right.' Isla looked at the flowers, nonplussed. She sniffed them, recoiling in surprise at the pungent odour of garlic.

'Wild garlic,' said Lily, chirpily. 'Such a powerful cleansing herb. I couldn't help noticing yesterday that there's some stuck energy in the salon . . .' She shook her head, pursing her lips thoughtfully, choosing her words. 'Well, it needs a little help. This ought to do the trick. Oh!' Her face lit up, and she pulled a bundle of dried leaves out of her bag. 'Let me do a smudging ceremony to clear the air!'

A hair salon stinking of garlic and sage was definitely going to create an atmosphere, thought Isla, but maybe not quite the sort Lily was thinking of. She smiled through tight lips, nodding politely and stepping back towards the door. 'Thanks so much, these look just beautiful.' That was polite enough. And she didn't say they smelt it – which, frankly, they didn't. The longer Isla held them, the stronger the rank raw garlic scent became.

'Wonderful. Now, I'm having one of our earth healing sessions tomorrow evening at the Clootie Well, if you'd like to join us? I know you're new here, and it can be challenging making real heart connections. The ceremony will help you to open your heart chakra.'

Isla grasped at straws quickly. 'Oh, I'd love to,' she lied, 'but I'm afraid I'm taking the girls from the salon out tomorrow night.'

Jinny, who, with her usual nosiness, had poked her head round the door behind Isla, gave an excited squeak. 'You are?'

Isla turned round. She was about to open her mouth to stop Jinny giving the game away, but Jinny had already darted back inside and could be seen hopping from foot to foot, clearly explaining to a dubious-looking

Shannon, who was very likely to come out and give the game away.

'Yes,' Isla continued as Shannon made her way towards the door. Isla raised her voice a little, enunciating the words clearly enough for them to be heard inside. 'Yes, I thought it would be nice to take the girls for a drink and a bite to eat to say thank you for making me so welcome.'

Shannon's face was a picture of confusion. She stepped backwards towards the computer, eyebrows furrowed, shaking her head. Isla, who had mastered the art of lip-reading years back – because making conversation with clients over the sound of a hairdryer was virtually impossible, and they liked to carry on talking all the way through their appointments – saw Shannon forming the words, 'Aye, you're not imagining things for once.' She hid a smile as Jinny gave her a shove in retaliation.

'Well, if you won't come tomorrow night, I would very much appreciate your expertise sometime.'

'I think I'm going to be quite busy, keeping this place going single-handed with my aunt away,' Isla began. But Lily was determined.

'Well, yes, but you have two and a half days when the salon is closed, and –' she lowered her voice again – 'there's not that much to do here, between you and me. I mean, obviously silence and alone time are vital for personal growth, but so is spending time in nature. And we have so *much* of nature up at Meadowview House.'

'That would be very nice,' said Isla, politely. She had to get away soon, or she'd be offering to take Jinny and Shannon on an eight-week holiday just to get away from Lily.

'Excellent.' Lily peered round Isla at the opening hours listed on the salon door. 'Shall we say next Sunday? Midday?'

Isla opened her mouth, then closed it again. She nodded, defeated. If she tried to say no, Lily would probably suggest she had some issues coming up with resistance and cast some sort of spell on her at midnight on the moors. It seemed easier to just give in. Maybe Lily would leave her alone after that – or perhaps her attention could be diverted on to Jinny, who definitely had latent hippy tendencies, despite her protests. Shannon had been teasing her just the other day about the crystal necklace she'd tied around her neck.

'Marvellous,' Lily beamed, holding her hand to her heart with her eyes closed before opening them again, waving her hand forwards as if her heart was blowing a kiss. The woman was quite mad. 'Thank Goddess. We're up at dawn, so any time after that on Sunday will be perfect. Of course, if you feel called to join us before dawn, that's absolutely fine too. '

Oh, help, thought Isla, stepping back into the salon.

Back at home, Isla sat down on the sofa with a coffee. She had absolutely nothing planned, there was a brand new book downloaded on her Kindle, and the rain was pouring in a comfortingly autumnal manner down the windows. She snuggled down under the crochet blanket her aunt had left her.

The phone buzzed as a Facebook notification flashed up on the screen. The mobile phone reception might be dodgy when you went to the far side of the village, but thankfully here in the middle of Kilmannan it was just fine. The salon's broadband connection (mainly used by Shannon and Jinny to keep up to date with the gossip pages of the tabloid newspapers) meant Isla felt a bit less isolated – and Helen's cheerful messages were something she looked forward to each day. It had been lovely getting back in touch after all this time.

Not long to go. You still all set? I spoke to Amira the other day – bumped into her at big Tesco. She's coming if we're coming. Safety in numbers . . .

Isla looked at the screen and frowned. There was a tiny, not very kind voice in her head that kept naggingly pointing out that if she turned up for the school reunion with Helen, Amira and – she knew what was coming next, she was just waiting to discover that he'd been unearthed from wherever he'd disappeared off to when they all scattered in relief on the day they got their final exam results – Costas, there was a danger that Isla's carefully constructed, look-at-my-perfect-existence image was in danger of falling apart. They'd all end up huddled together at the geeky table in one corner whilst the popular gang held court.

Isla typed in a reply:

Oh that's great news. Hope you've managed to get some sleep and Maisie hasn't had you up all night. We've recovered from the nit invasion. No idea how it happened but I ended up saying yes to a morning at her retreat place next week . . . tbh I think it was easier than saying no. It's amazing how persuasive these people can be.

Helen's reply came back straight away.

It's all that positive thinking stuff. She probably brainwashed you when she was having her hair done.

Isla smiled.

I'll make sure I wear sunglasses when I go up there next week then, to be on the safe side.

God, what was she thinking? It was lovely to have a friend back in her life. If that meant they would be sitting in the geek corner, so be it.

Chapter Twelve

'Och come *on*, make a night of it.'

Jinny hopped from foot to foot as she shoved the broom back into the cleaning cupboard. She pushed the door shut, still jigging back and forth to the tunes in her head that kept her running on a perpetual motor, and gave Isla her very best persuading face: begging eyes through a shaggy fringe.

'Shannon, can you put this appointment in the book for now, and transfer it over once I've finished this?'

Isla carried on typing in the last of the stock orders. With Jessie gone, she'd made the executive decision to stop using the harsh products from the bottom of the range – and, knowing she'd have to justify the expense, had encouraged Shannon to start bringing in some of the younger girls from town who normally escaped to Glasgow when they wanted a haircut. The salon had been fully booked all of Thursday, and Friday and Saturday looked like they were going to be chaotic, with girls from town desperate to get in and look their best for the disco in the old Pavilion dance hall that was taking place.

'I'm going to order an extra box of that intensive conditioning treatment,' Isla said, tapping the surface of the desk with a nail, thinking aloud.

'That's us full for tomorrow afternoon.' Shannon closed the salon diary with a decisive slam.

'You're doing really well.' Isla looked up. 'Both of you. Bookings are up, takings are up – and that has to keep Jessie happy about the changes we've made.'

'Yay,' beamed Jinny. 'So you'll stay out for a little drink after we've had dinner, then?'

'One drink after dinner,' conceded Isla, firmly. 'We've got a really busy day tomorrow – like Shannon just said, we're fully booked, so it's going to be all hands on deck, and I don't want to be late. I've got some admin stuff to do too.'

'One drink.' Jinny flashed her a bright smile, scooping up her bag. 'Come on, then. This'll do until tomorrow.'

Isla shook her head, smiling despite herself. Jinny was irrepressible, a bundle of enthusiasm and energy who never stopped from the moment she arrived (always ten minutes late, always promising that she'd be on time tomorrow) at the salon, until she hurtled out the door last thing, arms full of hair magazines that she studied every night in bed, determined to know everything there was to know about the latest fashions.

'Shannon, you coming?'

'Two secs.' There was a gurgle of water. Shannon – who had at first seemed so resistant to Isla's insistence on the daily routines that kept a salon running efficiently –

was now, boosted by the success she was seeing, taking on board everything Isla could teach her. Isla had watched as she'd begun to take a pride in her work that had previously been missing. Every night now, without fail, Shannon took it upon herself to clean and sterilize all the equipment, and always left the back room spotlessly tidy.

Isla gave her a smile as she appeared, wiping her hands dry on a paper towel.

'You're doing a great job.'

Shannon flushed slightly at the compliment. 'Reckon?'

'Yes.' Isla believed in working her staff hard, but she always praised them when recognition was due. Shannon was trying her best, taking time when it was her lunch break to watch Isla at work, asking questions about technique, making a real effort.

They'd started the evening with dinner in the little restaurant on the main street that looked out over the harbour, but it had been pretty clear to Isla that the girls were dying to get out and go for a proper drink. She'd allowed herself to be towed along to the grotty-looking hotel on the corner where Shannon's current love interest, Rab, (who, she informed them, as per her dating manual, she had no intention of acknowledging) was working.

The hotel bar was empty, save for a couple of American tourists who were sitting poring over a map of the island. They looked up, nodding a greeting.

Jinny and Shannon slipped into the corner, settling

themselves down on the faded red velour cushions of the bar sofa, pulling out their phones, catching up with what had been happening online in the half hour since they'd last checked.

'Two ciders and a gin and tonic, please.'

'You girls starting early the night?' The old man behind the bar gave her a knowing smile, cracking open the bottles of cider and clattering ice into glasses.

'Just an after-work drink to say well done,' said Isla, crisply.

'Aye, they all say that, hen.' He seemed pretty sure of himself. Isla gave him a polite smile, saying nothing.

'Here's to us.' Jinny clinked her glass with Shannon.

'Wha's like us?' Shannon replied, taking a huge mouthful of cider, following it with the kind of belch that would make a teenage boy proud.

'*Gie few, and they're a' deid.*' They raised their voices in unison. Isla sipped her gin and tonic and smiled at them politely. Girls in gaggles like this always made her uncomfortable, reminding her of school and being left out and laughed at for having the wrong clothes, the wrong hair, the wrong everything.

'All right, Isla?' Jinny looked at her, her heart-shaped face quizzical.

'Yes, fine,' Isla tried to sound unconcerned. 'You girls have done really well this week. I think Jessie will be really impressed when she gets back and sees how you're getting on.'

'Y'reckon?' Shannon looked dubious. She poured the

remainder of her cider into the glass, tracing patterns in the condensation that ran down the sides. It was a moment before she spoke, choosing her words carefully. 'You've got far more of a clue about that place than Jessie has.'

Jinny nodded, as open as her friend was guarded. 'Yeah, we've had literally twice as many customers this week as we would've had normally. And that's before everyone gets paid at the end of next week. You're already booked up for the whole of Friday afternoon, Isla.'

'Yes, but you're getting loads better now, Jinny, and when Jessie comes back there'll be another stylist so you won't even notice I'm gone.'

'Aye, and I'll be demoted to sweeping the floor, it'll be back to blue rinses and shampoo and sets, and Shannon won't get a chance to do any of the cool stuff you've been showing her.'

Shannon looked at Isla, eyebrows raised in confirmation. 'You know she's right.'

'I'll have a word with Jessie. I'm sure when she hears how things are going, you'll be fine.'

Shannon, who'd drained her cider in record time, looked doubtful. 'We'll see, I suppose. Another?'

Isla, who'd only taken a couple of mouthfuls of her drink, shook her head. Jinny nodded with feeling, despite having half a pint of cider still in her glass.

'If Jessie doesn't let Shannon do some proper cutting she's going to end up going off the island to work,' said Jinny, her usually cheerful face falling as she watched

Shannon's departing back, a flash of a purple dragon tattoo just visible below the torn shoulder of her T-shirt.

'I thought Shannon loved it here on the island, though?'

'She does. But there's nowhere else for her to go. The other salon that opened here closed again after about six months – everyone here is so stuck in their ways – and it's the only way she's going to get a chance to do something different.'

'What about you?'

'Och, no.' Jinny shook her head. 'I can't leave the island. My mum needs help with Mikey in the mornings, and all my brothers and sisters are here.'

'How many do you actually have?' Jinny had mentioned so many of them in passing that Isla hadn't managed to work out exactly how many family members lived in the big, sprawling house that looked out across the shore to the mainland.

'Well, you know Mikey. He's four – he's autistic, so Mum needs extra help with him. Emmy and Leah are eight – they're twins – and then there's Charlotte, she's eleven, and Philly, Leo and Rowena, who are triplets, and they're fifteen so they're a nightmare as you can imagine.' Jinny shook her head with the maturity and wisdom befitting an old lady of nineteen.

Isla counted on her fingers. 'Eight of you?'

'Unless Mum is planning on any more – and you can never tell, it depends on what mood she catches Dad in, and if he's around.' Jinny pulled a face.

'I can't imagine what it must have been like, growing up with that many brothers and sisters.' Isla thought back to her solitary childhood, weekends spent wandering around Edinburgh by herself, nights spent making her dad soup and bread after his long night of working shifts in his taxi. She'd read so many stories of huge, rambling families who lived on top of one another, but she'd never met anyone who lived in one. And irrepressible, happy Jinny, who was as easy-going as a labrador, was exactly as she imagined someone from a huge family would be.

'It's lovely.' Jinny smiled. 'Until it's hideous, when it's absolutely the worst thing ever. I seriously thought I'd escape to the mainland as soon as I could leave school, but when they made the basement into a little annex for me I decided I'd hang around for a bit. Then I ended up working weekends at Jessie's place, and I just sort of got stuck.'

'You don't want to be a hairdresser?'

'Oh, no –' Jinny looked worried that she'd offended Isla – 'it's not that I don't like it, it's just I like the other stuff more. The head massages and the therapies and stuff. I keep hoping Jessie might let me do a bit of experimenting on the clients. You're the first person who's talked about aromatherapy and all that stuff I like.'

Isla nodded. 'I think maybe if we try not to talk about it as experimenting, we might get somewhere with Jessie. They're clients, not lab rats.'

'Good point,' Jinny agreed. 'And I've been going off the island at the weekends to do my Reiki training and I'm almost ready to do my level three and then I'll be a Reiki Master,' she put her hands together in a prayer position and bowed, solemnly, before looking up with a giggle. 'I'm going to do a reflexology course next.' The words tumbled out in excitement.

'She talking about all that hippy-dippy stuff again?' Shannon set three drinks down on the table.

'Oh – I didn't want anoth –' Isla began, then held her tongue. It was kind of Shannon to buy her one. She didn't have to drink it all, anyway.

'It's no' hippy-dippy – you said yourself the Reiki helped your back.' Jinny leaned forward to take her drink, elbowing Shannon in the ribs.

'Aye, fair enough, but you'll have a hard job persuading Jessie to let you loose on any of her clients with it. She'd have trouble getting her head round giving a head massage during the shampooing.'

Isla felt herself exhaling in exasperation. There were more than enough people on the island to sustain the salon, and Jessie didn't seem to realize that if she just let go of the reins a little and let Shannon and Jinny do what they were capable of, she could relax and enjoy her time with Pamela and the grandchildren, leaving the place in their hands. Perhaps if . . .

'I'll sort Jessie out,' Isla heard herself saying. 'You two have done a wonderful job this last fortnight, and you don't really need me here at all.'

'You're not about to leave us, are you?' Jinny looked alarmed.

'No, I'm not going anywhere just yet. I've got another five weeks and four days,' said Isla, in a singsong tone, laughing.

Shannon raised an eyebrow. 'No' that you're counting down the days or anything?'

It was Isla's turn to blush. 'Well, it's nothing personal,' she began, taking a drink to give herself a moment to think. The truth was that she was beginning to enjoy the company of the two girls, their teasing camaraderie, and working together to make a success of Jessie's salon in her absence. She loved watching the girls learning – seeing their confidence grow after this short time was a real boost. She'd always enjoyed teaching the junior staff back in Edinburgh, but doing so had meant surrendering cutting time to one of the other stylists, all of whom were snapping her heels, determined to prove their worth and impress Kat. Without that element of competition and stress, she was relaxing and appreciating her work even more.

And she loved running along the seafront here in the evenings, with the salt-fresh air and the silence. Her runs were punctuated only by the sound of seabirds wheeling overhead – the silence that had seemed so alarming for the first few nights had become something she looked forward to. She'd stopped running with her headphones in, realizing she didn't need music to drown out her thoughts.

'It's just, I've got a deadline. I need to get back and get my career sorted out.'

'What's happening?'

'I'm thirty in September,' Isla found herself admitting. 'And I want to be at the top of my game by then.'

'But you were head stylist at Kat Black!' Jinny looked confused. 'Top stylist in the poshest salon in Edinburgh. You don't get much higher up than that, do you? Unless you're about to take on your own place – in which case, any chance of a job for us two?'

Shannon clinked her glass against Jinny's with a snort of laughter. 'Aye, I wouldn't mind a job in one of those posh salons on George Street. And a big fancy flat in town, and all.'

Isla winced.

'I had both,' she began. She'd finished one gin and tonic, and found herself sipping the second as she told the girls a truncated – and slightly downplayed – version of her story.

'. . . So I ended up getting the sack from Kat's place, and ended up here.'

'Good for us, mind,' said Jinny. 'No' so good for you. But there's no rush, is there? You're not about to turn into a pumpkin if you haven't got your dream job by the time you're thirty, are you?'

Isla shook her head. 'It's not that.' How on earth could she explain what had driven her all this time? She took another drink. The recent rekindling of her friendship with Helen seemed to have opened up some part of herself that had been closed off for so long. Back in Edinburgh, she'd never have opened up about how she felt. She'd lived with Hattie for years without ever discussing anything of consequence.

'Have you made a pact with the devil?'

Shannon looked at Isla over the top of her glass, her rainbow hair vibrant in the low evening sunlight that shone in through the window.

'No.' Isla took another sip. 'It's just –' She reached into her handbag, pulling out her purse, flipping it open.

'Awww, look at that. Is that you?' Jinny leaned forward, looking at the photograph that sat behind a plastic casing.

'Aye, it is. Look,' Shannon traced the picture with a crimson nail. 'I recognize the eyes. Is that your mum?'

Isla nodded.

'She's gorgeous. Looks like you.' Jinny looked up at Isla, who was surprised by the unexpected compliment.

'She died a few months after that photo was taken,' Isla began, cautiously. 'Cancer. She was thirty.'

'Ahhh,' said Jinny, with a single nod of understanding. Shannon looked at the two of them, nonplussed.

'Mmm.' Isla acknowledged Jinny with a small smile.

'I'm really sorry about your mum, Isla. That's horrible.' Shannon shifted in her chair awkwardly.

Isla, who had spent years making people feel better about the fact she'd lost a parent, gave her the same reassuring line she always trotted out. 'It's fine – it was a long time ago.'

It was a long time ago. That didn't stop it hurting, though, unexpectedly. Not on the obvious days like Mother's Day, when she'd expect it to sting; but when she worried about her dad's health, or when she heard a piece of music that sent her back in time to her childhood, or ate a cheese sandwich and drank a cup of tea and remembered the feeling of Sunday-night-ness when they'd all sit together, plates balanced on knees, and have tea in front of the television. And of course when she'd been at school and the children had picked her out, isolated her for being different, circled around her calling her names and being casually cruel, not for a second thinking how it might feel if they were the ones who didn't have a mum any more – *then* it had hurt. A hurt so raw in Isla's chest that she'd closed herself off against it, and against everyone else.

'You know,' Jinny began, choosing her words carefully, 'I think if something happened to my mum, she wouldn't want me living in a state of "what if".'

She was, Isla reflected, surprisingly astute for her age, underneath the whirling exterior and giddy nature. Maybe it was being the eldest of eight children that did it.

'It's not really "what if".' Isla's voice was quiet. 'It's more that – I want to get everything done that I can. I want to prove I can make it. I want to be able to turn around and say "Look what I achieved by the time I was thirty."'

She wasn't quite sure who she was proving it to. She could picture her dad's face, smiling at her fondly across the kitchen table. 'You do whatever you like, hen, I'll be happy.' He'd been cheerfully accepting when she'd decided to move out, take the place in the New Town with Hattie. He always maintained that all he wanted was for her to have a good life, enjoy herself. He never mentioned Isla's mum, though. She was the great un-spoken, a silent presence. And he'd stayed single all this time.

'Who are you turning round to?' Shannon sat back, an unexpectedly thoughtful expression on her face. Isla half turned in her chair, watching Shannon as she poked at an ice cube in her glass, fishing it out with a finger before crunching it up in her mouth.

'Gross,' said Jinny, pulling a face.

'Aye, but my dentist loves me,' said Shannon, in reply. 'Anyway, Isla –' she wasn't going to let it go – 'who exactly are you proving yourself *to*?'

Isla looked down at the photo of her mum, arms tightly wrapped around her chest. In the picture she was wearing a blue anorak with a fur lining. She could still remember the smell of it, and the smell of her mum's perfume, and the moment that picture had been taken, because afterwards they'd gone to the miniature railway and ridden on the train and had an ice cream and every-thing had been lovely, and she'd been treated to anything she wanted. It hadn't been for a long time afterwards that she'd realized: her parents knew by then. That the perfect day had been one they'd created deliberately, to preserve memories and leave them there for the future – for an Isla who'd have no mother, no siblings, nobody but her dad to look after her.

'It's not her, if that's what you're thinking. She was wonderful.' Isla smiled at her mum. 'But I need to prove I'm worth something. I spent years at school being treated like –' She stopped. That was a step too far, opening up too much. They didn't need to know that stuff.

'It must've been hard for you.' Shannon looked at her appraisingly.

'Mmm.' Isla nodded, taken by surprise. Working in a salon, though, Shannon must have heard so many stories over the years – and you couldn't do the job well unless you had the ability to listen, empathize, and do it all without judging.

'I was a right bitch when I was at school,' Shannon continued. Jinny got up, motioning to the now-empty glasses, and set off for the bar.

Isla, who had already looked at Shannon through the eyes of her teenage self and decided that she'd have steered well clear, tried to make an appropriately surprised but non-committal sound. It came out as a slight snort, which she turned into a cough. Shannon, undeterred, continued.

'Yeah, I'd have ripped the shit out of you, likes.' *No kidding*, thought Isla, looking at Shannon's sharp-edged face, the planes of her cheekbones standing out in the filtered late afternoon light. 'I wasnae all that nice to a couple of lassies in my class. Still feel bad about it now.'

'Really?' Isla, thinking of Jamie Duncan and Allison Graves and the whole gang who had made her life a misery, wondered if they were sitting somewhere having similar regrets. Unlikely, she thought.

'Yeah, the thing is – I was reading a thing about this in *Cosmopolitan* – we pick on anyone who isn't quite the same as us, don't we? I reckon you must have had a hard time, with having lost your mum and that.' Shannon gave a nod of acknowledgement as Jinny returned with a drink.

'It wasn't that much fun,' Isla conceded.

'Aye, well, you come across as dead stuck up and that, but you're actually quite nice, don't you think, Jinny?'

Jinny's face was a picture as she tried to simultaneously warn Shannon that she was being profoundly tactless, and emit sympathy and understanding in Isla's direction.

'Thanks,' said Isla with a wry smile. Shannon meant well, even if she did have a habit of galumphing in with both feet.

'She means we're glad you're here, and we're having a great time without Jessie – not that there's anything wrong with Jessie, of course, because she's lovely, but we've learned loads from you, and –' Jinny paused for breath.

'Anyway,' said Shannon with a broad smile. 'Here's to a good night out, and no hangovers the morn'.'

Isla, who had sworn after The Incident that she wasn't ever drinking anything again, had somehow drunk two stiff gin and tonics and was facing up to a third. She felt pleasantly warm, her limbs had loosened up, and she felt a huge wave of affection for these two funny girls – their odd ways, the fact they'd tried to make her feel welcome in their own unique manner. She raised her glass to Jinny and Shannon. 'Here's to us.'

The third drink finished, they decided to head on to the Anchor Bar, which overlooked the harbour. Thursday night in Kilmannan was surprisingly busy for such a tiny place and the pub was already filling up, the bar lined with customers. Standing alongside a girl in a pair of skin-tight shiny plastic trousers and a voluminous, gauzy top was a ruddy-faced farmer, still wearing a blue all-in-one overall, the trousers smeared with – well, Isla hoped it was nothing more disgusting than oil. There was a tractor parked outside, alongside a collection of cars as motley as the clientele. A battered old Volvo stood beside an immaculate silver Jaguar, lined up beside a rusty moped with the key still in the ignition.

'Two ciders and a gin and tonic, and can we have three bags of cheese and onion, Andy?' Jinny yelled over the top of the men who stood at the bar, then she somehow managed to dodge her way into the corner, where she beckoned Isla and Shannon to join her on the remaining three empty stools that sat around a stripped wooden table. The Anchor was clearly the place to be: there were

signs suggesting that later on there'd be live music playing, and the place was filling up.

'Edinburgh's got nothing on a night out in Kilmannan.' Shannon ruffled her hair carefully, applying a
further layer of dark-red lipstick using a tiny hand mirror
that she pulled from her pocket.

'I wouldn't know,' said Isla. 'I can't remember the last
time I went out.'

'With all that stuff at your fingertips? Clubs and bars
and restaurants and pizza at three in the morning?' Shannon sighed enviously. 'I'd be out every night if I could.'

'I go out once in a while with Hattie, my flatmate,' Isla
backtracked. It sounded a bit tragic even to her ears to
admit that the last time she'd been out before the drunken
texting episode was months ago. Back when she'd first
moved in with Hattie, she'd gone through a phase –
when she was Hattie's new thing, she realized, thinking
back – when she had gone out most weekends, watching
as Hattie got plastered on prosecco, making sure she got
home in one piece. She'd had fun, cautiously, and there
had been more than a few occasions when she'd ended
up in bed with some charming trainee architect or other,
and even a few months when she'd dated Philip, auction
eer son of Hattie's mother's best friend (or something
like that – everyone in Hattie's world seemed to know
everyone else, and they were all related and owned vast
tracts of land in the Highlands). But it had fizzled out,
and so had Isla's star. Hattie had moved on to Minnie, the
'absolutely darling' girl who was working alongside her

in the dress agency, and Isla had returned to her normal Friday night routine of bath, beauty products, book and bed.

'Well, a night out in this place will be a bit of a shock to the system, I reckon.' Jinny's eyes were bright now, three ciders down, and she was scanning the place over Shannon's shoulder, looking to see who else was around. 'I'll give you the low-down.'

'That's George MacKay, he's got the big dairy farm over the hill as you go out of town,' Jinny pointed to a stocky man in his late twenties, bright blue eyes above ruddy, wind-weathered cheeks. He was roaring with laughter, a pint in his hand. 'And that one with him is Jock Jamieson, he works at the forestry for the estate.'

The mythical Duntarvie Estate that everyone had mentioned. Isla was yet to meet anyone who lived or worked there. She'd driven out that way one afternoon, bored and restless, discovering a huge sign below one of two stone lions that rested at the gates to a long drive which led off into the distance. She'd pulled the car over to have a look, but driven away as someone had headed up in her direction in a dark-blue Range Rover – she was worried she was going to be arrested for trespassing.

Isla was having a good night. Not wanting to repeat the same mistake as last time, she switched to Diet Coke when she ordered another round of drinks, and watched with a vaguely maternal air (which surprised her) as

Jinny and Shannon got happily plastered on cider, dancing to the music of a passable covers band.

'I must get going.' It was half past twelve, and she had to be up in the morning. So did the girls.

'Aye, we'd better get a move on.' Shannon, her rainbow-spiked hair drooping in the steamy fug of the pub, fished under the table for her jacket. Somehow in the noisy, friendly crowd they'd shifted sideways, and their stuff had been left behind.

'Thanks for the drinks, Isla,' Jinny said, as she reached across over the head of a man who was looking down at his phone, pointing something out to the guy sitting next to him. It was so crowded, it was like playing sardines.

'Thanks for inviting me out.' There was a smile in Isla's voice as she spoke. The two men looked up as Jinny's bag swung down between them.

'We meet again,' said the fair-haired cyclist. A week on from the accident, he had a couple of steri-strips across a gash on his forehead.

Isla looked at him closely for a moment. Without the layer of mud, his hair was sandy blond and thick, pushed back from a tanned forehead sprinkled with freckles. His jaw was marked with stubble, and he had teeth Shannon's dentist would presumably find incredibly impressive.

'Whoa,' said a drunken voice behind her, as someone propelled her forward so that she found herself jammed between the cyclist's thighs.

'I'm sorry,' she said, trying to step backwards. There

was nowhere to go, the crowded bar having surged into the space that she'd previously filled.

'Don't be,' he said, looking delighted. He turned to his dark-haired companion. 'Roddy, this is –' and he looked at her with a slightly triumphant expression – 'Isla.'

Jinny emitted a tiny, excited squeak.

'Very nice to meet you,' said Isla, reaching out her hand to shake that of the dark-haired man. He ran his spare hand through his hair, ducking shyly, looking up at her through a flopping fringe.

'Roddy Maxwell.' He shook her hand firmly with impeccable manners, despite the chaotic surroundings. 'How d'you do?'

'Good, thank you.' Isla pulled a face as she was elbowed in the back once again by someone making their way past with a drink, which sloshed over her elbow.

'You girls coming, or what?' Shannon's deep voice carried across from the doorway where she stood waiting.

'I'll get out of your way.' Isla stepped backwards, carefully. As she did, her leg brushed against the blond man's leg and she felt a rush of something – gin, probably – going to her head.

'Jesus, Isla,' Jinny was actually twirling round in circles outside. 'You don't mess about. Straight to the top, eh?'

'What are you on about?' Shannon grabbed Jinny by the arm so that she had to stand still for a moment.

'Did you not see what happened in there? First I nearly hit bloody Roderick Maxwell in the head with my bag, and then two seconds later Isla's being introduced to him – quite the thing.'

'By who?' Shannon looked across at the bar window, where the silhouettes of drinkers could be seen against the light.

'I know he's a fast worker, but how the hell d'you know Finn MacArthur already?' Jinny cocked her head, looking at Isla with interest.

'Isla, you're a dark horse.' Shannon let out a low whistle. 'Mind you, with his reputation, I'm no' surprised.'

Isla shook her head, utterly confused. The drinks must have been a lot stronger than they seemed. 'What are you two on about?'

'Finn MacArthur. Total charmer, or a bit of a ladies' man, if you know what I mean, depending on who you talk to. Anyway, there's no' getting away from the fact he's gorgeous. Knows it, mind you.'

He certainly exuded an easy self-confidence.

Shannon hitched her bag over her shoulder and set off towards home, the other two following. 'Aye, and Roderick Maxwell is the Laird of Duntarvie Estate. His best mate. No' the sort of person that hangs around with hairdressers.'

Chapter Thirteen

Ruth was on her way back from the chemist, bag filled with the ridiculous pills that Doctor Lewis was insistent she take daily, when she passed the steamy window of the hairdresser's.

'Hello, Ethel.'

Her friend looked up from the magazine she was reading whilst waiting for her appointment.

'How're you this morning?'

'I'm fine, thanks, Ruth. Just trying out this hotshot new hairdresser we've got as a special guest.' She looked across at Isla, who was busy blow-drying Sandra Gilfillan's blonde hair. Sandra, who owned the hotel with her husband Murdo, had always been quite vociferous about the fact that she couldn't get a decent haircut on the island for love nor money, so it was testament to the spreading news of Isla's skill that she'd honoured them with her presence.

'I see herself is in the hot seat.'

'Aye,' Ethel gave a giggle. They'd been friends since school, and in all those years her laugh hadn't changed.

'Well, with the seal of approval from Her Majesty, this place will have bookings through the roof from all the ladies who lunch. I hope Jessie's ready for it when she comes back.'

Ruth had a sneaking suspicion that Jessie wasn't going to be so keen to get back to long days on her feet after a couple of months off playing granny. 'Well, we'll see.'

'Ruth.' Isla turned away from Sandra, smiling a greeting.

'All right there, Mrs Mac,' said Shannon, squeezing past her in the doorway, 'you're no' in today, are you?'

'No, just popping past on my way back,' Ruth explained, 'thought I'd say hello.'

'Well,' said Shannon, sliding Isla a mischievous look, 'We were out last night, and Isla seems to be getting on like a house on fire with your Finn.'

Ruth watched Isla frown at Shannon in the mirror, but was interrupted as she opened her mouth to speak.

'If I could just pay before this turns into a mothers' meeting.' Sandra stood up, preening herself like a fat hen, allowing Isla to slip her out of the gown and pick up her handbag as if she was born with a silver spoon in her mouth.

Once the payment was completed Sandra bustled out of the shop, almost knocking Ruth over in passing. Edging aside with her stick, Ruth said, 'Actually, Isla, I was wanting to have a wee word with you. I've been thinking that a wee bit of gentle exercise would do me the world of good. Do you fancy a little stroll tomorrow afternoon?'

Isla, who still looked perplexed, gave her another smile as she brushed down her top, which was covered in a scattering of Sandra's hair.

'That would be lovely. We close at half past twelve.'

'I'll get the bus along to town, then,' said Ruth, watching as Ethel was wrapped in a black salon gown by Jinny and bustled off to the sinks to have her hair washed. 'See you here tomorrow lunchtime.'

'I'll look forward to it.'

On the bus home, Ruth looked out of the window at children skimming stones on the beach and waited for the stop that was handily right outside her little cottage. Goodness knows what Shannon was playing at – she was a right little minx, that one, always stirring up mischief.

Safely indoors, she sat down on the sofa, feeling a bit out of breath. These new pills didn't seem to be doing a thing. Maybe a little snooze might help . . . Hamish hopped up with a chirrup of approval and settled down on her knee. As she dropped off, she hoped that Finn hadn't been up to his usual tricks. Isla was a nice girl . . .

Jinny flipped the CLOSED sign over in the face of a disappointed teenager, and her mum who was standing with hand poised to push the door open.

'Sorry, we're closed!' Jinny mouthed, motioning at the sign dramatically. 'And I'm off the island pronto, because I've got to get to Reiki training this afternoon and if I miss that next boat I'll be swimming across to the mainland, so tough luck, guys and girls . . .'

Shannon shook her head. 'You do talk a lot of bollocks, you do.'

'Well,' Isla closed down the computer screen, 'you guys need to have a think about what we're going to do, because I vote we start opening full days on a Saturday. We're turning people away, and that's crazy.'

Shannon and Jinny both groaned in unison. 'Noooo, we need our Saturdays.'

'You get more days off than anyone I've ever worked with. And think of the money. You'll get a pay increase, of course.' Isla hadn't actually run it past Jessie, but her aunt had been so vague on the phone the other day that Isla was sure it'd be fine. The salon's takings were up, word seemed to be getting around, and it was ridiculous to be closed on the busiest day of the week. Even in tiny Kilmannan people wanted to get dressed up on a Saturday night and head out to the pub, and not everyone could fit in – or for that matter afford – the journey to Glasgow on a Saturday, not to mention the cost of a salon over there.

'Ah well, if you're talking money,' Shannon perked up. 'That's a different matter.' Jinny nodded.

'OK, let's have a chat about it on Tuesday when we're back in. Meanwhile, have a good weekend, you two. Oh look, Shannon, someone for you.' Outside, face scarlet, arms full of flowers from the florist (which had turned out to be quite lovely, to Isla's delight), was Shannon's beau, the beleaguered Rab, who had been subjected to her determined study of *The Rules*.

'Awwwww,' said Jinny through a mouth stretched wide as she applied lipstick looking in the mirror. 'You can't say he's no' trying.'

Shannon looked cross. She pulled her ever-present handbook out of her bag.

'Is that no' due back at the library by now?' Jinny peered over her shoulder.

'Shut up. I renewed it.' Shannon snapped it shut, blushing slightly.

'There's nothing in there about what to do if they turn up with flowers. He's not supposed to be doing that bit yet.'

Isla burst out laughing. These girls. They'd made working here so much more fun than in any of the starchy, perfect salons back home. 'I think if I were you, I'd go along with it. There's a man out there with half the florist in his arms. I think that's a good sign.'

Shannon, by now as pink in the face as the hapless Rab, looked quietly delighted.

'All right. If this all goes wrong, I'm blaming you two.'

She headed outside, where Rab leaned across and gave her a sweet kiss on the cheek before they walked off, hand in hand.

Isla gave the place one final, routine check-over. Jinny hauled her bag full of books and goodness knows what else over her shoulder. 'Ready?'

They were closing the door when Isla felt something wet at the back of her leg, followed by a heaving, straining, panting noise. She turned around to see a scruffy-looking boy attached to a hefty Staffordshire Bull Terrier.

'Oh God, no, Leo,' said Jinny, in despair. She looked across the road to the harbour where the boat was already backing into position, ready to disembark the passengers from the mainland.

'Dad's had to go and fix a bike across at Jimmy Colhoun's place, and I've got a football match in half an hour. It's the tournament up at the school, I can't miss it.' Leo looked anxious. 'He says he'll definitely be back, but can you take Mavis until then?'

Isla hid a smile. Only in Jinny's world would a dog built like a brindled barrel, with a back broad enough to serve afternoon tea on, be called Mavis.

'I can't.' Jinny tucked her hands behind her back.

Leo pushed the lead in her direction. Mavis, slobbering, grinned toothily at him.

'Leo, I'm going on that boat, and there's no way on earth I'm taking a bloody dog to a Reiki session! Tie her up at football, come on . . . someone will take her for you.' Jinny's voice was pleading.

'He'll be back in half an hour. You can catch the next boat.' Leo looked at the lead in his hand, sizing up his options. 'I'll just leave her here . . .'

'She'll run away and steal steak pies from the butcher's if you don't take her, and then she'll get put down,' Jinny said darkly. 'And then Mikey will be upset, and it'll be all your fault.'

It was like listening to two children squabbling over a toy, only neither of them wanted it. Isla shook her head despairingly. 'Look –' she reached out a hand, taking the lead from Jinny's brother – 'I'll take her. I'm going for a walk anyway.' How difficult could it be?

'Have we got some extra bodies for our little walk, Isla?'

Ruth's appearance seemed to create enough of a disturbance that Leo shot off, disappearing in a second. Ruth patted Mavis, who snorted a greeting before dribbling on Ruth's handbag and attempting to steal her walking stick.

'Where are you going for your walk?' Jinny, half an eye on the boat, which was now preparing to load passengers, turned to Ruth.

'Well, Isla,' Ruth looked at her, 'I was thinking a wee stroll around the park behind the castle. Nothing too strenuous.'

'Excellent.' Jinny pulled her phone out of her bag. 'Mavis loves it there. I'll text Dad and tell him to pick her up there when he's done in half an hour.'

Leaning down to pat the dog, she hitched her bag onto her shoulder and hurtled off towards the boat, calling as she went, 'Thanks, Isla, I owe you one!'

Walking Mavis turned out to be slightly less relaxing than Isla had imagined. Ruth, who seemed a bit wheezy, couldn't manage anything more than a very slow pace with her stick. Mavis, who was enormously strong, was clearly used to slightly less sedate exercise and consequently spent the whole time pulling like a train until the muscles in Isla's arm were aching.

'Hello, Mavis,' said a woman being towed in the opposite direction by a huge, incredibly hairy German Shepherd. 'Are you taking some new people for a walk today? Look, Petal, Mavis has some new friends!'

Isla smiled politely as the dogs circled each other, their leads wrapping into a maypole pattern. She untangled it, and they moved onwards.

'So I gather you met my Finn,' Ruth began.

Isla opened her mouth to reply. Just then a brown and white spaniel, who wasn't on a lead, leaped up to them. It bounced over the top of Mavis's back, bounded around Ruth in a circle and headed back towards its owner, who was waving and calling from the far side of the park.

'Yes,' Isla began to reply, cautiously, having checked there were no other dogs. Mavis had slowed her pulling a little now, meaning she could concentrate on what she was saying. 'Well, you could call it meeting – he crashed his bike when I was out running.'

'Oh yes, that was a nasty one. He didn't hit you, did he?' Ruth turned to look at Isla.

'No, I was fine. He was lucky it wasn't worse.'

'Yes, well, as I said the other day when we were drinking tea, he has a habit of just getting by, that one.' She tutted, fondly.

At that, Mavis gave a bark of excitement and started

galloping on the spot, just giving Isla enough notice to gather her thoughts before she was towed halfway across the grass towards a tall man with shoulder-length hair who was waving happily at her.

'Wait there,' Isla called back to Ruth, who had already made herself at home on a wooden bench. 'I'll be back in a moment.' Ruth waved acknowledgement.

'Hello, beautiful,' said the man. Mavis rolled over happily, waving her paws in the air.

'You must be –'

'Paul. Jinny's dad.' He had a silver hooped earring in one ear. He reached out a hand that was streaked with some kind of engine oil, looked at it, and pulled it away in the time it had taken Isla to wonder whether it would be polite to just nod a greeting instead of shaking hands.

'Jin's really loving working with you. She's full of it every night. Lovely to see her so inspired.' He took Mavis's lead and wiped his hand on his jeans, absent-mindedly. 'You're a born teacher, from what I hear. She's been soaking it all up, coming home, telling us all about how I can run my business more effectively. You're a bit of a hit, from what I'm hearing.'

Isla felt herself blush. 'Well, she's a lovely girl. And she's determined to make something of herself, too.'

'Glad to hear it. The world needs more sparks like Jinny, if you ask me.' He ran a hand through his hair, pushing it out of his eyes.

'Well, anyway,' Isla turned, motioning to Ruth, who

looked quite happy on her bench, 'I'd better let you and Mavis get on.'

'Thanks for taking her. Really appreciate it.'

'No problem,' said Isla, happy to have handed her over. She was definitely a cat person. Her skirt was covered in dog drool and fur.

Walking back over to Ruth, Isla noticed that from here you could see the wide sweep of Kilmannan Bay. In the far distance, Jinny's boat was heading off to the mainland. The park was beautifully kept, neatly cut grass surrounded by a row of towering oak trees, underneath one of which Ruth sat patiently.

'I don't think I'll be in a rush to get a dog,' called Isla as she approached.

Ruth's infectious laugh rang out. 'Well, not one like Madam, perhaps.' She patted the space on the bench next to her. 'Come and have a sit down.'

'I thought you fancied a walk?' Isla crossed one leg over the other, turning to face her.

'Och, that's enough of an exercise for me. I tell you what, though, I quite fancy a cup of tea at the cafe outside the castle, if you'd like to join me? My treat.'

'I'd love to.' Isla noticed Ruth was still a bit out of breath, even after sitting down for a rest. 'Are you OK to walk, or do you want to give it a bit longer?'

'Oh, don't worry about me, I've just got a bit of a wheeze.' Ruth shook her head. 'Look at that.' She pointed with her walking stick to the edge of the bench, where some tiny blue flowers were growing. 'D'you see those?'

Isla peered down at them. They looked like miniature bluebells, but finer and more delicately drawn. 'They're pretty – what are they?'

'Harebells. When I was a wee girl, this field wasn't a park at all, but a big meadow – the secondary school behind you wasn't there, of course, because we just had one school in the town, where the little art gallery is now.' Ruth looked thoughtful. 'I used to sneak up here when I could get away with it – I had a lot of brothers and sisters, and I was in the middle, so I always got stuck with all the worst jobs, looking after the little ones.'

Isla smiled. It was amazing to think that Ruth, at eighty, had lived her whole life here on this little island. Even though she had to grudgingly admit that the place wasn't as grim as she'd first thought, eighty years seemed like a long time to be stuck here.

'I was a reader and a daydreamer,' continued Ruth, 'but my mother didn't have a lot of time for that sort of thing. I used to bring my favourite books up here and lie under that oak tree over there and pretend I lived somewhere beautiful. My favourite was *Anne of Green Gables* – I loved the way she renamed all her favourite places.'

'Oh, I loved her too!' Isla had suspected from the offing that Ruth was what Anne would have called a kindred spirit.

Ruth put her gnarled, age-spotted hand over Isla's, looked at her and smiled.

'Then I shall share a secret with you. I always thought Kilmannan was such a hard name for such a pretty place.

188

When I sat here surrounded by harebells and daisies I renamed it Wildflower Bay. I never told a soul that until now.'

Isla felt a wave of fondness for Ruth. She loved her dad so much, but she'd grown up without a woman in her life – her gran had died years ago, and Jessie had been out of the picture for years, until now. And suddenly, here she was on this weird little island, with the girls in the salon making her laugh, and Ruth confiding secrets. 'Well, I won't tell another soul either. I think it's a beautiful name.'

Ruth gave her hand a squeeze. 'How about that tea and cake, then?'

Chapter Fourteen

The driveway up to Meadowview House was almost two miles of rutted, gravel-strewn unmade road. Isla had read all about the history of the place in the tiny museum that adjoined the ruined castle in the centre of Kilmannan. It had been built in 1895 by Timothy Lord, a Shakespearean actor, who had retired in disgrace after being sued by the husband of his mistress. There by the lake, miles from anywhere, he roamed around his land dressed in tartan jacket and plus-fours, pipe and tweed hat in hand, drunk more often than not. The easy-going islanders had been content to let him get on with it, taking him – as the girls in the salon told her – as they found him. He'd even had busts of Shakespeare, Keats, Johnson and one of himself made, and they sat atop stone plinths at the entrance to the sprawling grounds.

Isla drove along slowly, trying hard to avoid potholes, weaving her little car from side to side, cringing at the metallic thud of stones pinging up onto her precious red paintwork.

She slowed the car a little at a particularly deep pothole, realizing there was no way around in this case. Something in her rear-view mirror caught her eye. A muddy green Land Rover was approaching at some speed, and there was nowhere for her to pull over.

She jolted the car through the pothole, trying to speed up to a racy five miles per hour. It was no good. With an ominous *clonk*, the low-slung underside of her car hit an unexpected heap of gravel. The Land Rover behind her beeped and flashed its lights.

'Sod off, you impatient git,' said Isla through gritted teeth.

The horn beeped again. Isla didn't dare look up into the rear-view mirror in case she caught the driver's eye. Clearly driving cautiously was some kind of major violation of the Countryside Code. She saw the lights flash again, three times, and the horn blasted loudly. Oh God, there was no way she could pull over. The verge sloped steeply up towards the trees on one side, and down into a ditch on the other. She shook her head fruitlessly.

'What the *hell* do you want me to do?' she hissed.

The horn sounded again. Isla snapped. Slamming her foot on the brake (which – she realized later – given that she was travelling at five miles an hour, didn't make a major statement) she jumped out of the car, leaving the door open and the engine running.

'What the bloody hell do you expect me to do?'

'Afternoon.' Finn MacArthur smiled at her lazily. One hand was on the steering wheel, the other arm draped out of the open window, where his fingers beat out a rhythm on the mud-encrusted door of the Land Rover.

Isla, heart thumping with fury, glared at him. He was so *infuriatingly* laid-back.

'I was going as fast as I could. My car isn't exactly designed for the crappy roads you have in this god-forsaken place.'

Finn's face broke into a wide smile. He was enjoying this, the shit. Isla balled her fists by her side, taking a deep breath to try and calm her temper.

'That's why I was trying to get your attention.' Finn raised one sandy eyebrow at her, his blue eyes sparkling with amusement.

'If you see that Douglas fir up there –' Finn pointed in the direction of a group of identical-looking Christmas-type trees, unhelpfully – 'there's a wee clearing to your left. Pull the car over, I'll give you a lift.'

'You don't know where I'm going,' said Isla, hearing the frost in her voice. Irritating git.

'Aye, I do,' grinned Finn. 'This is a dead end after Meadowview House. The road was blocked off years ago.'

Oh, bugger right *off*, thought Isla.

'I can't just leave my car there. What if it gets stolen?'

'By whom?' Finn's smile grew even broader, laughter deepening the lines around his eyes.

'I don't know,' said Isla, truculently. 'God knows who lurks around these woods at this time of day.'

'A sunny afternoon in the middle of nowhere?' There was laughter in his tone.

He had a point, but she wasn't going to concede it. 'I don't know what people do for entertainment around here.'

'The only people you'll see this far into the woods are drunk teenagers who've sloped off to get off with each other on a camping trip. And they'll be in bed, hungover, at this time on a weekend.'

'Fine.' She turned on her heel and stalked back to the car.

It seemed to take forever to rattle along to the little clearing – Isla was convinced she'd miss it and so was crawling along so slowly that the engine was whirring uncomfortably in first gear. Eventually she pulled into the grassy space, switching off the ignition and locking the car.

'Sorry about the mess,' Finn said, throwing a handful of newspapers onto the back seat. 'This is my work truck. It ends up being a portable office. I've got a load of orders there to hand in to the estate later.'

'It's fine.' Isla sat primly, both knees pressed together, hands folded on her lap, trying to look disapproving. The Land Rover made short work of the rutted road, squealing and juddering as it made its way across the uneven surface. She ought to make some attempt at conversation but there was something about Finn that made her clam up. All her usual failsafe starters had deserted her. If she wasn't careful she'd end up asking if he was going any-where nice on holiday.

'Are you—'

'So what's—'

They both stopped at the same moment.

'Sorry—'

'You go ahead—'

Isla began again, 'What's—' just as Finn said, 'I'm—'

They both laughed.

'Your turn,' said Finn, as he swung the truck down the little hill, through the pillared stone gateway, and past the old stables.

'So, do you help Lily out with retreats when you're not working?'

Finn looked at her sideways with an expression of horror.

'She's not my – Jesus, no.' He shook his head, looking alarmed.

'I just assumed she—'

'Jesus Christ Almighty.' Finn pulled the car to a stop, turning to face Isla, his expression the perfect mixture of horror and amusement. 'Lily?'

'You're not together?' Isla had assumed that the beau-tiful Lily would have been his type.

'Never.' Finn ran a hand through his hair, leaving a piece standing on end. Isla thought inconsequentially that he could really do with a trim, and wondered who cut his hair.

'No, I'm just dropping off some carvings I've made for

the retreat she's running.' He motioned to the back seat, where a large cardboard box sat. 'You?'

Isla felt a bit foolish. 'I was press-ganged into coming along.'

'You got roped in by accident, yeah?'

She laughed. 'Something like that. Yes.'

'Lily's got a fairly –' he paused for a second – 'er, powerful personality, don't you agree?'

'It's her aura, I reckon.' Isla gave him a smile, relaxing slightly. Finn started up the engine again.

'Dunno what it is, but she's on something. I reckon it's that herbal tea. She's non-stop. And as for Lucien the demon offspring . . .'

It was a relief to discover it wasn't just her (and Jinny and Shannon) who had private – and fairly uncharitable – thoughts about Lucien's behaviour.

'He's a bit high-maintenance, isn't he?'

'I think Lucien's behaviour means his reputation precedes him. My mate Susan's wee girl goes to the same nursery school and by all accounts he's just as – what's the word?'

'Creatively physical, Lily called it.' Isla finished his sentence.

'If by "creatively physical" we mean "demonic fiend who tries to poison the nursery lunches by putting UHU glue in everyone's sandwiches" . . .'

'He did not.' Isla giggled.

'Not a word of a lie.' Finn looked at her deadpan as

he pulled the car up outside Meadowview House. Lily approached as they were getting out.

'Ah, Finn. *And* Isla. That's funny, I was talking to Melody, my rose quartz crystal, this morning, and she said both your names to me.'

Finn slid Isla a sideways glance, his face completely neutral. Isla concentrated hard. It sounded like Lily had just said –

'Oh, yes,' Lily continued airily, picking up on their confused expressions. 'Yes, my crystals all talk to me, all the time.' She pulled a lump of something green and sparkly out of her cardigan pocket. 'This is Questa.'

'Hello, Questa,' said Finn politely. His expression was inscrutable.

'Oh, she won't reply,' said Lily, as if talking to a six-year-old. 'It's Sunday, you see. I always give them Sunday off. It's a day of rest. The Sabbath.'

'Absolutely.' Finn would be bloody good at poker, Isla thought. He nodded in agreement.

'Now. We're running a little behind.' Lily motioned across to the garden beyond the house, where a red-faced woman could be seen digging over a weed-infested vegetable patch. Two men, meanwhile, were painting the woodwork of the windows that looked down over the lake. 'We've been offering ourselves to Gaia and giving thanks for the splendour of our physical being.'

Isla found her voice. 'Oh, and now you're doing a bit of DIY?' It seemed like an odd way to spend a retreat week on an island, but each to their own, she supposed.

'DIY?' Lily smiled at Isla kindly, again as if talking to someone rather simple. 'Claire and Sandy have blessed the earth with rue and vervain, and now they're creating an offering by clearing the ground ready for it to be blessed with fruitfulness.'

'And vegetableness,' added Finn helpfully, pointing with a completely straight face at something green that could have been potato plants.

Isla suppressed a snort of laughter. Finn elbowed her in the side almost imperceptibly.

'Yes! Yes. Oh Finn, you are just *such* a blessing to this place. Such a joy, isn't he, Isla?'

'Mmph.' Isla bit the inside of her cheek. She could feel a giggle threatening to escape.

'And lovely Phillip and Stewart are creating beauty, which is part of my desire to rebirth them back to an essential state of balanced masculinity.'

Finn's eyes widened and Isla's giggle erupted into a snort, which she turned into a cough.

'Ah, some clearing, Isla. Do you have unspoken conflict? Some emotional resistance? Coughs and colds are always a sign of blockages in your throat chakra.' Lily reached into her pocket, handing over a pale-blue stone. 'This will help.' She held it up against Isla's throat. 'Hold her there.'

Isla obediently placed her hand over the stone.

'Now, Finn. Have you brought my lovely totems?' Lily turned back towards the pickup truck.

'Yep, all in the back there. I'll grab them if you let me know where you want them. They're quite heavy, mind.'

Isla stood waiting, blue stone (apparently female) at her throat. She wasn't quite sure if she was doing it right, or if she was supposed to move or not. After a couple of moments she pocketed the stone, hoping Lily wouldn't notice.

Finn had intended to do a flying drop-off of his slightly unorthodox cargo. He smiled ruefully as he slid the box out of the back seat, feeling his arms tauten against the strain. As he did so, a sharp pain shot up the side of his torso. Bloody ribs.

He gasped at the unexpected pain, the box slipping slightly from his grasp.

'You OK?' Isla had joined him beside the Land Rover, her pale face a picture of concern. She reached across, taking the other side of the box.

'Yeah.' It came out more as a gasp than a word. He'd been pushing himself far too hard all week, with a manic week at the forestry office with Roddy, trying to sort out an audit that was already overdue, and then evenings down at the workshop getting this lot finished in time, with Lily calling regularly to check on his progress.

Isla stepped in front of him. 'Let me take this side for you. You go forwards, I'll go back.'

She was a curious one. Assertive, and clearly used to getting her own way, but there was a shyness hidden behind the dark-brown eyes. She was so prickly, and yet here she was jumping to help him out.

'Thanks.'

With the strain taken off his aching torso, Finn was able to study Isla as she stepped carefully backwards, head turned over her shoulder so she could see where she was going.

As she'd been every time he saw her, she was immaculately dressed – today in grey jeans and a pale vest and cardigan, a silver locket nestled in the hollow at the base of her neck. He felt a stab of desire mingled with something else – something he still hadn't managed to put a name to. There was something about this prickly, defensive girl he liked a lot. Whatever it was, it was enough that it was stopping him from making a move, where normally he'd have stepped in immediately.

Isla stumbled on a tussock of grass. 'Shit, sorry.'

Lily stepped aside, making space for them in the wide-open hallway. They deposited the box on an oak table.

'Right, that's your lot.' Stepping back, Finn rubbed at his side. It was bloody painful.

'Let me have a look at that.' Lily hovered a hand down his side, not touching his body. Isla watched as Finn opened his eyes wide in an expression of mock terror.

'You'd really benefit from our healing session this afternoon. It's a shame you can't join us.'

Isla looked at him with a slightly hopeful expression, but he was thinking he could make a run for it now, head back to the house, get on with sorting the paperwork for this audit, watch a bit of crap TV, eat a pizza, check on his ma.

He caught her eye, and gave her the tiniest raise of an eyebrow. Under her carefully neutral expression he caught a glimpse of pleading.

'Oh, go on then. I could do with getting in touch with my inner hippy.'

Lily tutted good-naturedly. 'It's much more meaningful than that, Finn. But I'm delighted you'll be joining us. As is Melody.' She indicated a large lump of crystal that sat on a shelf.

'Oh yes, I see what you mean,' he agreed. Isla's nostrils flared in amusement.

'I knew you'd understand,' said Lily, in a pleased tone of voice. She was apparently completely impervious to sarcasm. 'Now, I'll just go and gather the others and we can begin.'

Isla looked at him as Lily swept off into the gardens. 'Are you insane?'

'Apparently. And I'm not alone. Surely you've got better things to do on a Sunday afternoon than this?'

Isla pulled a face. 'Not really. I promised myself I wouldn't go back to Edinburgh for the first few weeks because I thought it'd make the time pass more quickly.'

He'd forgotten she was only here briefly.

Isla stood awkwardly at the edge of the circle. They had gathered on the grass, barefoot, as instructed by Lily, the sun glinting on the water of the loch in front of them. Isla couldn't have felt more self-conscious if she tried. Finn, barely disguising his amusement, stood opposite, a wooden totem in his hand.

'Everyone, gather.' Lily's tone was reverent. 'Come closer.' The group all shuffled forward.

Lily brandished her wooden phallus above her head, closing her eyes for a moment. She took a deep breath inwards, exhaling through pouting lips. Isla caught Finn's eye for a moment, and his eyebrows flickered upwards in a silent expression of amusement.

'The Palad Khik is a phallic representation of Shiva.' Lily lowered the wooden carving, nestling it in her hands in a slightly alarming manner. Isla, realizing she wasn't taking this seriously enough, bit the inside of her cheek in the same way she'd done earlier when the giggles threatened.

'It's an amulet – a symbol redolent of fertility and positivity. And it's the totem for this retreat. We are blessed with two residents of the island here with us today, which adds an element of grounding and a sense of place.' Lily looked from Finn to Isla. The others smiled at them welcomingly. Isla, resident on the island for a whole three weeks, tried to look appropriately at one with her environment.

'Now, for the first part of today, we are going to start with an expansive opening. We are holding space for both womanhood and manhood – yin and yang. This is a ritual for our evolution and for the soul growth, a chance for our true potentiality to come forward. An opportunity for learning and expansive power and . . .' Lily paused to draw breath. If it hadn't been such a long way back to her car, Isla would have contemplated making a run for it. But it was a good mile away down the track, and she suspected that if she did try and leg it, Lily would suggest she needed some additional deep therapy to explore her issues with abandonment, or something. So she stood still and waited.

'Neil, Claire, if you can just lie down where you are, we can begin the process. We are starting with a circle.'

Both Neil and Claire lay down obediently, side by side.

'Now, if you can just shift yourself around, like this,' Lily took hold of their heads and tugged them into position, 'and if the rest of you can join us, we are going to begin with a crown chakra connection.'

Finn slid a look at Isla. 'What the . . .?' he mouthed, silently.

'I don't know.'

Somehow Isla found herself lying on the grass, her head touching Claire's on one side and with Finn close by on the other.

'Lovely.' Lily leaned down. Isla caught a whiff of lavender oil from her long skirts. The multitude of bracelets on both her wrists jangled gently. Lying so close to Finn, Isla felt acutely aware of his presence, as if there was a magnetic charge from the earth drawing them together.

Lily adjusted them: 'A little bit closer, like this –' and

in that second, Finn's head was touching Isla's, and the circle was complete. Isla felt a jolt of something quite unexpected shoot through her. It was a long time since she'd been this close to any man. Isla lay completely still, barely breathing, hyper-aware of every movement her body made.

Lily instructed them to close their eyes. The air filled with an eerie, low-pitched humming noise, which became lower and deeper, taking up the space around them until it seemed to resonate within Isla, deep inside her body. She drifted away, time and space lost in the sound.

A gentle touch on her arm woke her. God – had she fallen asleep on the grass? She opened her eyes and sat up with a start, gasping in surprise.

'Shhh.' Lily motioned, open-palmed, to the rest of the group. They were all still lying, eyes closed. 'Take your time.' Isla curled herself into a cross-legged position, kidding herself that she was looking with equal interest at everyone in the group. But she found herself drawn to Finn's face, long eyelashes sweeping down onto his dark tanned skin, his cheeks shadowed by fair stubble. He had a look of the Viking about him, she realized – the island ancestry showing. As Lily laid a gentle hand on his chest, he was the last in the circle to wake. He opened sleepy blue eyes, looking up at Isla with surprise before sitting up, running a hand through his dark blond hair.

'God. Did I fall asleep?'

'That's exactly what I thought,' Isla smiled at him. 'No, your secret's safe with me.'

'I must've been knackered.'

The rest of the group were yawning and stretching their arms wide. Despite her quirky manner, Lily clearly knew her stuff. Everyone seemed far more relaxed and the group were all smiling at one another as if they'd shared something far more hypnotic than a meditation circle.

'The singing bowl has therapeutic benefits for everyone.' Lily held out a heavy metal pot. 'And now that we are relaxed, the next thing we need to do is get everyone into pairs. Sandy and Phillip, I would like to see you two working together. Claire and Stewart, Paul and Ann-Marie, if you could all come with me, I'll settle you into your working space.'

Everyone stood up and followed Lily obediently to their positions.

'What are we doing now?' Finn looked across the unkempt lawn. Another couple had been placed on the water's edge and were sitting, facing each other, cross-legged.

'I have no idea.' Isla put a palm down flat on the soft, new grass. She looked down as a tiny black-and-yellow ladybird made its way across the back of her hand. She could have quite easily made her excuses and left now, but – well, she was surprisingly keen to see what came next, and if she was honest with herself she was enjoying being in Finn's company, despite the dire warnings she'd had from Shannon and Jinny about his reputation as the island Lothario. He seemed surprisingly down-to-earth – but then, Isla realized, it was more than likely that he didn't find her remotely attractive, so that wasn't really much of a shock.

Finn didn't seem to be in any rush to get away, either.

'Here we are. Now, you two are perfect just as you are. Finn, if you can just turn yourself around so you are facing Isla directly, and we can begin.' Finn swung round on the grass so he too was sitting cross-legged across from Isla.

'A little closer. I need you in contact for this one.'

'Sorry.' Finn's knee brushed Isla's, and she felt her cheeks flushing.

'It's fine.' Her heart was hammering against her chest now. This was a bit more than she'd expected. He was close enough that she could feel the warmth of his body touching hers.

'Now this is very simple. As you are all first-time participants, we aren't going to do the whole eleven minutes. We will simply begin with seven.'

Seven minutes of meditation was more than Isla had ever managed in the past, and seven minutes of meditation whilst knee-to-knee with a surprisingly handsome man – even one who wasn't remotely interested in her – was going to be a bit of a challenge, but Isla nodded politely. She closed her eyes in preparation.

'Oh no, we need your eyes open for this one. This is the gazing exercise.'

Finn widened his eyes at Isla in horrified amusement. 'What are we gazing at?'

'Each other,' said Lily, simply. She looked around, assuring herself that everyone was in place. 'When the ting-sha bells ring, we begin. And I will ring them again to signify the end of the session.'

'Is it too late to make a run for the pub?' Finn hissed at Isla. He clearly felt as uncomfortable as she did.

'What's a ting-sha?' she hissed back, just as the unmistakable sound of the bells chimed out clearly in the silence of the afternoon sunlight.

How hard can this be? Isla thought. *All I have to do is look into his eyes for seven minutes.* Finn's eyes were blue, with a hazel-brown ring around the circumference. At the corners were laughter lines that suggested someone who didn't take life – or himself – too seriously. His eyebrows were dark, and framed his face well – not overgrown, not bushy – Isla saw male clients come in all the time looking for a haircut and only as they prepared to leave, their session at a close, would they say, almost in passing, 'you couldn't do something about . . .' and they'd wave to a monobrow, or Denis Healey eyebrows that were threatening to take over the whole of their face, and . . .

She shifted in her seat. It didn't matter how she tried to keep herself busy with stream-of-consciousness chatter in her head: the truth was that having Finn gazing

directly into her eyes was stopping her brain from working properly. It also seemed to stop her looking into his
eyes. It was like a game. If he was focusing on her, she
couldn't seem to focus back, and when that happened
she felt strangely vulnerable. It was also strangely hard
to look into both eyes at the same time. She dropped her
gaze for a second, looking back at him, taking the advantage. It wasn't supposed to be combat, she remembered.
His pupils relaxed and dilated. Her heart was thumping
so loudly in her chest that she was certain he could hear
it. Uncomfortable, she looked away. When she looked up
again he was still there, looking steadily into her eyes.
Time seemed to have stopped. They'd been there for
hours. She felt for a moment like she was going to cry,
and in the same moment she saw something – a look of
sadness within the depths of Finn's blue eyes – and suddenly, inexplicably, Isla found herself wanting to reach
out and hold his hand. He shifted his gaze for a second,
looking down before raising his eyes to meet hers again,
the tiniest sparkle of amusement there now. He was challenging her, a tiny flicker of the eyebrow suggesting she
wouldn't make it. *You'll see*, Isla thought, raising her chin
in defiance. She looked at him, feeling the corners of her
mouth twitching in amusement.

The bells rang out.

They sprang apart, both sitting back slightly. Isla
closed her eyes for a second.

'Well . . . that was intense.' Finn shifted his weight
back onto his arms, arching his back in a stretch.

'And hug your partner,' Lily's voice sang out.

Finn reached across, almost hesitantly. It was strange, but it somehow made sense – Isla leaned into him, feeling his arms wrap around her for a fleeting moment, the heat of his skin beneath his T-shirt. His heart was thumping, too. She pulled back.

'How did you find that?' Lily bent down beside them, taking their hands and holding them for a few moments. This was all getting a bit too close for comfort. 'No need to talk. No need.' She smiled at them peacefully. 'My guides tell me you're harbouring a long-held hurt, Finn, my darling. Release it, and you can move on to achieve your full potential.'

Finn cleared his throat uncomfortably, making a vague noise of agreement. He folded his arms across his chest in a subconscious gesture, one so obvious that even Isla picked up on it. Lily raised a silent, but slightly admonishing eyebrow.

'And Isla. Sweet Isla.' Lily gave her hand a little shake as she held it, as if to loosen her up. 'You have so much to offer. You must open your heart.'

With that, Lily stood up, and made her way down the field to the next couple.

'I'm sure she was meant to give us a chance to tell her how it went.' Finn grinned at Isla. 'That was freaky. D'you reckon we can make our escape yet? I don't know about you but I could murder a pint of something non-herbal and definitely not organic.'

As if she – or her spirit guides – read his mind, Lily

suddenly called out cheerfully, 'Come on, everyone, let's go up to the house for some delicious refreshment.'

'*Grrrrargggh!*'

Isla jumped sideways just in time as Lucien, the demon child, hurtled towards her, brandishing a huge wooden – was that a *penis*? He disappeared into the trees behind her.

'Lucien, sweetheart, we need that totem for the meditation circle in a moment, darling. Can you just pop it back in the peace yurt?'

There was no reply, but some distinctly un-peaceful crashing and yelling from the undergrowth was followed by an ominous splash, which suggested something untoward was going on.

'Lucien?' Lily's voice had a faint air of desperation.

'Shall I nip over and see what's going on?'

'That would be wonderful, Finn. Bless you.' Lily smiled at him beatifically, inclining her head to one side. 'He is *such* a sweetheart,' she added, watching his disappearing back as he strode into the woods. He was clad in a pair of faded, beaten-up jeans, a grey T-shirt clinging to a muscular back that Lily was clearly quite taken with 'So good with Lucien. He adored him the moment he met him – I took him down to see Finn at work in his studio. *So* good to see a man with both yin and yang in perfect balance.'

Isla managed not to snort with laughter. Lily's expression suggested she'd be quite keen to balance Finn's yin and yang herself. She was looking at him as if he was the only cream cake at an organic tofu buffet.

'Anyway, Isla, I can't thank you enough for coming up here. I'd *love* to exchange knowledge with you. I'm hoping to manifest my own holistic range of therapeutic products, but with your knowledge in the meantime, it will be *marvellous* to get an idea of the sort of things the right people are using.' She set off towards the house. Isla, slightly bemused, followed her.

'Well, yes, I—' she began.

'Lindenflower and honey tea?' Not waiting for a response, Lily poured a sludge-green liquid into a chipped mug and handed it across the table. 'Have a seat. I do love it when everyone gathers here in the kitchen. So important for the house to have a real *soul*, don't you think?'

'Yes, I—'

'Oh, look, there's Finny now, having fun with Lucien.' Lily motioned outside, where Isla could see Finn, dripping wet and covered in mud, carrying a flailing Lucien under one arm and the wooden phallus in his other hand. It didn't look particularly enjoyable.

'*So* good for him to have an adult male to sport with,' beamed Lily. 'Not that I want him to grow up with unnecessary prejudices about gender, of course.'

'Of course.' Isla sipped the tea. It was utterly revolting.

'Just give me two moments,' trilled Lily. 'I'm going to pop outside and see if Finn needs any help.'

I bet you are, thought Isla.

'Excuse me.' A voice came from outside so Isla left the kitchen.

A plump and very pretty blonde-haired woman of about thirty stood with her partner – at least, Isla supposed they were together, as they were clamped side by side, looking uncertain.

'Are you here for the silent retreat?' the man whispered to Isla, first looking from side to side, a guilty expression on his face.

'Matthew, it said on the email – we're not *in silence* until after dinner.' The woman looked at Isla, shaking her head with an all-men-are-idiots expression before turning back to him. Definitely together. She hissed at him crossly, 'I told you that already in the car. Honestly.'

'Oh.' His voice was unexpectedly deep. He was, Isla noticed, dressed in a manner that suggested an overgrown toddler, or as if his mother had suggested he make an extra-special effort for the occasion. Dark beige chinos were neatly ironed, the hem doubled over above spotlessly clean navy boat shoes and the kind of almost-invisible socks you wore to the gym. His top half, complete with a childlike, slightly rounded tummy (Isla couldn't help wondering if he'd growl if she poked it, like her old teddy bear) was clad in a very new, very neat blue and white striped cotton top. He looked very sweet, very earnest and utterly sexless. Especially, Isla was surprised to find herself thinking, in comparison to Finn, who'd strode off towards the Land Rover a moment ago, flashing her what had looked like a grin of complicity. He'd swung up into the back of the trailer, having thrown a pile of log offcuts in carelessly, vaulting over the back on tanned arms, T-shirt hitching up to show that muscled back which clearly had no need of gyms or – Isla shook herself. *For goodness' sake.*

'So,' said the woman, rousing Isla from her thoughts, 'if you're not here for the retreat – d'you work here?'

'Me?' *God forbid*, thought Isla, suddenly very grateful for the salon, with Jinny's mad ramblings and Shannon's gruff manner. 'No, I'm just here to visit. I'm not from the island. I –' She paused for a moment, noticing that Lily was climbing back over the gate that led down to the paddock full of Highland cows. What on earth was she doing now?

A bucket in one hand, long skirt trailing almost to the ground, clad in a rainbow T-shirt and wellies, she was marching back across the drive.

'Ah! Wonderful.' Lily's clear voice reached them.

'Is *this* the owner?' The man looked at Isla with an expression of concern. The woman reached across wordlessly, lacing her fingers through his.

'You must be Felicity and Matthew.' Lily stamped towards them, putting down the bucket a few feet away with a clatter of metal on gravel.

Felicity nodded. Matthew pulled at the neck of his Breton-striped top as if adjusting a non-existent tie.

'Splendid.' Lily motioned to the bucket. 'Cowshit. Wonderful for the roses.'

Isla caught Felicity's eye. The split-second expression said more than enough. *Get me out of here*, it said. *Who is this woman?* it said. *I could have been on a spa week in Berkshire with luxury treatment rooms*, it said.

Isla gave a sympathetic grimace that she hoped expressed what she was thinking, which was, 'Beats me, I should be having breakfast in Starbucks right now.'

'Lovely Isla is not just a hairdressing *artist*, but she is an absolute walking *encyclopaedia* of natural hair products, aren't you?'

Isla, feeling slightly panicked that if she didn't escape soon she might end up railroaded into taking part in a silent retreat, smiled vaguely and stepped sideways, trying to look for Finn. It was a long walk back to her car, and he was her only other source of escape.

'Right, then.' Lily actually clapped her hands, like a schoolteacher. 'Why don't you two come along and meet the others who made the earlier boat.'

Felicity and Matthew followed her, expressions slightly guilty. 'I told you we should have left earlier,' Felicity hissed. Matthew glowered back at her.

Lily had already picked up the bucket of manure and was marching towards the house, singing a folk song completely unselfconsciously, and completely off-key.

'Phillip, Ann-Marie, Paul, Sandy –' Lily began, waving a bangle-jingling arm in an arc towards the four people who were sitting at the kitchen table, with the pot of Lily's revolting-smelling leaf and herb tea in front of them – 'this is Matthew.' Where were the others? She guided him with a firm hand in the small of his back to a chair on the far side of the table. He sat down with an obedient plop, like a well-trained Labrador.

'And this –' with a well-practised movement, Lily had somehow detached Felicity from her partner's side – 'is Felicity.'

Felicity sat down, looking deeply uncomfortable and giving her partner a wide-eyed silent glare of horror.

'If you'd all like to take a moment to introduce yourselves.' Lily reached across to the wooden dresser behind Isla, which was festooned with fairy lights and an assortment of religious icons, feathers, and smouldering incense cones. She handed Stewart a painted wooden stick decorated with sparkling threads and glitter. 'Stewart, you have the talking stick. I'll just sort things out with Isla and I'll be right with you. Two shakes of a mermaid's tail.'

Isla, trying not to giggle, caught Claire's eye as she turned to leave. 'Help me,' mouthed Claire, silently.

Lily had clearly been hoping they'd hang around for the whole day, but there was only so much yoghurt knitting Finn could take. She'd let them go on the condition that he and Isla promised to take part in the wishing ceremony at the Clootie Well at the end of the week. They'd both nodded dutifully, before grabbing their things and jumping into Finn's Land Rover with indecent haste.

'Well, that was . . . unexpected.' He put the car into

gear and they crunched down the drive, wheels spinning.

He looked across at Isla. An afternoon in the sunshine
had brought out a smattering of freckles on her high
cheekbones and her pale face was flushed with colour. It
had been a pretty weird experience. He'd only stayed
because he was strangely drawn to this prickly, stand-
offish girl who seemed to have nothing good to say about
the island he loved so much.

There was irony in her voice as she spoke, a half-smile
playing on her lips. 'You aren't a fan of "nurturing the
goddess"?'

He snorted with derision. 'Not when it seems to con-
sist of doing Lily's gardening by the light of the moon,
no. You?'

'I'm all right for gardening, I think.' Her tone was dry.

'Yeah.' He looked across at Isla. She had a still quality
that reminded him of one of the deer he sometimes came
across in the forest when working: silent and watchful,
huge dark eyes fringed with long, sweeping lashes. At
any second she seemed likely to dart away – and yet she
was as far from a country girl as you could get, dressed
even today in a close-fitting black vest top, cropped black
jeans and an expensive-looking pale cardigan.

'You city types don't go in much for that sort of thing,
do you?'

She laughed. 'I've been known to "nurture the goddess" in my dad's back garden, but only under duress.
I'm not exactly a gardener.'

'You didn't fancy "nourishing your surroundings as an offering to the goddess Kali"?'

Isla flashed him a genuine smile. 'You mean painting the hall of Meadowview House? Whilst listening to whale music? Or making herbal tea from cowshit?'

'Or dancing naked under the moon whilst playing the drums? Or wrapping yourself in ribbons and offering yourself to the sea goddess?'

Isla burst out laughing. 'No. None of the above.'

She shook back her hair as she spoke, so it fell back into place. He noticed that it shone like a fresh conker, perfectly cut – somehow, despite having lain on her back in the middle of a field, she still looked immaculate.

'Lily isn't stupid, is she? She's got them paying for a retreat *and* doing her house maintenance. I might try something like that at the salon.'

Underneath that prickly exterior was a sharp sense of humour. He liked her. Staring into her eyes, he'd found himself wondering what was going on inside her head – despite the closed-off impression she gave, there was a depth of emotion there beneath the surface that fascinated him.

'D'you fancy it, then?'

Isla recoiled in surprise. 'Redecorating? No, I think I'm all right for that this weekend, thanks.'

He shook his head briefly, frowning. If Roddy could see him now, he'd be pissing himself laughing. All the usual well-worn lines he'd worked over the last however many years (and, God, he realized, it was a lot of years) – they were deserting him, and he was clutching at straws like a clueless fifteen-year-old, tripping over his words.

'I meant that drink.' He shifted the steering wheel slightly, avoiding a huge rut in the driveway. 'The Fisherman's Arms in Port Strachan. It's quiet this time of day.'

Why on earth had he said that? It made him sound like he was on the pull and he was definitely, absolutely not on the pull. Not this time. He didn't quite know why but what he wanted to do was sit down and talk to her, find out more about what made her tick, find out what she thought of the island—

'Oh.' She looked flustered, eyes darting from side to side, back stiffening. She was searching for an excuse not to come; he recognized the signs clearly enough.

'If you're busy, it's fine, don't—'

'Yes, yeah – I – just—'

He killed the engine. They'd reached the halfway point where Isla's car sat tucked neatly to one side in the lay-by.

'Another time, perhaps?' She turned, the car door half open. Her eyes darted up to meet his for a second, and then she slipped out of the Land Rover and was gone.

Finn pulled back and waited, watching as Isla's little convertible bumped cautiously down the rutted track. He ran a hand through his hair, heaving a sigh of irritation. He'd no idea what had just happened there, but he was in no mood to go home. Roddy wasn't around, he didn't fancy a drink on his own, and all Lily's hippy-dippy shit had left him feeling decidedly weird. That circle meditation thing had made him feel like he was on another planet and he'd found himself thinking about childhood, and memories of Shona, and things from another life – things he'd kept locked away safely for years. And the eye-gazing thing had been completely freaky – maybe Isla felt the same way he did. Seven minutes in silence, looking into her eyes, had left him with more questions than answers. Behind that guarded mask she wore there was so much lurking – Lily had been right about that, saying Isla had so much to offer.

It was insane that he was even thinking about all this stuff. He still couldn't work out why on earth he'd hung around when Lily had offered him the chance – he shook his head. No, all right, he knew exactly what was the reason – or who. What he couldn't work out was why he felt like this.

Maybe spending the rest of the afternoon down at the workshop would clear his head – yeah, that was it. He started the engine, turned on the radio loud enough to blast out the unwelcome thoughts that were crowding in, and headed back. It was probably all this stuff with Roddy and Kate and the baby, messing with his head.

Chapter Fifteen

'Sit yourself down over there, Netty, I'll be with you in a moment.'

Shannon waved her next client in the direction of the two chairs, speaking with two hair grips pursed in her lips (*unhygienic*, thought Isla, reminding herself that she must point out to Shannon that it wasn't acceptable practice).

The woman collapsed onto the chair with a grateful sigh, tucking her shopping bags to one side. She closed her eyes for a moment, rubbing circles on the skin of her temples.

Not waiting to be asked, Isla fetched a cup of tea from the pot Jinny had just made a few moments ago.

'Oh, thanks, hen,' Netty looked up with a smile. 'You read my mind.'

'All part of the service.'

Isla returned to the desk. The salon was quiet this morning, probably because the sunshine was pulling the usual pop-in clients away from their day-to-day routine. Everyone seemed to be out in their gardens, making the most of what had so far been a pretty dull, grey start to the summer – which was unusual, everyone kept telling her. Jinny was busying herself with a stock-check of supplies, planning to make an order. Isla, meanwhile, was attempting to make the computer booking system as simple as possible, in the hope that when Aunty Jessie returned she might make use of it, rather than ignoring it and scribbling everything down in pencil in the scruffy-looking diary that sat on the reception desk. It was covered in doodled flowers and patterns courtesy of Jinny, and the pages were curled and dog-eared – it was hardly the most professional piece of equipment.

As the weeks passed it was becoming clear to Isla that the salon, which had previously just ticked along nicely, could in fact be bringing in a lot more money. Both Shannon and Jinny were keen to learn, worked hard, and had some good ideas. Of course, there was always the possibility that Jessie would get back and be appalled by the changes that had taken place, but if they had everything in order and could show the results . . .

She tapped away at the spreadsheet. She'd brought in a version of the same computerized booking program they used back at Kat's salon. Once it was in place, it was pretty much foolproof, but she just had to get it set up exactly so . . . The hum of Shannon's hairdryer lulled her into a meditative state as she clicked away, completely absorbed in the task. Jinny was pottering around out of sight. The salon was a hive of quiet industry.

'Isla?' Shannon turned away from her client, who was an old school friend of hers.

Isla looked up from the desk, putting down her pen.

'Seeing as we're not busy, and Netty doesn't mind being a guinea pig, can you show me how to do a chignon?'

Shannon really was throwing everything she had into her job now. She'd stopped pretending not to be interested in what Isla was doing, and now that they were starting to get younger, more experimental clients in – the ones who'd previously have visited Glasgow, but who'd realized that with Isla in situ, they could have their hair done for a quarter of the price – she was soaking up every piece of knowledge she could.

'Go on then.' Isla pushed her chair away from the desk. She smiled into the mirror at Shannon's friend. 'Hi, Netty. We prefer to think of you as a model, rather than a guinea pig . . .'

Thirty minutes later, with a delighted Netty striding out of the salon transformed and glowing with the confidence a new hairstyle can bring, Isla returned to the desk.

'Hi.'

'What?' Isla looked up, startled, at the customer who'd just come in. 'Sorry, would you mind giving me two seconds, I'm just –' she clicked save, hoping that she'd made the right adjustments to her spreadsheet – 'fixing something. Can I help?'

There was a thud from the back room as Jinny jumped

down from the folding steps she'd been standing on. Following that, a small squeal of excitement. Following *that*, Jinny appeared as if by magic at Isla's side, where she stood, virtually vibrating with silent excitement.

'Yes, hopefully.' The woman had a fuzz of dark hair that looked in desperate need of some taming serum. 'I'm Kate – Kate Maxwell.' She held out a hand, rather uncertainly. Isla, disguising a look of surprise, shook it. Prospective clients didn't usually start off on *quite* such formal terms.

Isla clicked on the mouse, opening up the booking page. 'Are you looking for an appointment?'

'Well, yes and no.' Kate ran a self-conscious hand over her dark curls, making no appreciable difference to the unruly mop of hair. Isla smiled to herself – as a hair stylist, one grew accustomed very early on to people apologizing for the state of their hair. It was the first thing everyone did as soon as they walked in. She'd see girls who'd swear blind they hadn't cut their own fringes (which hung unevenly at jagged, kitchen-scissored angles) and women who'd come in with disastrous home colour jobs that they'd swear blind had been done at a salon elsewhere. It didn't seem to occur to any of them that she was there to do a job, and the job was making their hair look the best it could.

She'd always wondered if dentists got the same thing with teeth. She gave the woman a reassuring smile and waited patiently for her to stop fluffing up her curls with an apologetic expression. Shannon had paused with comb in mid-air, trying to look as if she was contemplating the work she had just begun, but Isla could see that her ears were pricked up and her gossip radar was activated. The client didn't seem to mind. She too was looking on with interest, and another woman in the waiting area had put her magazine to one side and was sitting examining her nails with an innocent expression.

'I live up at Duntarvie House?'

She sounded English – southern, and quite posh. Still none the wiser, Isla looked at her and then up at the clock on the wall, slightly pointedly. She had another quarter of an hour before her next client came in, and at this rate she wasn't going to get the computer sorted.

'Right . . .' Hands poised above the keyboard, eyebrows raised, Isla looked at her expectantly.

'I'm, um –'

God, thought Isla, *spit it out already*.

'We've been having weddings up at the house and I – well, we – well, I really – thought it might be a good idea to come and have a chat with you?'

The house. Not just any house: the big house. The castle-like Duntarvie that the girls had mentioned in awestruck tones – the one that Shannon and Jinny had shown her the photographs of in the much-thumbed copy of *Hello!* magazine.

Of course, this must be the lady of the house. It was typical that she'd be English, Isla thought. *Coming up here, stealing our land . . .*

'Well, I'm only here for a few weeks,' Isla explained.

'That's fine. I'm really keen that we should try and support business on the island, and I know Jessie's not the most –' Isla must have given her a look, because she paused uncomfortably – 'I mean, I know she's your aunt, and I'm – well . . .'

Shannon strolled across, folding her inked arms across her chest and drawing herself up to her full five foot three, skinny-jeaned legs akimbo. 'You mean, Jessie's not exactly *on trend*, shall we say?'

'Mm. Yes, well –' Kate flushed pink – 'something like that. But I heard you were around for a while, and I know Shannon is doing great things, because she cut my friend Susan's hair and it looks amazing.'

Shannon gave a nod, as if accepting praise where it was rightly due. 'Aye, she's got good hair, Susan.'

This is all very well, thought Isla, *but I'm not sure how Jessie's going to take to having her pet stylist poached by the lady of the manor.*

'So what are you thinking?' Isla laced her fingers together and looked at Kate expectantly.

'Well, the thing is, we've got a wedding this weekend.'

Isla raised her eyebrows in surprise. Mind you, they hadn't officially agreed to opening the salon on Saturday afternoons yet . . . 'Right,' she said encouragingly, and Kate's words all came out in a rush.

'The thing is,' she repeated herself, before lowering her voice, 'they're a bit of a nightmare – er, I mean they're a bit *high maintenance*, if you know what I mean?'

Isla nodded with feeling. 'Oh, yes. Yes, I do.'

'Well, they've just changed their minds at the last minute. Apparently the bride's decided that instead of flying up her own stylist from London she wants something simple, and they've decided at the last minute that they want everything sourced from the island if possible. Including the people.'

Given the speed at which things typically moved around here, Isla imagined Kate had her work cut out.

'I know it's late notice. I am *really* sorry. And I feel really bad, because – well, at least Jessie's not here, because –' Kate lowered her voice – 'I don't even get my own hair cut here.'

'Mmm.' Isla looked at Kate's hair again, thoughtfully. 'So who does, er, who is your stylist?'

'Me?' Kate looked slightly uncomfortable. 'I, um ' She pulled her dark curls back off her face, twisting them around her hand, forming a thick rope, 'I have to confess I haven't had mine cut for ever. I've trimmed it with scissors, but I suspect I'm not meant to say that, am I?'

Isla shook her head with a wry smile. 'Not really.'

'The last time I had it cut properly was for the wedding.'

'Which wedding?' Jinny, who'd been ferreting through the piles of reading material in the little waiting area, held up the copy of *Hello!* that was her pride and joy. 'You mean this one? The one your house is in? You know I couldn't *believe* you had them there in your house – it was so amazing. Were they really nice in real life? I reckon they were really lovely. My wee sister Rowena reckons that he's having an affair with Margaret Powell, because she read something in the gossip pages of the *Mirror*, but if you look at this picture . . .' She paused for breath. Shannon rolled her eyes.

'Actually, I mean my *own* wedding. I kept meaning to, and then it was just ages and it got a bit embarrassing, and then the place I went to here in town closed down and—'

'It's fine.' Isla was used to this part, too. Sometimes mothers would come in to have their children's hair trimmed and she'd watch them rushing in, hurrying through the process, clearly feeling awkward about the state of their own hair. 'Anyway, Shannon is extremely talented, and I think she'd be a perfect candidate for event hair.'

'Oh my God.' Kate's eyes widened slightly. 'Yes, that sounds great. Lovely. I'll give you a shout.'

Then she backed out of the salon door, giving the cloud of hair one last – fruitless – smoothing-down.

'*Extremely talented!*' Shannon blew on her fingernails and polished them on her T-shirt with a smug expression. She did a little shimmy and then stopped midway, looking at Isla with genuine surprise. 'You've never mentioned that before.'

'You've got a real eye,' Isla admitted.

'Right, well, you heard it here first.' Shannon turned back to her customer. 'You'd better take advantage of me

before I'm away down to London to work for Toni &
Guy.'

'She seems quite down-to-earth, considering she lives
in a castle,' Isla remarked to Jinny.

'Aye, I think she is. She's not posh – well, she's got
that posh accent, but that's just English, not proper posh.'

'So how did she end up here?' Isla was fascinated by
the idea of this mysterious castle. She'd been out running
past the huge stone entrance gates, with the lichen-covered
stone lions that guarded the driveway; but beyond the
walls the gardens seemed to be thick with trees and
rhododendrons, and despite running all the way round
(exploring on foot, Isla called it to herself, knowing perfectly well that she was just having a bit of a nosy), she
hadn't seen anything else.

'Oh, she got a job working for Roddy Maxwell. He'd
been going out with Fiona Gilfillan – her dad owns the
hotel up on the hill, near the golf course? – until Kate
came along. My mum knows her a bit. She's nice.
Normal.'

'You have to be, to live here,' Shannon joined in from
across the other side of the room. Netty twirled her chair
around, the better to take part in the conversation

'Aye, the thing about living here is, you have to get on
with everyone in your own way. There's no' a mistake
you make that isn't round the whole island by the next
morning, if you know what I mean.'

Isla, thinking of her drunken disaster the night she'd
lost her job, felt a huge wave of gratitude that she hadn't

been on Auchenmor when it happened. 'I suppose that makes everyone think twice?'

Netty, Jinny and Shannon burst out laughing.

'No; it means we have to *own our mistakes*, as whats-her-face from the hippy retreat would probably call it. You can't pretend you haven't been an arsehole if you've been an arsehole. You just have to take the mickey-taking on the chin.' Shannon spoke with a fair bit of authority in her voice.

'She's right,' said Netty. 'I could tell you some stories about almost everyone on this island, but we tend to let bygones be bygones. We've all got our secrets and our stories.'

'Wouldn't live anywhere else, though,' said Jinny. 'I might joke about getting a big posh job like yours, Isla, but I love this place too much.'

'Aye, me too,' said Shannon, surprising Isla, as she turned back with comb in hand. 'You might have your posh shops and your fancy restaurants and all that stuff, but this place gets in your blood.'

Chapter Sixteen

The rest of the week passed quickly. Jinny was completely beside herself at the thought of working up at Duntarvie House. Shannon was trying to play it cool, but her every spare second was spent with her head in a hair magazine, brow furrowed in concentration, scribbling sketches in a notebook.

Isla and Ruth had another walk together, this time along the shore road. They didn't go too far – Ruth was a bit stiff, claiming she'd slept awkwardly. Isla wasn't convinced: Ruth was still wheezily breathless, and leaning heavily on her stick. Isla wanted to talk to Finn about it, but didn't really feel it was her place. And she hadn't seen him since the retreat at Lily's – it was surprising how easily you could avoid people on an island this small, if you wanted to. Maybe he felt a bit awkward about the gazing ceremony thing – or maybe because she'd said no to a drink, he'd decided to steer clear. She'd been out running in the evenings after work, but supposed his bike was still out of action.

*

On Friday evening Isla lay on the sofa in the flat, messaging Helen. She'd been for her usual run along the shore, bumping into the same couple she met there every night, smiling hello. She'd paused at the rocky outcrop along from Finn's cottage, hands on her knees, catching her breath, watching the last ferry sail and smiling to herself as a dog walker threw sticks into the sea for a determined little West Highland terrier. She'd half wondered if she might bump into Finn – then told herself she wasn't interested in him in any case.

Helen's message flashed up:

Looks like the reunion's going to be everything we ever dreamed of and more. Seriously, Isla, I'm not sure I want to go through with this. Maisie's barely sleeping at night, I look like death warmed up, and I don't think my self-esteem needs the hit.

Isla typed her reply:

Nonsense. I'm not having you chicken out. You look gorgeous in that dress you've chosen. I'll be with you. It'll be fine. What's the worst that can happen?

The idea of walking in alone was hideous. If Helen didn't go . . . A reply pinged back.

We can undo years of therapy?

Isla smiled.

It's not that bad. It's a school reunion. People go to them all the time.

Yeah. You seen Grosse Pointe Blank? I tell you what, if we can take guns I'm definitely up for it.

We're adults. We've moved on. They can't still be arseholes.

You think? Did you see Jamie Duncan's coming?

Isla's stomach dropped to the floor. So far she'd been checking the page every day, wondering why there was no mention of him on there. How she was supposed to go in there and prove a point to him, when he appeared to have fallen off the face of the earth, was proving problematic. But now he was definitely coming . . . She scrolled down the page on her phone, looking at the list of attendees. No sign of his name.

You sure? He's not on the list.

No, Big Dave said in a thread somewhere that he was coming. Apparently Jamie doesn't do Facebook.

Weird. Anyway, look, just because he's coming

(Isla felt a little teenage whoosh of excitement in her stomach as she typed this)

doesn't mean YOU aren't. He probably isn't even friends with Allison and all that gang any more.

:-/

Don't pull faces at me. We're going to go in there and wow them with our fabulousness . . . OK?

. . . right. Oh God, the baby's crying. Got to go.

Isla stood up from the sofa and stretched. Outside her window, the sky was bruised purple. She needed to start getting ready to head out to Lily's wish-making cere-mony at the Clootie Well. She wrapped herself up in a jumper and scarf, thinking as she did so that this weather was ridiculous for the time of year, and that normal places didn't have weather like this in the middle of summer. Stepping into the street, she thought, *if Finn doesn't turn up to this and I'm on my own, I'm going to feel like a complete mug.*

She hadn't had any intention of going at all, but she'd bumped into Lily at the little post office, and Lucien had been so loud and demonic, and Lily had been so weirdly persuasive (Isla had said to Helen in a message later that she was beginning to think Lily was part witch) that she'd ended up saying yes just so she could get away.

She followed the carved wooden signs that led up beyond the close-cut parkland – a gang of teenagers hanging out by the swings in the distance making her edgy as she passed, the hangover from years of catcalling still with her – and through a leafy archway to a narrow path lined with hawthorn hedges, a few last flowers still dotted here and there under the leaves.

The sound of bagpipes startled her as she followed a

bend in the path and stepped out into a little clearing where a group of people stood.

Finn had no idea how he'd ended up agreeing to play bagpipes for Lily's Clootie Well wish ceremony. The woman was completely barking mad, and he could have been out for a drink with the boys – even Roddy had been let off the leash for the evening, an increasingly hormonal and stroppy Kate having decamped to her mum's cottage for a girly night of watching DVDs and eating their weight in cake. Finn had had a drink in the Four Bells and then sloped off, explaining that he'd promised to do this as a favour. He'd picked up the pipes and shoved them in the back of his Land Rover before heading up the back road to the well.

He'd just struck up a first low note when he caught sight of Isla, stepping out from the narrow path and into the clearing. Dark eyes wide, wrapped in a soft brown fluffy jumper with a scarf tied around her neck against the chill of the evening, she looked apprehensive, pausing for a second as she caught his gaze. Thank God he was occupied with something or he'd be standing there, blushing and tongue-tied like a bloody teenager.

'Isla, how wonderful. Take a ribbon.' Lily's voice was so powerful that it could be heard clearly over the deep humming of the pipes. Finn raised an eyebrow in greeting at Isla, who looked back in surprised recognition.

'Once Finn has welcomed in the spirit of summer with song; we're going to bless the goddess of fertility, and then everyone is going to take a ribbon, tie it to a branch – as you can see, the tree is quite laden with wishes already – and make their own special wish.'

Isla stood there, a ribbon in her hand, looking as awkward as Finn felt. Outside her comfort zone she looked younger, somehow. He finished the tune. Placing the pipes down carefully, he made his way over.

'Can't get enough of this sort of thing?'

She gave a half smile, handing him a spare ribbon. 'Something like that. Lily sort of press-ganged me into it.'

'Yeah, she's fairly persuasive, I'll give her that.'

'You could put it like that. I think if I hadn't said no, I'd have been savaged by Lucifer – I mean Lucien.' She started laughing.

'He's terrifying. I reckon he's already making voodoo dolls in his bedroom at night.' Finn looked at Isla sideways. 'How else did she get us here on a Friday night? I knew I felt something pulling me here.'

'Divine forces,' she whispered, giggling.

'Demonic ones.' He spoke in a low voice, realizing as he did so that Lily was beckoning them forward. 'We've been summoned.'

'Shh.' Isla tried to look serious. She bit her lip. Finn looked away. God, she really was beautiful.

They took their place at the back of the motley-looking group. Nobody else here was from the island – not surprising, because the locals were out having a beer or sat at home with a takeaway. This lot must all be the latest retreat visitors. They looked the sort. One couple looked as if they'd been to the outdoor shop beforehand and got themselves kitted out for the occasion: they were clad in matching outfits of convertible windproof walking trousers and sensible walking boots, with close-cut matching haircuts, and scarves tied neatly round their necks against the unseasonable chill. Behind them, two women stood hand in hand. He'd noticed them giggling earlier, and Lily giving them a warning look. They must be the naughty girls of the group. He caught the eye of one of them, and she pulled a face. They stood waiting their turn, then tied a ribbon each around the branches of the tree. The Clootie Well, Lily explained, was a hawthorn tree around a natural spring, where a nature spirit or goddess with healing powers was thought to reside. Locals would travel to the well and tie cloths – or cloots, as they were known – around the branches, as offerings to the goddess.

Lily then attempted – fairly fruitlessly – to get everyone to take part in a dance of celebration for the oncoming harvest as Finn played another tune. After the participants had settled, relieved, onto blankets in a circle, she produced a bundle of slim dark-green candles and, lighting them from one in her hand, passed them around to everyone present.

'May the goddess mark our wish. Peace be with you.' She took a place in the circle and then turned to her left, shaking hands before placing a kiss on the surprised cheek of the sensibly clad man. His eyebrows shot upwards and his cheeks flushed pink.

The handshakes spread around the circle and then, as the ceremony seemed to be over, Lily made her way over to Isla with her hands clasped together in excitement.

'Isla, you walked up from the town, didn't you? Come back to the retreat with us – we're having a celebratory midnight supper. Lovely Jacob here has prepared the most gorgeous kale and lentil stew.'

Having recognized an opportunity for a quick getaway, Finn had already shoved his bagpipes over his shoulder. The keys to the Land Rover were in his hand. He had to act quickly.

'Another time, maybe? I've promised Isla I'll give her a lift back.'

'Yes.' Isla, still sitting cross-legged on the blanket beside a small, round, fuzzy-haired woman whose eyes were closed, shot him a grateful look, picking up the baton instantly. 'I'd have loved to, but I've got to be up first thing to open the salon and—'

'Why don't you drive up for a quick bite? We won't be late, and it will be *such* fun.'

Isla met Finn's eyes again. Hers were wide with horror and she gave a minute shake of her head.

'Let's see how we go. Got to get these pipes home. If the damp gets into them, it can cause all sorts of problems.' Unthinking, he reached out a hand. 'Isla? You ready?'

'Absolutely.' She took it, and he pulled her up from the ground. The fuzzy-haired woman opened her eyes in surprise.

'I'm really sorry.' As they reached the Land Rover, Finn felt suddenly awkward, opening the door and shoving off a pile of crisp packets and water bottles so she could sit down.

'No,' Isla's voice was emphatic, 'I am *so* relieved. I had visions of being press-ganged up there and force-fed lentil curry, when all I want is a bag of chips.'

'Me too.' Turning on the ignition, he looked at her and smiled. 'D'you fancy—'

'God, yes.'

The Land Rover bumped along the narrow track that led down to the back road to Kilmannan.

'Is that really true, about bagpipes getting damp?' Isla looked at him, head cocked slightly to one side.

'Total bollocks.'

'I thought as much.'

'Just as well our Lily's not a mind-reader.'

They parked the Land Rover on the harbour and walked together along the road to the tiny fish and chip shop.

'You're early for a Friday.' Jim, used to Finn's habits of picking up a bag of chips on his way home from a night in the pub, looked up from behind the counter. 'No' out wi' the lads tonight?'

Finn motioned outside to the harbour wall, where Isla sat looking out at the evening sky. It was getting dark at last, the sky streaked lilac and purple.

'Ah right, say no more.' Jim handed over two bags of chips, wrapped the old way in paper.

'No, she's just a –' Finn shook his head. Whatever he said, with his reputation there was no way Jim would be buying it.

'Fancy a walk along the beach?'

'I'd love to.' Isla took the chips and they set off together, side by side.

After a few moments of silence, they both spoke at once.

'So how are you finding island life, then?'

'Have you recovered from the bike crash?'

'You go first,' said Isla, sitting down on one of the smooth rocks that jutted out of the sand and looking up at him. She patted the stone beside her, inviting him to join her.

'My rib's still a bit buggered, but it's getting there. How about you? How long have you got left?'

Why the hell did I ask her that? Finn thought. *Nice to meet you – so when are you leaving? Brilliant.*

'Another few weeks. I'm going back to Edinburgh soon, for a school reunion.'

'Interesting. They're usually a bit of a car crash, as far as I've heard. You got any skeletons ready to come out of the closet?'

My God, this was getting worse. *Why not ask her if she's got any old flames hanging around while you're at it, man?* He shook his head.

Isla looked at him sideways. 'No, definitely no skeletons. Do you?'

'Well . . . ' He kept his tone light as he stood up,

stretching out his back. The rib was still hurting like actually.

'You look sore.' Isla stood up. 'Shall we walk over there? Ooh, look – is that a seal on the rocks down there?'

'Yes – come on, if we walk slowly I'll show you. We don't often get them on this side of the island. Too many tourists.'

Night was falling quickly now. As they approached the seal, it plopped into the water. Isla laughed. 'Too quick for us.'

'I'll take you out and show you some another time, if you like. My friend Roddy's got an observation centre over the other side of the island.'

'That'd be lovely.' She looked at him sideways again. 'So, about these skeletons. I'm guessing you can't have any, because everyone here knows everything, right?' She popped a chip into her mouth and carried on walking.

'Well . . .' And then it all came out, somehow. There was something about Isla; she had a peaceful way about her.

'Ruth – Ma – you've been spending quite a bit of time with her, haven't you?'

Isla smiled. 'I love her. She's amazing. You're lucky to have a mother like her.'

'Ah.' Finn stopped for a moment, turning to look at Isla. Sometimes people would work out their ages and do the maths. Isla either hadn't thought of it, or was too

a long time – until I was fifteen
mum.'

Isla nodded, as if everything had

Finn shook his head and explained. How
been fifteen, his whole world had shifted side-
wa,   en Ruth had sat him down and told him that his
big sister who lived in Australia wasn't his sister, but his
biological mother. That the reason he'd been born in
Inverness was so that nobody on the island would discover that a fifteen-year-old Shona had given birth. How
Ruth had brought him up as her own; that they'd done
what they thought was the right thing. It was a different
time, Ruth had explained to him. But he'd been absolutely furious when he discovered, and refused to speak
to his sister, taking out all his teenage anger and confusion on her when she tried to call from Australia,
where she'd moved away to start a new life.

'That must have been so hard for her. And for you.'

'And for Ma – Ruth,' Finn conceded. 'She tried to do
the best she could to fix everything, and somehow she
just got caught in the middle. But I couldn't let Shona just
turn up, aged thirty, and start trying to act like my
mother. I already *had* a mother.'

'And nobody on the island knows any of this?' Isla
reached out to put a hand on his arm. He felt the warmth
through his sleeve, turning to look at her.

'Roddy does. And I imagine he's told Kate, because I

didn't tell him not to. But that's it. Shona came back to visit ten years ago, and it wasn't a success.'

He still felt guilty about it. He'd been twenty-five, old enough to know better, but he'd behaved like a spoilt child. Shona had gone home to Australia devastated – and a horrible, petulant part of Finn that he didn't much like had felt glad that she felt bad.

'Can't you sort things out with her now?'

'I've tried – a bit,' he admitted. But it had been a pretty pathetic attempt. Ruth had mentioned something about Shona coming back for a visit, and several times he'd gone to pick up the phone, or write an email – but he didn't know where to start.

'There's always time,' said Isla. She brushed a strand of hair out of her eyes, looking directly at him.

He looked back into her brown eyes. Kindness and compassion shone back at him.

'I suppose you're right.'

'I usually am.' With a flash of a smile, Isla turned away and headed back up the beach towards home.

Chapter Seventeen

'Oh my God, this place is *massive*,' Jinny hissed under her breath at Isla as they made their way into Duntarvie House. Isla, who made a rule of trying to stay cool in situations like this, mouthed 'I know', aware she was just as wide-eyed as Jinny. Even Shannon's habitual cool had been replaced with jittery nerves. She'd insisted on checking their kit bags about five times before they'd loaded everything they needed and driven to the far end of the island and through the wide stone gateposts that marked the entrance to the Duntarvie Estate.

'Oh great, you're here. The bride's had her make-up done already. She's in here.'

Kate was wearing a pale grey dress that set off the colour of her eyes. She led them through into a beautiful little drawing room decorated with hand-tied posies of wildflowers and foliage – all, as she told Isla whilst munching on a celery stick ('Sorry, I can't stop eating them – it must be a craving, or I'm missing some vital celery nutrient'), sourced from the estate and put together by Helen, the florist from town. She lived in one of the pretty little estate cottages they'd driven past on the way into the castle itself, and had done an amazing job. If this was just the room they were getting ready in, the wedding room itself must be breathtaking.

Isla looked up. The ceilings were unbelievably high, the walls decorated with a pale eau-de-nil wallpaper that gave the room a calm air, and—

'She's made me look like a bloody china doll!'

There was a crash as the door was shoved open and a furious woman burst in, wrapped in a white satin robe.

Isla, who had plenty of experience of exactly what weddings did to people, stood well back. Kate – who, she noticed, had a packet of celery hidden on a bookshelf – stepped forward.

'Rose, this is Isla, who is our stylist, and Shannon, who'll be—'

'Shannon is our head stylist,' said Isla, filling in quickly. 'She's here to make sure you get exactly what you want, Rose, so if you just pop yourself down there, perhaps Jinny can get you a drink?' Isla motioned to Jinny, who darted over to a table on which a tray of freshly poured Mimosas stood waiting. She reached out to get one, but her hand was knocked out of the way by a photographer, who held out a warning finger. 'Two seconds,' he whispered, pulling back out of the way and disappearing out of sight.

Shannon was in her element. Rose, who'd been hatchet-faced and furious just a second ago, was now cooing with amazement over Shannon's mermaid tattoo. Shannon, meanwhile, had already begun curling and pinning Rose's hair in front of the ornate, beautifully scrolled mirrors that had been arranged in front of matching Louis XIV chairs.

'Is there a bridesmaid?' Isla stepped back and whispered to Kate. 'I thought we were doing her hair, too?'

Kate widened her eyes. 'Long story.' She bit into a piece of celery. 'It *was* her best friend, but they had a falling out, and then she decided on her sister, who is still upstairs getting ready –'

Isla looked up at the clock. She wasn't leaving much time.

'– but then she decided it would be the best friend, after all.'

'So where is she?' Isla's bag was sitting beside the second, empty, ornate chair. Jinny, meanwhile, was doing the worst ever job of being unobtrusive. She was hovering around Shannon like a gnat, offering her hairpins and combs, whilst Shannon, displaying an admirable level of patience and professionalism, was swatting her away discreetly.

'Jinny, do me a favour? Check and tell me how many rollers I've brought?' Isla felt a bit guilty at setting her a pointless mission, but with tensions already running high and the bridesmaid nowhere to be seen, the last thing she needed was Shannon turning round and shoving Jinny into the expensive satin curtains.

Kate lowered her voice again. 'Well, the bridesmaid's

upstairs. She's not – well, she doesn't exactly need much hair styling.'

Isla raised a questioning eyebrow.

'When they fell out, she went off and had her hair shaved off for charity.'

Isla had to hide her giggles beneath a hand. 'I don't know how you do this.' She waved a hand around. 'Wedding stuff would send me mad. How d'you cope with all the Bridezilla stuff?'

'Bridezillas?' Kate scoffed. 'I tell you what, after a couple of years at this, I can tell you the Groomzillas are a million times worse.'

'I didn't even know that was a thing.' Isla shrugged.

'Oh God, neither did I. And I speak as someone who behaved as a complete arse at my own wedding.'

'I don't believe that.'

'I'll tell you about it sometime.' Kate smiled. 'It all worked out in the end –' she ran a hand over the small bump which was emphasized by the empire line cut of her dress – 'but God, I was hideous.'

'Tea.' A tall, stately-looking woman entered the room, bearing a huge pot on a silver tray.

'I knew I'd timed that right,' said a voice behind her.

'Mum, there you are! Look at Shannon's tattoos, aren't they amazing?' Rose, now as pliant as a kitten, turned to her mother, beaming.

'Lovely, darling. Is this seat for me?'

'Looks like I'm on,' Isla said to Kate, positioning herself behind the mother of the bride.

Chapter Eighteen

As soon as Isla missed the first boat off the island on Monday morning, she had a sneaking suspicion that everything that could go wrong on her day off was about to.

Rolling off the next boat, she turned left, making her way through the little harbour town on the mainland and onto the comforting familiarity of the dual carriageway. She put her foot down. Feeling the little car take off, its engine roaring in relief at being able to hit above forty miles an hour for the first time in weeks, she tried to shake off the feeling that surprising her dad with a trip home was a bad idea. Lily, no doubt, would waffle on about the power of instinct; Isla just thought she'd gotten out of bed on the wrong side. It took a certain amount of bad luck to sleep through two alarm clocks and miss a boat that sailed past your own sitting room window several times a day. But Isla had been exhausted – she'd been flat out for days.

Why she'd taken it into her head to go home for the day when she was so tired was beyond her, but something about the cosy environment of Duntarvie House, and the fact that everyone else was surrounded by people they loved, had brought on a wave of homesickness.

She made it to Edinburgh just in time to get snarled up in a snail-like queue of tourist traffic, and tried to remain calm as she edged the car forward, managing five miles in half an hour. When she finally turned the corner down the A-road that led down to her dad's place she was desperate for the loo, dying for a cup of tea, and cursing herself for being spontaneous.

She pulled up outside the house, realizing as she did so that she'd made a mistake. Within two seconds, out of nowhere, a crowd of small boys on bikes had appeared and were circling the car, eyes wide with admiration.

'That your car, missus?'

The bravest of the gang looked up at her through a mouthful of crisps. 'Gonnae gies a shot in it?'

'I don't think so, no.' Isla set the alarm and strode up the front path to the door, opening it with her own key when there was no reply to her knock. 'Dad?'

The house was empty – surprisingly tidy, considering her dad hadn't been expecting her – but there was definitely nobody home. Out of habit, she opened the fridge; inside, to her amazement, were both vegetables *and* fruit, and the milk was skimmed. Maybe her lectures were finally sinking in.

'Oi!' Coming out of the house, relieved that at least she was no longer desperate for the loo, she found the car had been invaded. She'd been right to suspect that the moment her back was turned, they'd be all over it. 'Hands off.'

'Awww,' said the crisp eater, removing his backside from the bonnet, where he'd perched to take a selfie.

Isla tried her dad's mobile, but it went straight to voicemail. Next stop was the flat. Maybe Hattie would be around. They could go for a late lunch. Isla was dying for sushi . . .

'Hi, honey, I'm home,' she called, echoing Hattie's familiar cry as she opened the door to the flat. It felt like a lifetime ago that she'd packed her bags and left Edinburgh, but it was only weeks. Island time seemed to operate differently. It was amazing to be back here in the chaos and the bustle, and yet – Isla bit back a gasp of horror as she took in the state of the place. Without her there to keep Hattie's chaos under control, the sitting room looked like a bomb had exploded. Last night's curry takeaway cartons were open on the table – Isla sniffed cautiously, hoping they were from last night – and the kitchen counters were a sea of spilt milk with cereal-bowl boats floating on top.

At least she knew that her bedroom wasn't going to be—

Stepping into the room she'd left immaculate, Isla realized that she'd been foolishly optimistic.

The spotless white sheets she'd saved for and bought from the White Company, the fluffy afghan throw that lay across the end of the bed . . . they were thrown to one side, hanging drunkenly off the edge of a bed that had clearly been recently slept in. The dressing table where her candles and silver jewellery bowls sat in a tribute to minimalism was stained with something sticky, which was spilt across the top and had dripped down one leg of the table, and – Isla closed her eyes, stepped backwards out of the room, and pulled the door shut behind her. *It's only stuff*, she repeated to herself. It could all be replaced. And it's Hattie's house, and if she wants to live like a *disgusting spoilt repellent stinking bloody pig* (Isla took another calming breath, ineffectually), that was fine. BLOODY HELL.

She shut the front door of the flat behind her with such force that the bang echoed through the stone hallway. Still no reply from her dad.

It was late evening when he returned home. He was definitely looking healthier – wearing a freshly pressed shirt, and tidier than she'd seen him in a long time.

'You should've given me more notice,' he said, enfolding her in a hug. 'I'd have been here.'

'It's fine,' said Isla, who'd spent an enjoyable few hours re-watching her favourite old John Hughes films, texting Helen about what they were going to wear to the reunion (which was now a terrifying few days away) and eating the apparently neglected chocolate biscuits from her dad's biscuit tin.

'But you're back on Saturday for that school reunion thing, aren't you?' said her dad, loosening his tie.

'Where did you say you'd been?' Isla looked at him shrewdly.

He waggled his eyebrows at her, teasing. 'I didn't.'

'Oh, come on, what've you been up to? A night out with the boys?'

He gave a vague nod, and pinched a biscuit.

'Get your feet off that table, young man. You're no' too old to go over my knee.'

Finn ducked his head as Jean, housekeeper and *grande dame* of Duntarvie House, slapped him jokingly over the head with a newspaper. She was lovely, but bloody terrifying. He could remember Roddy getting a cuff round the ear more than once as a young boy. You didn't mess with Jean. Roddy might've grown up without his mum, but Jean had more than made up for it with her mixture of stern discipline and love.

The house hadn't changed that much since Roddy and Kate had started hiring it out as a venue for posh weddings. OK, there were parts that looked a lot more spruced-up than they had done when they'd messed around there as teenagers; and where the huge dining hall had once stood full of disused furniture, the wood floor now shone with wax polish. There were now whole areas of the big house from which the pack of mud-covered dogs – Roddy's black Labradors and Kate's spaniel, Willow – were completely banned.

But in the kitchen, the huge table remained the heart of the house, and Jean still bustled about by the Aga, and

Roddy still took himself off to sit by the fire in the book-lined study, where Kate would curl up on the sofa and snooze. She was exhausted at the moment.

'Right, Finn, make yourself useful. Set the table for me. Roddy, can you nip out to the greenhouse and get me a lettuce and a handful of cherry tomatoes for the salad?'

Kate made to stand up. Dressed in jeans and a loose-fitting shirt, she still wasn't really showing. She looked utterly radiant, though – her cheeks flushed pink beneath the ever-present freckles, dark hair knotted back in a ponytail.

'So.' She looked at Finn with an expression he recognized all too well. 'What's this I hear about you spending last Sunday up at the retreat place with a certain glamorous new hairdresser?'

'Oh God,' Finn rolled his eyes. Every time the island gossip mill churned out the latest news, he was amazed by how quickly things got round. 'I was delivering a load of carvings.'

'Carvings, my foot,' snorted Jean, sliding a warm quiche onto the table, oven gloves in hand. 'That's no' what I heard. Fertility dances with huge big wooden—'

'Is that right?' Kate snorted with laughter. 'Going for the subtle approach, are we, Finn?'

Finn found himself protesting. 'She's not that sort of girl.' He wasn't in the mood for being teased about Isla being another potential notch on his highly decorated bedpost. She wasn't like that; she was different.

'Oh, yes,' said Roddy, coming back into the kitchen.

He ran the lettuce under the tap, shaking it in a colander before turning to look at Finn with amusement. 'Where have we heard that before?'

Finn shook his head good-naturedly. He could take a bit of piss-taking, fair enough. He deserved it.

'Ah,' Kate turned to Roddy, laughing. 'Finn's losing his touch. Time was, you'd have worked your magic on her and she'd be up here having lunch with us before you sloped off to bed for the afternoon.'

'It's not like that. There's nothing going on.'

Jean assembled the salad, tossing it in a bowl, looking at Finn shrewdly. She placed it down on the table. 'Help yourselves. Kate, there's plenty of celery if you're still after it.'

Kate shook her head, pulling a face. 'Don't even mention the word – the thought of it makes me want to throw up now. But if we had a watermelon, mind you . . .'

'You'll be lucky if you can get one of them at the Co-op. Could you not crave something we can grow outside?' Roddy put a hand on his wife's arm. The baby seemed to have brought them even closer together.

The three of them chatted and laughed their way through the meal, as they'd done many times before. The weddings had been enough of a success that Roddy and Kate had made the decision to take a break whilst the baby was born, so they could focus on family life and not have to deal with the stress of anxious pre-wedding preparations taking up every moment. They'd still have the estate to run, but it would take some of the pressure off.

'And there's something we wanted to ask you,' Kate said, curling her feet up underneath her. It was another chilly afternoon, and the fire was lit in the big sitting room. The dogs lay, panting with the heat, sprawled on the rug in front of the hearth.

'Go on.' Finn hoped they weren't going to ask if he'd take over more admin on the forestry side. Since handing over the reins to Dave, he'd really been enjoying getting back into working on his woodcarving. It had been years since he'd had the time to do it, and strangely, working on Lily's unorthodox commission had really got him back in the creative mood. He'd taken a real pride in making each of her carvings as unique as possible – they mightn't be the sort of thing he'd sell to a gallery, but since then he'd started a huge figure of Pan, sculpted from a piece of wood he'd had sitting in the workshop for years. God, maybe Lily was having more of an influence than he realized.

Roddy reappeared from the kitchen, a pot of coffee and biscuits on a tray.

'We were wondering if, now you're doing a bit more of the stuff you love – would you make us a cot for the baby?'

'An heirloom,' explained Kate. 'We'd like to have something we can pass down through the generations.'

Finn raised his eyebrows, indicating the vast room of the castle in which they sat.

'Yeah, all right, smart-arse – besides the castle and all that shit, obviously. Anyway, it would be really lovely if it came from you.'

'I'd love to.'

'So, about this hairdresser girl . . .' Roddy raised an eyebrow.

'She's got a name, you know.' Kate shoved him on the arm. 'She's really nice, actually. I like her.' She shot Finn a look. 'Don't go doing your usual—'

'Bugger off.' He threw a piece of bread roll at her head. 'First, there is absolutely nothing going on – we're just friends.'

Roddy burst out laughing. 'Right, I've heard that before.'

'She's not like that, honestly. She's quiet. She's funny, when you get to know her. And she's kind. She gets on really well with Ma. They've been going out for walks together.'

He caught Roddy and Kate exchanging glances.

'And is she kind to animals, too?' Roddy passed him a coffee.

Finn chose to ignore that comment.

Driving home over the moorland road, Finn pulled over and killed the engine, looking out over the hills and to the islands beyond. Everything around him was changing, but this place remained the same, unmoving. Kate and Roddy were establishing themselves as a family. Even Jean was making noises about retiring, taking some time to travel the world with her husband. Already the island gossips were out in force: Finn's reputation preceding him, it would be seen as a done deal that the only reason he'd hung around up at the retreat was in the hope of getting his leg over. And OK, fair enough – in the past, that might've been his intention. But this time, he wasn't sure it was enough. Isla had made him open up, talk about his past, think about what had happened with Shona, his – his mum. Maybe it was time to have a proper talk about everything.

Part Three

Chapter Nineteen

'Oh my *God*.'

Isla looked up from her coffee to see Jinny exploding through the front door of the little hair salon. There was a crash as she knocked over a cardboard display of products, which she dismissed with a wave of an arm that was brandishing a glossy magazine.

'We're in *Hello!*' Her hair flying, Jinny threw a plastic bag down on the floor – another four copies of the same magazine slid out – and spread herself across the reception desk, flicking through the pages furiously.

'What's going on here?' Shannon sauntered in behind her, cool and measured as always, sizing up the situation. She smoothed down the long-line vest top she was wearing over a black miniskirt, peering across to see what her friend was so excited about. Isla smiled to herself. The girls had worked hard at the weekend. Had Jinny known that the photographers who'd been manoeuvring around them on Saturday were working for *Hello!* she'd have been delirious with excitement – which was precisely why Isla, who'd found out whilst chatting to Kate, had decided not to breathe a word. Rose, the bride, had enough society clout to guarantee a few pages of coverage. Isla hadn't expected the feature to appear in the magazine this week, but Jinny's delight had made keeping quiet well worth it.

'Ahhhh!' Shannon shrieked with excitement, abandoning her usual couldn't-care-less demeanour. 'There I am! Look, Isla! Oh my God, *look*, Jinny's in the corner of that one, helping you fix Rose's mum's hat in place.'

'I'm famous.' Jinny did a little twirl on the spot, ending in a curtsy. 'Autographs are available on request – oh my God, this is so amazing, can you believe it? Our salon, featured in a proper magazine like real hairstylists?'

Isla shook her head, laughing. She peered over Shannon's shoulder. They were all in there – and she was mentioned in the caption. Well, that was one in the eye for Kat Black and Chantelle. She wondered if they'd pick up the magazine over coffee in Edinburgh and notice. And – she gave a shiver of anticipation and nerves – the reunion was two days away. Well, that would be one in the eye for the mean girls from school. She crossed her fingers behind her back and sent up a little petition to Lily's goddess of the Clootie Well: *please let them pick up a copy of this week's edition*. Maybe she'd sneak up later and tie a wish to the tree, just in case.

'This is *literally* the absolute best day of my life ever. I can't believe it. I can die happy.' Jinny hopped up and down.

Shannon was still peering closely at the picture, as if

she couldn't quite take it in. 'Can you imagine what Jessie's going to say to this?'

Isla looked up as the door rattled open and their first client of the day walked in. 'I'll give her a call later. Meanwhile, you two, we've got hair to do.'

Chapter Twenty

'You're sure you don't want me to put a nice colour in?'
Shannon spoke to Isla's reflection. It was Saturday morning, they'd finished up early, and Isla was feeling so sick
with nerves that she could barely speak. Her stomach
was twisted in a knot.

She shook her head.

Shannon ran her hands through Isla's wet hair. Jinny,
meanwhile, was spinning round on the next chair, dithering over what Isla should wear, a prized copy of *Hello!*
still close at hand. She'd been utterly delirious with glee
for the past two days – every single client had been
shown a copy, the newsagent had ordered in extras from
the mainland, and Jinny was determined that Isla should
take one with her to the reunion.

'Just stick it in your bag, casual-like. And when they're
all, "So I'm manager of Marks and Spencer, what do *you*
do?" you can just pull it out –' she flicked it in the air, as
if brandishing a sword – 'and be like "Yeah well I'm in
Hello! magazine actually, so stick that in yer pipe and
smoke it."'

Isla, who could imagine Jinny turning up to her own school reunion in ten years' time and doing just that – except, of course, that there wasn't a soul on the island who didn't already know about it – laughed. There was absolutely no way she'd do anything like that. To be honest, she was seriously contemplating backing out. She knew that both Helen and Amira wouldn't take much persuading.

'How about I make it a bit asymmetric?' Shannon ran her hands down Isla's hair, thoughtfully. 'I mean, it's in gorgeous condition and that, but it's a wee bit . . .'

'Safe?' Jinny piped up, helpfully.

Shannon pulled an awkward face. 'Er, yeah.'

Isla, who prided herself on her smooth, gleaming, neatly kept bob, grimaced at them in the mirror. They were probably right. 'OK. Nothing majorly radical.'

'Nah,' said Shannon, picking up the scissors, 'you're safe with me.'

Isla closed her eyes. It was true, she did feel confident in Shannon's abilities. The younger girl had a real talent that had just needed to be brought out, and the last few weeks had done that. Isla had loved teaching her, and she'd been a brilliant pupil. How she was supposed to go back to being Jessie's second-in-command, Isla couldn't imagine – but Shannon adored island life, and wouldn't want to move away.

When she'd first arrived here on Auchenmor, the idea that someone would want to stay here voluntarily had been impossible for Isla to comprehend. As time had passed, though, and she'd grown used to island time – where things got done, but you had to allow at least twice as long as you would in the city, and nothing was in a hurry – the friendliness that had at first spooked her had come to seem reassuring. Now, when she popped to the florist for armfuls of gorgeous flowers to make the little flat more welcoming, she stood and chatted with Helen about what she'd brought over from the market. She popped to the greengrocer's for fresh, locally grown vegetables instead of wilting bags of pre-packed salad from the supermarket, and pottered around the shops with Ruth, helping her with her shopping and stopping for tea and a bun on the way home.

'Isla?' Jinny placed a cup of coffee on the little ledge below the mirror. 'You asleep?'

'No.' She looked up at the girls, who had paused for a moment to admire Shannon's handiwork. 'Just thinking.'

'About the school reunion? I can't imagine being thirty.' Jinny scrumpled up her face, looking in the mirror. 'D'you think I'll be wrinkly by then?'

Shannon shot her a look. Isla rubbed between her eyes, where frown lines, product of years of concentrating hard as she cut hair, had begun to form.

'Don't listen to madam there,' Shannon said, with uncharacteristic reassurance.

'Ooh, no,' said Jinny, backtracking. 'I didn't mean *you* are wrinkly, I just . . .'

Isla laughed. 'It's fine. I wasn't really thinking about

the reunion – to be honest,' she found herself confessing, 'I feel a bit sick thinking about it.'

Shannon made a couple of final adjustments before standing back with her scissors, head cocked to one side, mouth pursed thoughtfully. 'Right, let's dry this off and see what you think.'

'You are looking *gorgeous*.' Shannon sat back on her cutting stool, looking at Isla's reflection in the mirror. She'd done a beautiful job of her hair, Isla had to admit. Jinny was desperate to do her make-up, but there was no way that it would survive the journey back to Edinburgh. It would have to wait, and she'd do it in her dad's bathroom before Helen arrived to pick her up. She had the two o'clock ferry to catch if she was going to make it back to Edinburgh in time.

Chapter Twenty-one

With a final smoothing down of her hair, Isla slipped into the back of her dad's cab.

'Right then, Cinderella – let's get you to this ball.' He turned in his seat to smile at her before starting the taxi with a growl of the diesel engine. Isla strapped herself into the back seat, smoothing the belt over her black dress. She'd decided to go classic and understated, with her habitual black – a slash-necked dress which, she realized, looking down, rode up her thighs more than she expected when she was sitting down. She'd have to stay standing up the whole time, or tuck her legs under the table.

She took a breath, trying to calm herself. Despite the perfect hair, the manicured nails, the expensive shoes and bag, she felt like she was ten again, heading off to the primary-school disco in a dress she thought was gorgeous. Closing her eyes, she remembered the scene. Allison and the gang had rounded on her, laughing and pointing, saying the frilly edge and pretty polka dots made her look like she'd come in her nightie.

Oh, God. A tidal wave of last-minute panic hit. She looked down at her phone. It still wasn't too late to pull out, to tell Helen that she couldn't face it. They could go out for a girly dinner instead, catch up over a bottle of champagne . . . Isla paused for a moment, shaking her head, remembering the last time she'd mixed an Edinburgh night out with alcohol. No. There was no going back.

The horn sounded as her dad pulled up outside Helen's house. Amira, who was meeting them at the reunion, was the brave one. At least Helen and Isla would be walking in together. With a deep breath, Isla put her phone back in her bag and braced herself for the fray.

'You look amazing!' Isla moved her handbag, making space for Helen. She'd highlighted her huge, beautiful eyes with dark shadow and her hair was pinned up loosely, waving tendrils curling around her neck. Helen put an instinctive hand up, doubt flashing across her face.

'So do you.' Helen sat down, and they set off.

They sat in nervous silence, both looking out of the window, the radio playing incongruously cheerful tunes through the speakers. With a groan of the handbrake, the cab pulled up.

'Right, girls –' Isla's dad had hopped out of the front seat and opened the door for them, like a chauffeur – 'you both look cracking. Go in there and knock 'em dead.'

*

The function suite of the Muirton Arms hotel looked like it hadn't changed in the last fifteen years. A shiny silver plastic banner hung across the wooden door, emblazoned with the word 'Congratulations!'

'What are we congratulating?' Helen, tugging at the hem of her skirt, looked at Isla and pulled a face.

'Ourselves,' Isla replied, taking another deep breath and trying to control the overwhelming urge to flee, 'for making it here. We can leave any time.'

'We can leave any time.' Helen chanted the response.

Inside, by the front door, a very blonde woman with her hair pinned up in a loose bun stood holding a sheet of name stickers.

'You'll have to excuse me, I'm terrible with names and faces . . .' She didn't look up as she scribbled something on a clipboard. 'I've no idea how Charlotte roped me in to working on the door.'

Isla peered at the woman's chest, trying to make out her name as Helen ran through the list, finding her name and sticking it to her chest. Who on earth was Tina?

'Isla.' Tina looked up at her with a smile of recognition. 'Oh yes, I remember you, we sat next to each other in Chemistry.'

Tina – Christina. Quiet as a mouse, hair to match, top of the class for science, kept herself to herself – this blonde, glamorous woman in teetering heels was Christina?

Inside the function room there were balloons hanging from the light fittings, a tray of drinks sitting on the bar, and huddles of people standing awkwardly around. It looked like a middle-management conference had been relocated to an eighteenth birthday party. Half the men were in suits, the women balancing in unfamiliar heels. Helen reached across and took two glasses, handing one to Isla.

'I know you said you weren't drinking, but this is just in case.'

Isla took the glass of wine and sniffed it, wincing. It smelt sour, the reek of alcohol making her eyes water.

Helen continued. 'Amira's just texted, she'll be here in a second. She decided she wasn't coming in until we were definitely in the building.'

'In case we chickened out?' said Isla, raising her eyebrows in amusement.

'Well, would *you*?'

'Oh my God, Isla Brown!' A voice from across the room sounded out like a foghorn.

A gaggle of women spun round, the unmistakable Allison Graves at their centre. Isla felt her heart thudding, and her stomach turned over with panic.

'Here we go,' said Helen. 'Brace for impact.'

Isla felt her cheeks lift into an automatic rictus smile of recognition, and the pack moved in for the kill.

'I saw you in *Hello!* magazine.' Allison Graves, her hair still just as red, her wiry figure very definitely not just as wiry (she had a decidedly matronly bosom in her red lace dress), flapped her hands in amazement.

'Aye, Kerry saw it as well,' nodded one of the other

women, who Isla recognized as Lynne, one of the old gang who'd routinely terrorized her. 'Did you bring it with you? Isla, you could've given us a wee autograph, you're famous.'

Isla looked wildly at Helen, who was being embraced by someone in a navy-blue velvet tunic.

'No idea,' mouthed Helen, wide-eyed.

'Not exactly famous,' said Isla, virtually dumbstruck.

'Last I heard from my mum was that you were working in that posh hairdresser's up on Hanover Street.' Allison clinked her glass against Isla's with a grin of complicity. 'No' bad for a lassie from our wee town, eh?' Allison turned to the others, nudging Isla with a beaming smile.

Isla, completely floored, just nodded, and swallowed a mouthful of the disgusting wine.

'Isla?' Allison nudged her. 'Anyway – I'm sorry, I was a right bitch to you when we were at school. Bygones, eh?' And to seal the deal, Allison insisted on buying her a drink, admiring her outfit, and dragging Helen over to compare childbirth horror stories.

Isla was completely derailed by the fact that everyone was so bloody nice and grown-up, and had so obviously moved on from the people they were at school: it was all, wasn't it lovely to see such-and-such got married to that boy from the year below, and what a pity Malcolm couldn't make it, but did you know he's got an undertakers' firm in Melbourne now?

It was weird, but the moment of triumph just wasn't

there. There was no delicious revenge to be had, because everyone was older, fatter, greyer in places. Jinny would giggle at that. They were turning into their parents. And where the hell was Jamie? She'd been watching the door surreptitiously all the while, as she listened and nodded and made polite noises in the right places.

She escaped to the loo for a moment to gather her thoughts and check her hair in the mirror – Shannon had been right, the cut was still classic, but the swing of the asymmetric style gave it a modern edge. She ran a comb through it quickly, and headed back outside. Amira, looking as surprised as Isla felt, waved a quick hello from across the room.

'Isla Brown. How're you doing?' A bald man with a round face and a stomach to match turned round from the bar, a pint of beer in his hand.

'Hi.' Isla smiled vaguely, half-scanning the room over his head.

'Dinna recognize me without the hair, eh?' His voice was familiar. Isla felt a sudden lurch in her stomach.

'Jamie?'

He nodded, beaming. 'Can I get you a drink?'

Chapter Twenty-two

Desperate for all the news, Shannon and Jinny were earlier for work on Tuesday morning than they'd ever been.

'Morning!' they chorused in unison.

Jinny filled the kettle. 'Just thought we'd make you a cup of coffee and you can tell us *all the gossip* from the weekend because we are absolutely *dying* to know what happened.'

'I'll tell all after work.' Isla – who had spent the previous day walking across the beautiful Selkie Bay on the far side of the island and watching the seal colony bobbing about in the water, speaking to nobody – still wasn't ready to talk. 'Right now, I just want to act like it didn't happen.' Her tone was final.

Shannon, wisely, kept her mouth shut. At five o'clock she flipped the closed sign over and locked the door before turning round, hands on hips, to face Isla.

'So?'

Jinny dried her hands on a towel and hopped up onto the desk, lips pursed in anticipation of gossip.

Isla, surprising herself, said: 'I don't suppose you two fancy a drink?'

Shannon and Jinny didn't have to be asked twice. They grabbed their bags instantly and shot to the door in a Pavlovian manner at the mere mention of the words.

'Right. Two ciders for us, one gin and tonic for you. It's therapeutic. Don't argue.' said Shannon, seeing the expression on Isla's face. Isla didn't protest further. She took a large gulp and sat back, feeling the alcohol hitting her bloodstream almost instantly. She hadn't eaten all day.

'So what the hell happened?'

'Oh God.' Isla nursed the first drink of several, and began.

'And then,' she explained to Shannon and Jinny, who still saw almost everyone they'd gone to school with virtually every day, and for whom the idea of a school reunion was completely alien, 'then, just when it couldn't get worse, Jamie Duncan turned up.'

'That's the one you had a bit of a thing for, right?' Jinny waved across for Shannon's boyfriend Rab behind the bar to get them another round, and bring it over. This was far too important to miss.

'Yes,' groaned Isla.

'AND?' chorused Jinny and Shannon.

'Oh God. I was trying to make an early escape – Helen was feeling the same as me, like we'd done our time and that was quite enough, thanks very much – when he launched himself at me outside the ladies' loos.'

'Ooh,' said Jinny, breathlessly.

Isla shook her head. 'No.'

All those years of daydreaming about the day her prince would come, and it hadn't occurred to her that the years might not have been kind to Jamie Duncan – heart-throb of the estate, first boy to kiss a girl in year six, cool-est boy in school with an earring when nobody else was allowed one. When the round-bellied, balding, leering, *wedding-ring-wearing* Jamie had pounced, having arrived late and clearly several pear ciders down, Isla had side-stepped deftly, leaving him swaying against a wall.

'Oh my God.' Shannon made vomiting motions.

'Ewwww.' Jinny pulled a face.

'Yeah.' Isla downed her third gin and tonic in a oner. 'Yeah.'

'So, you can strike him off the list then,' said Shannon, pragmatically. 'You need to have a look at my copy of *The Rules*.'

'The library's copy, don't you mean?' said Jinny.

'Shit, you're right.' Shannon frowned. 'I got another overdue warning about it about three weeks ago.'

'So what's next?'

'The Three Bells?' Isla, slightly unsteadily, got to her feet. Jinny gave a squeal of excitement and led the way.

Finn had only nipped in to the pub for a quick scampi and chips on the way home because he couldn't face another microwave dinner for one. He'd bumped into Dave – who'd shamefacedly admitted he'd nipped in for a pint on foot on the way back from the estate office, just so he could avoid the hell that was bath and bedtime with his three small children – and they'd ended up making it two, and a long talk about what to do about staffing and long-range plans. It wasn't even eight o'clock when the door of the pub opened with the distinctive clattering bang that suggested this wasn't the first of the many island pubs that someone had visited that evening.

'I think maybe you should have a Coke instead; just pace yourself a bit,' said Jinny. He looked up to see her and Shannon from the salon, followed by Isla, who was slightly cross-eyed, and with her long limbs all over the place doing a passable impression of Bambi on ice.

'Ooh, snooker,' said Isla. 'I'm rubbish at – oh *hello*, Finn.'

Dave, just leaving, gave him a knowing look. 'Oh, aye?' Finn shook his head. Bloody hell, had she been on the hair-curling liquid or something? She was plastered.

'Isla.' He pulled out a chair and she flopped into it, elbows on the table, chin in her hands, gazing at him with slightly unfocused eyes.

'I'm getting her a Coke.'

'Coffee and water would be better, I reckon,' Finn called out to Shannon, who was heading to the bar.

'I don't drink,' explained Isla, helpfully.

'Right,' nodded Finn. 'I can see that.'

'You've got nice eyes. Mind you, so did Jamie Duncan.'

Jinny, sitting on the other side of Isla, shook her head at a questioning Finn. 'Don't ask. Long story.'

Shannon returned with an espresso and a pint of water. She turned back to the bar to order drinks for herself and Jinny. 'Want anything?' she asked Finn.

'I'm good, thanks.'

They sat in silence for a moment. Isla swayed gently on the chair.

'God, I *really* want a Pot Noodle.'

Shannon returned with drinks, sizing up the situation in an expert manner. 'Jinny, do you want to wait here, and I'll get Isla home? Isla, I reckon you need a bit of a sleep and a couple of painkillers for the morning.'

'I could just have a snooze here. S'quite comfy.' Isla's head nodded forward.

'I'll walk you home.' Finn stood up. 'You got the keys to the flat?' Isla nodded. He caught a brief look between Shannon and Jinny. 'I'll come back and let you know she's in safely. Deal?'

Isla tucked her arm into his quite happily. She was a fairly lightweight drunk compared to some of the lumpen buggers he'd had to help haul home from the pub on a Friday night over the years. There'd been one memorable occasion when Paul MacEwan, a dairy farmer from the far side of the island, had been so plastered and was so enormous that they'd had to roll him into the back of a pickup truck and wheelbarrow him through the farmhouse door. In comparison Isla was floating along by his side, quite cheerfully.

She stopped suddenly, pulling him round. 'You're nice, Finn.'

'Thanks. You are too, Isla. Now, let's get you home.' He started walking again.

'No.' She stopped dead. 'I mean I *like* you.' Her eyes were wide. She was gorgeous, completely plastered, and had no idea what she was saying. Unfortunately. Finn realized with a jolt that he wished desperately that they were having this conversation on a beach in the rain, and completely sober.

And then it was too late, and Isla had reached forward – she was tall enough that she didn't even stand on tiptoe, just snaked her arms around his neck and tried to kiss him.

'Woooah!' shouted a group of boys cycling past on BMX bikes.

'No,' said Finn, pulling back, holding Isla at arm's length. 'You're going back to Edinburgh in a few weeks.'

Isla looked at him for a moment, cocking her head to one side. 'I suppose I am.'

He nodded. God, this was hard.

'Ooh, I *really* want a Pot Noodle.'

'Let's get you home.'

'She's in the flat, quite happy, off to bed with a bottle of water and two ibuprofen.'

Finn stood over Jinny and Shannon, who had been deep in conversation with their arms waving animatedly.

'Aye, she's going to need them in the morning.' Shannon shook her head, mouth pursed in mock disapproval. 'D'you want to join us for a drink?'

It was the last thing he wanted. Looking up at the light glowing from the salon flat, he sighed and set off for home.

It took Isla a moment to remember why there was a half-drunk bottle of water and a packet of ibuprofen by her bed. Oh, God. She headed for the kitchen to make coffee, realizing when she opened the fridge that the milk was out of date. Pulling on a pair of leggings and a hoody, she ran down the stairs to the salon fridge.

As she turned back to make her way upstairs, something outside the door of the salon caught her eye. It was too early for deliveries – the first ferry hadn't even made it into the harbour.

Isla pulled open the door, bending down to discover a gift bag. Inside was a Pot Noodle with a pink Post-it note stuck to its top.

'Friends?' it said.

'Love me tender . . .'

The sound of Bruno's deep voice as he sang along to his favourite Elvis track made Ruth smile. She'd decided on a whim that morning to hop on the bus along to town, and, pleasing herself, had hopped straight off and in for a plate of scrambled eggs on toast and a pot of tea. Surprisingly the cafe, which was usually packed at this time of year, was almost deserted.

'There you are, my darling,' Bruno beamed at her. He'd been on the island for donkey's years, but the Glasgow accent still bore a hint of his native Italy. He'd kept a teenage Finn out of trouble, giving both him and his best friend Roddy part-time jobs working there in the holidays – Finn washing dishes behind the scenes, Roddy out front making coffees for the tourists who came in off the boat in droves back then, oblivious to the fact they were being served cappuccinos by the future Laird of Duntarvie. Ruth smiled to herself, remembering. She sat back on the red leather seat of the old-fashioned booth and relaxed. This was the life.

'Ruth!'

Talk of the devil – Kate, Roddy's wife, came through the door, smiling as always. She was a lovely girl, a real breath of fresh air. Smelling of roses and carrying an armful of flowers wrapped in paper, Kate leaned across the table, kissing her on the cheek.

'How are you?' She put the flowers down on the empty table opposite. 'I've just nipped in for a sneaky bit of Bruno's chocolate cake.' She looked down at her stomach.

'I'm fine,' Ruth smiled, motioning to the empty space beside her. 'Are you staying here, or taking it back up to the big house?'

Kate sat down with an exhalation of breath. She

looked from side to side in a jokily conspiratorial manner, lowering her voice. 'Don't tell anyone, but Jean's up there making mushroom quiche for dinner, and the *smell* –' Kate pulled a face, making Ruth giggle. 'And she's got it into her head that I'm eating too much rubbish, so between her and Mum they've cleared out all the things that taste nice in the house, and I am *desperate* for cake.'

'I won't tell a soul. Let me get it – my treat. Bruno,' Ruth called across, 'can I have a nice big slice of that chocolate cake, please?'

Jean was a lovely woman, but fairly set in her ways. Poor Kate; Ruth could remember being dreadfully sick when she'd been expecting Shona.

'Here you go.' Bruno frowned slightly as Kate reached across and took it gratefully.

'Ohhh,' she sighed, blissfully.

'That solves the problem. If any of the food police come in, we can tell them you're just having a wee taste of my cake.'

'You are an angel,' Kate beamed, her mouth full.

Later that afternoon, with the salon closed as usual for the Wednesday half-day, Isla was just pottering around when she heard a knock on the glass. Looking up, she felt her cheeks flush scarlet.

'Hi.'

'I'm *so* sorry about last night.' There, it was done.

'It's fine. It was nothing.'

Oh good, thought Isla, *we can just pretend it didn't*

happen. She brushed away a slightly miffed feeling that she'd hoped it might be slightly *more* than nothing to Finn; but then, with his reputation he probably dealt with people making passes at him three times before he'd even made it to work in the morning.

'I wondered – as you're closed this afternoon – if you fancied a trip over to the other side of the island? See the seals?'

'I'd love to. Give me five minutes.'

They parked in a lay-by overlooking the bay. In the distance, purple against the sky, was the huge sleeping giant of Eilean Mòr, the island that stood several miles across the sea beyond Auchenmor. The air was still, and filled with the sweet, coconut scent of the yellow gorse bushes.

'If we walk through this field,' Finn explained, 'we can take a shortcut down to the rocks where the seals hang out. I'm not the expert – Roddy's the one who knows all the marine biology stuff – but it sort of rubs off on you when you grow up with someone like him.'

'You two seem really close.' Isla clambered over the stile that led into the field.

'Yeah, we are. Neither of us had any siblings – well,' he looked at Isla, his face clouding for a second, 'I didn't know I had any, let's put it that way.'

'Have you thought about what you're going to do about Shona?'

Finn shook his head. It was clear that he didn't want

to talk about it, and Isla was happy to enjoy the peace and not push it.

'You're lucky to have Ruth, anyway. I love spending time with her.'

'She loves you.' Finn gave her a nudge. 'I think I've been replaced in her affections, actually.'

'Hardly. You're her blue-eyed boy.' Ruth had chatted away about how proud she was to see Finn back in the workshop, doing the creative work he loved. Isla had promised to call round after the reunion and let Ruth know how it had gone. It was an unlikely friendship, but they enjoyed each other's company enormously.

Finn and Isla walked down towards the beach together in a comfortable silence, the sea birds swooping overhead. As they stepped onto the rugged black stones, Finn pointed out the first of many seals basking in the sunshine. It was amazing that just hours away the city was gearing up for Festival time – and she'd soon be back there, with all this just a distant memory. Until recently the idea of wanting to come back to Auchenmor ever again had horrified her, but of late, as her friendship with Shannon and Jinny – and, Isla admitted to herself, with Finn – had grown, she'd realized that once Jessie was back, she could see herself coming over for the occasional weekend. The bustle of city life was in her blood, but the island had an unexpected charm that she'd grown to love.

She and Finn sat down on a couple of rocks and he produced some chocolate, which tasted delicious in the salty air. They sat together for a while, looking out to sea, before he spoke.

'So, not long now. What are your plans for when you get back to Edinburgh?'

'I honestly don't know.' Isla shook her head. 'Maybe I'll open a meditation retreat like Lily, get a load of guests in to redecorate the place, charge them a fortune.'

Finn laughed. He scooped up a handful of tiny pebbles, letting them run through his fingers and down into the rock pool at their feet.

'Well, you've transformed Jessie's place for her. Maybe that could be your thing. You could set off around the Highlands, create a chain of high-fashion salons and scare all the old ladies out of their blue rinses and perms.'

Isla frowned. 'I don't think so.'

'What did you want to be when you grew up?' Finn shifted around to look at her, his gaze open and direct.

'Me?' Isla looked at him, thoughtfully. He was a good listener, Finn. He looked you right in the eye, made you feel like he was really interested in what you had to say. It was part of his charm – she winced slightly, remembering the other night. 'Um, actually, when I was younger, I wanted to be an English teacher.'

'Interesting choice of career, then, hairdressing.' Finn's eyes crinkled as he laughed.

'Yeah, well, it wasn't really a choice. It just sort of happened.'

'You've done a brilliant job with Shannon. Ma was telling me you've taught her loads.'

'I like teaching the girls far more than anything else,' she admitted.

'So go back to college. Train as a teacher. It's not too late, y'know.'

Isla looked at him with surprise. She'd shelved that plan a long time back.

He raised a quizzical eyebrow. 'Just a thought.'

Isla fell back into silence, watching as a tiny crab made its way from one edge of the rock pool to the other. Overhead the gulls wheeled, their calls rising and falling on the wind. Eventually, they set off for home, Isla still lost in thought.

It had been a quiet afternoon, but a lovely one. When Finn reached across to give her a kiss on the cheek, Isla surprised herself by turning it into a hug of thanks.

Chapter Twenty-three

Finn drove back over the hill to Kilmannan, Isla by his side. He was going to drop her off in town and nip back for a chat with Ma – talking to Isla, he'd realized that there was no point putting it off any longer. Flicking on the indicators, he turned across the junction, catching sight of a rainbow-coloured flash of tattoos and brightly dyed hair climbing out of a beaten-up old Corsa.

'That's Shannon,' said Isla, leaning across to wave. 'What's she doing at Ruth's place?'

Finn let down the window, slowing the car to a stop. 'You OK?'

'Yeah, Ruth left her purse on the counter when she nipped in earlier.'

Finn switched off the ignition, suddenly feeling the need to check on Ruth. 'D'you mind if I just pop in? Shannon, I'll take it – thanks.'

'No probs,' said Shannon cheerfully. She handed the purse over and clambered back into the Corsa. It roared off, leaving a black cloud of exhaust fumes in its wake.

'I'll come in with you,' said Isla, 'say hello. We're

meant to be getting together tomorrow evening – I'll just make sure she's still OK for meeting after work.'

Finn smiled at her as he pushed the door open. She genuinely loved spending time with Ruth – maybe it was growing up without her own mum around, but they'd formed a bond that was really sweet.

'Ah, hello, you two.'

Finn frowned down at the sofa where Ruth was sprawled, half-lying, half-sitting, still wearing her coat.

'Are you OK, Ma? What's going on? I've got your purse here – Shannon said you left it in the hairdresser's.' He placed it on the mantelpiece and squatted down to Ruth's level. She looked paler than usual, the wheeze on her breath evident.

'Vertigo,' she said, hefting herself upwards, 'that's all. I think I had a little spell when I got home, so I just sat myself down for a moment. Nothing to worry about.'

Isla sat down beside her, smiling. 'Shall I take your coat?'

'Och, yes, go on then.'

Watching Isla as she tenderly helped his ma back into place, Finn found himself asking, almost without thinking, 'Ma, I was about to take Isla back into town before I came back – would you mind if she –' Isla looked up at him, dark eyes on his – 'I mean, Isla, d'you fancy staying for a bit of early supper?'

'That would be very nice.' Ruth smiled up at him. She looked tired.

The little kitchen in the cottage hadn't changed in

years. He filled the kettle and discovered that she'd made a pot of his favourite Scotch broth. Switching on the gas ring, he turned back to the fridge and started with surprise at finding Isla just behind him.

'Sorry.' She flushed slightly. 'I thought maybe I could give you a hand?'

He shook his head. If Roddy and Kate could see him now, they'd be teasing him mercilessly. He was as jumpy as a bloody kitten with Isla around.

'That'd be lovely. If I cut this bread, d'you want to butter it for me?'

They worked side by side, Isla's arm brushing his from time to time. She was ridiculously beautiful and beyond distracting. He felt a pang every time her remembered that she was only going to be here for another few weeks. Maybe he could try just staying friends with her, make sure she was looked after . . . He snorted with sudden laughter.

'What is it?' Isla turned to him, pushing her hair back from her face.

'Sorry, just thinking about something funny that happened the other day,' he lied. He couldn't tell her he'd laughed because the idea of Isla – feisty, sharp-edged, no-nonsense – needing someone to look after her was completely preposterous.

'Finn,' Isla lowered her voice to a whisper, putting down the butter knife for a moment, 'd'you think Ruth's OK? She looks a bit pale to me.'

'Yeah.' He'd hoped he was being paranoid in thinking

that. He sighed. 'I dunno; you know what she's like. She'll say it's nothing.'

'I've never met anyone with such an aversion to doctors. Seriously, you'd think they were all trying to kill her off.'

'I'll maybe try and persuade her to pop in to the surgery tomorrow.' Even as he spoke, he knew it was highly unlikely to happen. He tipped the soup into three deep bowls.

'I can hear you two whispering away in there,' came a voice from next door, 'and you'd better not be gossiping about me, or I'll come in there and skelp your backsides.' There was a cackle of laughter.

Ruth, sitting on the sofa, was quietly pleased that she'd been caught out having a small nap in her raincoat. At Bruno's earlier she'd had a lovely chat with Kate, who'd agreed that Isla was the best thing that had happened to Finn in a long time and that it was a pity the two of them couldn't blooming well see it.

It was lovely to hear those two pottering about in the kitchen together, and she was fairly sure she'd managed to fob them off with the excuse that she'd suffered a bit of vertigo – she had her friend Ethel to thank for that one, Ethel having recently been laid low with dizzy spells that had kept her at home for a few days. Ruth had finished her chat with Kate and decided that that was enough for one day, and had been very grateful to accept a lift back home in Kate's car.

Taking her flower-sprigged walking stick in one hand,

she pushed herself up out of the sofa – it was too damned close to the ground, that thing, which was precisely why she never usually used it. Straightening the embroidered tablecloth, she laid the table neatly before sitting down at her place.

Finn dropped Isla back in town after they'd eaten.

'Will you pop in and make sure Ruth's OK on your way back?'

He'd already planned to – he had something he wanted to say, something he hadn't wanted to talk about in front of Isla. 'Course I will.' He was struck again by how much she evidently cared for Ma. With Shona half a world away in Australia, it was nice that they'd created such a bond. Hopefully, even if Isla was back in Edinburgh getting on with her city life, she'd keep in touch. He suspected, somehow, that she would. There was a small part of him – he gave a wry smile, realizing as he did so that he could hear Roddy saying 'yeah, very small' with his eyebrows raised in amusement – that really hoped she'd make a regular habit of visiting the island once she was gone.

'Back so soon?'

The sound of the television greeted Finn as he stepped into Ruth's cottage. Hamish ran down the hall to meet him, hoping for more food. 'You've just had biscuits and cheese, you greedy bugger,' said Finn, leaning down to scratch behind the cat's ears. He lifted his head to address

Ruth, his tone deliberately casual: 'Yeah – just thought I'd check you didn't need anything before I headed back.'

'Not at all,' came her sing-song island accent through the gap in the sitting-room door.

'Not even a quick cup of tea?' Knowing the answer, he'd begun filling the kettle already.

'Here you are.'

Ruth was sitting, quite happily, on her armchair. A crochet blanket, one of many she'd made over the years, was tucked around her knees. She had the television remote control to one side, and her walking stick balanced ready by the fireplace on the other. One bar of the electric fire was on, despite it being midsummer.

'It's nippy in here this evening,' she said by way of explanation, catching him looking.

He sat down, pushing up the sleeves of his shirt. It felt quite warm to him, but he wasn't eighty, he supposed.

'Ma.'

'Mm-hmm.' She looked at him expectantly, and turned down the volume of the quiz show she'd been watching.

Finn stood up and picked up the photograph of himself and Shona by the seaside. He turned it over in his hands, examining the frame, before replacing it on the mantelpiece.

'Look, I've been thinking. Isla lost her mum, and she loves spending time with you.'

'Yes.'

'Well.' He cleared his throat. 'I've been thinking.' He was sounding like a stuck record.

Ruth sat waiting, her face wise and patient as ever. It crossed his mind that at her age, she didn't really mind waiting for things. But she'd been waiting far too long for this, really.

'I want to try and sort things out with Shona when she comes over.'

'Well, that is good news.'

'I hope so.' He swallowed, closing his eyes. The clock ticked on the mantelpiece, and the low murmur of the quiz show carried on in the background. For a moment he looked again at the picture of Shona, who'd been faced with an impossible decision years ago, when a teenage pregnancy would have scandalized the island. She'd had to make some pretty grown-up decisions, and live with them.

'I want her to know I'm not angry at her any more.' Saying the words, he realized he had no idea why he'd harboured such an irrational grudge for so long. He had not only Ruth, his ma, who'd brought him up, loved him, supported him – but Shona, who'd stepped aside and made a difficult choice that she'd stuck by until they felt he was mature enough to take it on board. And then he'd thrown it back in her face, rejecting her. That must have hurt badly – and yet Shona was still reaching out. It was time for him to stop acting like an overgrown teenager and face up to his past.

Chapter Twenty-four

'Well?' Ruth looked at Isla expectantly.

'Are you sure it's not too cold for you?' Isla cast a glance at the sky, where plum-coloured clouds hung threateningly overhead. This shocker of a summer was certainly keeping the tourists away: the island was practically deserted, and Bruno's cafe, usually packed with day trippers, had been almost empty earlier.

'I'm waterproof. And Doctor Lewis said a walk every day is good for the circulation. As long as you don't mind slowing those long legs down to my pace.'

'I'm happy to stroll.' Isla gave her a nod of agreement, and they continued down the path towards the woods.

They walked along in silence for a while, the air thrumming with the expectation of rain. Birds were gathering in the trees, and beyond the metal railings that flanked the woodland path Ruth could see cows gathering beneath the sheltering branches of a spreading oak. There was a storm coming, right enough, but there was something about this weather she'd always loved.

Despite a good bit of tactful probing over cups of tea,

Ruth had managed to extract not one piece of information about what had happened at Isla's much-anticipated school reunion.

'You know . . .' She paused for a moment, leaning on her stick. A good night's rest had helped – and this morning, strangely enough, she'd slept until eight – but she was puffed out, and her legs were aching, the skin stretched taut with water retention. 'I used to come along here as a girl when I was courting. I bet the young ones still do.'

'I didn't do anything like that as a teenager,' Isla admitted. Ah, that was more like it, thought Ruth. There was something about walking and talking that brought people out of themselves – especially girls like Isla, who were so private.

'Too busy with your books?'

'Hardly.' Isla gave a hollow laugh. 'No, I was the most unpopular girl in school. Wrong clothes, wrong hair, wrong everything.'

'Och, you must've had a few friends? You're such a lovely girl.'

Isla pulled a face.

School in Ruth's day had been very different. She'd been top of her mixed class from the age of eleven, desperate to go off to the teacher training college, but her family hadn't had the money to send her. Instead she'd got a job working at the local chemist, where she'd focused her brain on learning everything there was to know, trying not to envy her school friend Ethel, who was sent off to Glasgow and came back to teach the children in the little island school a few years later. When she'd been married, though, she'd given it all up in favour of staying at home and keeping house.

Ruth rather envied Isla, with her determination and her ambition. If she'd been thirty in this day and age, she liked to think she'd have been just as driven. She sneaked a glance at Isla, who was walking alone, chin tipped up as always, that slightly guarded expression on her face. It was a long time since the schooldays that had left such a mark – Ruth privately wondered if raking over old coals by going all the way to Edinburgh for a reunion had been a good idea. But it wasn't her place to say anything, so she'd just listened as Isla had explained her plans to go; and now she was biding her time, waiting to find out what had gone on.

'Ouch!' Isla bent down to untangle a bramble cable that had wrapped itself around her shoe. She looked up with the first smile Ruth had seen that day. 'Well,' Isla conceded, 'it's been lovely getting back in touch with Helen and Amira.'

'Now that sounds very nice.' Ruth looked at Isla sideways. It was like getting blood from a stone with this one. But she was good for Finn – he'd always been one to have female friends hanging about, but Isla was different. Ruth approved of her. She'd make a good – ah, there was no point in going down that road. The two of them would need their heads banging together first, and she was too old for that nonsense.

There was a crack of thunder, and the first drops of rain splattered through the trees. Ruth had known this was likely to happen, which was partly why she'd suggested this route – it was sheltered, and it was only a ten-minute stroll from home. Taking Isla by the arm, Ruth led her towards the little stone shelter that stood in the middle of a clearing, surrounded on all sides by beech trees. Inside was the same stone bench she'd sat on a hundred times, from childhood adventures through teenage courting to times when she'd had an argument with George and stormed out in temper early in their marriage, sitting out waiting for him to come and find her – and times when she'd cried until there were no tears left. These stone walls were held together with secrets.

'Sit yourself down there.'

'Are we safe out here? What if there's lightning?' Isla frowned up at the sky through the canopy of dripping leaves.

'This place isn't going anywhere. I've sat out here in the rain more times than you've had hot dinners.'

'I didn't think anyone actually said that any more.'

'Neither did I.' Ruth looked at Isla, laughing.

She reached into her handbag, watching with delight as Isla's eyes popped in surprise.

'I was a Girl Guide, I'll have you know. Prepared for any occasion.' Unscrewing the lid of the silver hip flask she'd stashed earlier, she handed it to Isla, who took a cautious mouthful.

'Sherry?'

'I know, if I was a true Scot it'd be whisky, but I can't stand the stuff. It'll warm you up soon enough, anyway.'

Isla handed it back and Ruth took a sip herself before passing it back to Isla.

'Well, I've tried not to be nosy, and I wasn't going to pry in front of Finn. So what happened? Did you see the dreamboat who made your life hell all those years ago?'

Isla burst out laughing, surprising both Ruth and a couple of wood pigeons who were nestling overhead. They whirled upwards in a flutter of indignation.

'He's a balding plumber with three children who lives in East Kilbride.'

'Divorced?'

'Not even slightly.' Isla giggled. 'But he tried to persuade me to go outside with him for old times' sake.'

Ruth felt her eyebrows shoot upwards. 'And did you?'

'No, I did not,' Isla recoiled with indignation. 'I was perfectly nice, I made polite conversation, I listened to all the girls who spent years making my life hell asking for hair advice, and telling me how impressed they were with my career; and then I left.'

'So you didn't get the big film-star moment, after all that?'

'No.' Isla reached across, taking the hip flask from Ruth's hands silently. She took another swig, screwing the lid on tightly before looking up, her eyes dark and thoughtful.

'No,' she sighed, 'and I can't quite believe I spent all those years waiting to prove a point to the people they used to be. It didn't occur to me that they'd have moved on.'

'As you had,' Ruth reminded her, gently. She reached across, putting a hand on Isla's knee, feeling how thin she was beneath the expensive material of her trousers. She'd been living for too long on her nerves. The girl needed a hot bath, a decent meal, and some mothering.

'I don't think I had,' admitted Isla. 'Anyway, I realized that it was time to get a bit of a grip on myself and sort my life out – work out what I want for me, not for anyone else.'

'That sounds like the most sensible thing I've heard all day.' Ruth looked up at the sky. 'So what's next?'

Isla looked thoughtful. 'I've spoken to Jessie – she's back over next week, for a couple of days – about how well Shannon and Jinny are doing.'

'You've done a good job with those two.'

'I haven't done much,' Isla said modestly. 'But I'm hoping Jessie doesn't think I've lost the plot completely with the changes we've made. I'd like to see Shannon being given a chance to run the show a bit.'

'And what about you?'

Isla gave a slight shake of her head. She picked at a leaf, tearing away the greenery until she was left with a handful of shreds that she shook onto the ground below their feet.

'I don't quite know.'

Ruth looked at her shrewdly. 'Ah, your time on the island's had a bit more of an effect on you than you expected, hasn't it?'

'Well,' Isla leaned sideways, affectionately, linking her arm through Ruth's, 'making friends with you has been the best bit.'

Ruth felt herself beaming with happiness. She gave Isla's arm a squeeze of affection. 'The feeling, my dear girl, is completely mutual. You know, with Shona on the other side of the world I missed out on having a daughter to spend time with. I've treasured our time together.'

Isla smiled back at her. 'I'd have liked to meet Shona.'

'Och, I'm certain she'd love you. And you'd certainly smooth the waters when Finn meets up with her after all this time. Maybe you could take a wee visit through?'

'Perhaps,' said Isla.

'Well, I don't want you being a stranger when Jessie gets back. I think, as much as Auchenmor needs you, you need time on this little island.'

Ruth looked up at the sky through the trees. The darkness had lifted as they'd chatted, and there were a few streaks of pale blue showing now.

'I think that's the worst of it over now. Shall we make our way back?' She turned to Isla and smiled conspiratorially, lowering her voice slightly. 'I don't think Doctor Lewis needs to know we spent half our walk sitting on our backsides, do you?'

*

Ruth smiled to herself as she watched Isla make her way down the path. She wasn't going to say a word to Finn and risk jinxing herself, but she hoped that their friendship was a bit different. Finn had a lot of good friends on the island, but Ruth liked Isla most of all.

She pottered around the kitchen, making herself tea, keeping an eye on the time. Shona had promised to give her a ring on Skype when she got up, to make some arrangements for her trip. She was so glad that Finn was open to the idea of building bridges with Shona. She wasn't going to get Shona's hopes up too much when they spoke, but it would be a relief for Shona to know that she'd be in for a far warmer reception when she got here this time. And it had lightened Finn, too. He had a definite spring in his step. Or maybe, Ruth thought, that was just the effect Isla was having.

He'd popped in for a surprise flying visit on the way to check on something up at the estate earlier, giving her a quick kiss on the cheek. 'What was that for?' she'd asked, laughing.

'Because I can,' he'd smiled, heading back down the path to the Land Rover. 'I'll see you tomorrow, OK?'

Chapter Twenty-five

Hamish was waiting on the doorstep, prowling to be let in. He hopped up onto the window ledge beside the front door as Finn pushed down the handle, realizing as he did so that it was locked. Instinctively, he checked the time. He'd promised to get Ruth to the doctor for her appointment at ten – why the hell had she gone without him? Hamish miaowed, crossly, jumping up at his arm, rubbing himself against Finn.

'Hang on, hang on.' Where the bloody hell had he left his key? He hadn't used it in God knew how long – the house was always open. Why on earth had Ruth locked the front door?

Finn turned back to the car. Where were the spare keys? The Land Rover was a complete tip, as ever. Rummaging through the glove compartment, he heard a familiar jingle and pulled them out.

'Ma?'

He knew as soon as he said her name. There was a stillness in the air, somehow. Nothing had changed, and yet . . . He stepped over the letters that lay untouched on the mat.

'Ma.' His voice was quieter now. He could hear the pleading in its tone.

Pushing open the door to her little downstairs bedroom, he felt a coldness run through his veins. He closed his eyes, wishing it all away.

Ruth was sitting up in bed, propped up against pillows, her eyes closed, the bedside light on. A cup of tea sat by her side, the gentle mutter of Radio Scotland playing quietly beside her bed on the digital radio he'd bought her last birthday to replace the ancient transistor she'd had for donkey's years.

She looked utterly peaceful – she could have been dozing.

But she was gone.

Finn sat down on the bed beside her, feeling her cool hand, closing his eyes again. She was gone, and there was nothing he could do.

Hamish jumped up onto the bed beside him, tail curled in a hopeful question mark. Unthinkingly, Finn stood up, made his way to the kitchen, and tipped biscuits into the cat's bowl. He looked at his phone for a long moment before dialling.

'Isla.'

'Hi, Finn. I'm just about to do my first client. Can I give you a ring back at lunchtime? We still OK for later?'

'D'you think you could do me a favour?'

*

Isla had left her client with Shannon, telling her something had come up. She'd arrived at the bedroom door, her face white with shock, and held on to Finn for a long moment before following him inside.

'You don't have to go in.' He'd felt protective of her, somehow.

'I want to –' she'd looked young, and brave, and frightened – 'if it's OK?'

'Of course it is.' He'd pushed open the door. He hadn't moved anything, and Ma had still been sitting up there in bed, paler now, he realized, than when he first walked in. He'd willed her to wake up, tell him to get on with work, stop hanging around wasting the best of the day, tell him to pop the kettle on, do anything –

'Oh, Ruth,' Isla had gasped, her hand to her mouth. Silently, tears had filled her eyes.

Finn had held out an arm and drawn Isla in close. They'd stood together, his face buried in her hair, taking strength from each other.

Doctor Lewis had come out from the surgery. 'She was a lovely woman,' he'd said with a sad smile, signing the death certificate, and adding to Finn, 'I'd like you to come in to see me at the beginning of the week, so we can have a bit of a chat – it's been a lot to take in.'

Now Finn, sitting on the sofa, was watching a cup of tea go cold.

'D'you want me to ring Roddy for you? Or Kate?' Isla sat down beside him, having seen the doctor out.

'They're off the island today – Kate's having a scan at

the hospital in Glasgow.' Isla nodded. He felt a sudden pang of guilt. 'But that's not why I rang you. I just thought—'

'I didn't think it was.' Isla put a hand on his arm. The truth was, he'd rung her because she had been the first person to come into his head. She'd been the first person to come into his head a lot of the time, recently. And Ruth was very fond of her, too – he inhaled sharply.

'You OK?' Isla looked at him, concerned.

'Just trying to take it all in. You didn't –' He looked at her, suddenly feeling anger. 'She didn't tell you she was suffering from heart failure, did she? You didn't know she was sick and not tell me?'

Isla shook her head, stung. He was grieving, and lashing out; she knew that instinctively. She remembered when her mum died, how everything was brushed under the carpet. The only emotion she'd had left, the only one she'd seemed to be allowed, was anger. She'd smashed a cup by accident in the kitchen one night, and, realizing that it somehow made things feel better, had picked up every single piece of crockery on the draining board, crashing them down on the tiled floor, furious tears streaming down her face. She'd expected to get into trouble but her dad had just quietly sent her to bed and swept it all up. The next morning when she got out of bed there was a brand new set of dishes in the cupboard, and nothing was ever mentioned about it again.

So it wasn't surprising to her that the first thing that Finn would do was lash out.

'Honestly, I promise – if she'd said something, I'd have told you.'

She'd known something was up – the swollen ankles had been getting worse, and the breathless wheezing – but Ruth had made it clear that she didn't want to discuss what she'd have called 'any of that nonsense'.

Finn hung his head, shaking it slightly. 'I'm sorry, Isla. I don't know why I said it. I just –'

'It's OK. You don't need to explain. You loved her, and she loved you so much, and . . .' Her voice was choked, and she felt the tears spilling over again. Oh, Ruth.

Finn rubbed his forehead, pressing his brows together, screwing up his face in thought. He looked up at her, his whole face registering shock and sadness.

'I'm going to have to ring Shona now, let her know. And the rest of the family.' He put his head in his hands for a moment. 'Oh God, Isla. What a bloody mess.'

Chapter Twenty-six

'Isla?'

Shannon, who'd stayed on after work to tidy the salon in preparation for Jessie's visit back to the island, shook Isla's arm. She'd been staring out of the window and into space again, something that she'd done a lot of in the few days since Ruth's death.

'Hmm?'

'I was wondering if we should lock the back room before Jessie gets back?'

'Jinny's room?'

The little back room – which had previously been filled with ancient stock and out-of-date equipment – had been cleared out one weekend by Jinny and Shannon, who had borrowed Jinny's dad's pickup truck and taken most of it to the little scrap yard on the hill towards Scalpsie Bay. Jinny had taken it upon herself to paint the room a pale violet and hang bright sari material – which she'd bought from the market in Glasgow – on the walls. With the addition of some of her Buddha statues and some fairy lights, she'd made the little space beautiful.

Isla had signed off the expense of a massage table, saying she'd deal with Jessie later, and Jinny, delighted, had started doing the occasional holistic treatments on their regular clients.

'No,' Isla decided on the spur of the moment. 'Leave it with me. I'll handle Jessie.'

Shannon looked dubious. 'She's not going to like it.' She shook her head. 'She says all that stuff has no place in a hairdresser's and if people want that kind of hippy nonsense they can go up the hill to the weirdo retreat place.'

Isla stood firm. They'd worked hard, and she wasn't going to back down now – and anyway, putting it off until Jessie was back on the island full time, rather than popping over for a few days' visit, wasn't going to make it any easier. She couldn't help thinking that Ruth would approve of that, too.

'Well,' Jessie looked around the salon, taking in the changes, 'you've got this place looking like a new pin.' She gave a nod of approval. 'I knew I'd be leaving it in good hands with you, Isla. Have these lassies been behaving for you?'

Isla looked at the girls, who were both dressed neatly in black today – they'd decided that with Jessie coming over for a visit, they were going to pull out all the stops. So whilst Shannon's hair was still peacock blue and her tattoos spun in a riot of colour down her arm, her black jeans were spotless, her silk vest ironed perfectly. Jinny's tiny frame was engulfed in a voluminous, flowing black dress, her hair ironed straight, no jangling bracelets on her wrist, but huge, ornate Indian silver earrings that hung down to her shoulders.

'We thought as the shop was closed we could give you a special treatment,' said Jinny, twisting one leg behind the other, pulling out a chair. Shannon poured a cup of tea and handed it over.

'What's this?' Jessie sniffed the cup, surprised.

'It's an ayurvedic blend,' Jinny beamed, looking pleased with herself. 'Designed to rebalance your chakras and bring body and soul into alignment.'

Oh God, thought Isla, *you're going too far*. She looked over Jessie's head at Jinny, pulling a face.

Jessie took a sip, sitting back in the chair. 'Very nice,' she said, her tone surprised.

'We've made a few – changes,' Isla began. 'I mean, you've probably heard from Calum . . .'

'Och yes, he tells me the place is heaving and I tell you what, it was a surprise when I took a look at the accounts on the computer. What have you been doing, Isla? Have you been printing money out the back room or something?'

Isla saw a fleeting glance of panic exchange between Shannon and Jinny.

'Not quite, Jessie, but –' *No time like the present*, thought Isla. 'Actually, before Shannon does your hair, Jinny's got something up her sleeve to show you.'

Jinny gave a tiny squeal of excitement. Released from

her silence, she whirled across the room, opening the
door with a flourish to reveal the brand new treatment
room. There was some spa-type music playing quietly,
and the scent of essential oils wafted out from a burner.

'If you'd like to come this way, madam, and slip off
your shoes, you can settle yourself down on the bed for
a treatment . . .'

Forty minutes later, Jessie emerged looking completely blissed out and not quite on the same planet. She
sat amenably whilst Shannon blow-dried her hair ('There
now, you look gorgeous – off you go for a date night
with Calum, and maybe his luck will be in tonight . . .'
Shannon said at the end, causing Isla to fix her with a
glare that said 'don't push it').

'You're looking braw, hen,' said Calum, winding
down the window as he pulled up outside the salon.

Jessie turned around and gave them a wave, pausing
just as she was about to climb into the passenger seat.
'I'm away to be a lady who lunches, girls. Have a lovely
day.'

Isla closed the door of the salon and turned around.

'Yes!' shouted Shannon and Jinny, fists in the air in
celebration.

'Well, I think we could call that one a success.' Isla
gave them a massive smile, and the three of them hugged
in delight. She was fairly certain that Jessie – who'd con-
fided to Isla that she was enjoying playing granny far too
much to come back to working in the salon full time –
wouldn't be getting under Shannon's feet for too long,

but she wasn't going to say anything just yet. Right now, just knowing that they'd passed the first major hurdle was enough.

'So what are you two up to with the rest of your day off?' Isla locked the salon door.

'I'm away to the park for a picnic with Rab,' said Shannon, hitching her bag over her shoulder and waving as she saw his little car pulling up at the end of the street. She'd finally given up on *The Rules* and the two of them seemed to be getting on enormously well, spending all their spare time together. He was another reason Shannon would have for wanting to stay here on the island, Isla realized. With Jessie seemingly quite happy, things seemed to be working out for both the girls.

'Jinny?'

Jinny gave an impish grin before pulling on a motorbike helmet that looked ridiculously huge on her tiny frame. She'd recently been given an old moped by her dad, and took great delight in trundling around the island at thirty miles an hour, beeping excitedly to everyone she knew, waving an arm that caused the scooter to waver alarmingly on the road.

She flipped open the visor. 'I'm taking myself off on a secret mission,' she explained, wrinkling her nose with delight. 'I'm going up to Lily's place because she's looking for someone to do some extra treatments on the retreat clients, and I met her in the street the other day, and we got talking.'

'Oh Jinny,' Isla couldn't help laughing. Jinny and the

crazy Lily were probably the perfect combination, and her retreat clients would absolutely love Jinny's quirky nature. 'That's brilliant. So what's the secret mission, or can't you tell?'

'Och no,' said Jinny, shaking her head. 'The secret mission was going up to Lily's place to talk about working there part-time. I was a bit worried that you'd be concerned I couldn't fit in working at the salon and up at the retreat, and –' she put a hand to her helmet, where her mouth would have been had it not been masked – 'I've just told you the secret!'

Isla shook her head, still laughing. 'I'm sure we can work around you. It sounds like a brilliant idea.'

Everything was getting sorted, and Ruth was gone. With a sudden wave of tiredness, Isla decided to go up to the little flat and have a rest. There wasn't anything else to do.

She'd just settled down on the orange and brown sofa with a book and a drink when the doorbell chimed. Pulling herself up with a groan, she looked out of the window – she didn't get visitors, as a rule.

The only person besides the girls it could be was Finn, but he'd popped into the salon that morning, surprised to see it open, checking she was OK. He'd looked tired and drawn, and she'd hugged him goodbye as he headed off to the funeral directors' to discuss Ruth's funeral service. When Isla turned back both the girls had been studiously looking away, pretending to busy themselves with last-minute preparation for Jessie's arrival, but she'd felt their stares. Isla knew they were dying to know what – if anything – was going on. The idea that she and Finn could just be friends seemed impossible for them to comprehend.

She headed downstairs, not having been able to see a thing from the window.

'Hello, darling.'

Her father was standing there looking pleased with himself, a couple of M&S bags in hand.

'Thought I'd take a day off, see how my girl is doing, seeing as Jessie's over for a couple of days.'

'She knew you were coming?' Jessie hadn't said a word.

'Aye, I said we'd maybe pop in later on and say hello, but she tells me she's off out for a fancy meal after having her hair done in some posh salon?'

'Come upstairs.' Isla paused to give him a huge cuddle. He was exactly what she needed.

'I nipped to the shops before I came, picked up a few bits – I know you said you were fed up because the food here is terrible.'

'Oh, Dad.' Isla peered into the bag, seeing he'd stuffed it full of meals for one and packets of her favourite sweets and their shared favourite, ginger ale. 'Actually, I've discovered there's some amazing shops here, and places that sell stuff so fresh it's straight off the farm, but –' she pulled out a packet of Percy Pig sweets, tearing them open – 'these are gorgeous. Want one?'

He shook his head, patting his stomach. Isla looked at

him properly, realizing as she did that he'd lost even more weight. He looked great, better than she'd ever seen him – much more like her old dad that she remembered from the years when her mum was still alive.

'Nope, I'm watching the calories.'

'I'm amazed.' Isla shook her head as they sat down on the sofa. 'All those years, I've been nagging you to stop eating biscuits, and as soon as I go away—'

'Aye, well, I decided it was time to make a few changes.' He looked a bit uncomfortable, reaching into his pocket for his phone. 'In fact . . .'

Oh God, Isla thought. *Please don't be moving to Australia to start a new life, or something like that.*

He cleared his throat awkwardly, looking down at his phone screen. 'The thing is –'

He handed the phone across to Isla. There was a photograph of a smiling middle-aged woman with kind eyes. She was half-kneeling, dressed in outdoorsy clothes, hugging a huge black German Shepherd dog.

'That's – well, she's – I met someone.'

Isla looked down at the picture and back up at her embarrassed-looking father, who looked desperate for approval. She put the phone down on the sofa, reaching across and wrapping her arms around him. 'Dad, she looks lovely.'

He pulled back, looking at her directly. 'You don't mind?'

Isla looked at him, wrinkling her brow. What on earth did he mean?

'I just – well, I didn't ever want you to think I was replacing your mum. But when you came over here, I was lonely without you popping by after work and dragging me out for walks on the canal.' He laughed. 'Anyway, I went into the cab office one day and Estelle – that's her name – was new. She's working on the control desk. We got chatting, and—'

'Mind?' Isla squeezed him tightly again. 'I've never seen you looking this well and happy, Dad. And you've been on your own far too long.'

'Ah, darling,' her dad said into her hair, 'you're such a sweetheart.'

'I love you, Dad, and I want you to be happy.'

'And that's what I want for you. Now tell me, my Isla, how are you doing?'

Isla, who wasn't sure exactly how to answer that, hid her face in his shoulder and thought.

Chapter Twenty-seven

Finn paused for a moment, his hand on the door of Ruth's little stone cottage. The sun was beating down on his back, and he felt irrationally angry that the summer – which she loved so much – had arrived at last, but too late. The lavender bushes by the front door were beginning to flower, and the smell made his head spin with memories.

'You OK?' Isla reached out, putting a hand on his shoulder.

'Yeah.' He shook himself briefly. 'It's a bit weird, I don't know why—'

'It's all right. That's why I'm here.' She smiled at him gently. The sun had brought out freckles on her nose that made her look much younger, and somehow, more vulnerable. She was hurting too – and with that reminder, he braced himself, and opened the door.

Nothing had changed inside. A shift in energy, perhaps – a sense of everything having stopped. But the house still smelt sweetly of Astral hand cream and the floral scent that Ruth had worn, and in the sitting room the crochet blanket sat folded neatly on her armchair beside the remote control. The bed where she'd slipped away had been stripped, the mattress lying bare. Annabel, Ruth's neighbour, had wanted to do that ('one last wee favour,' she'd said, rubbing his arm in sympathy, 'dinna worry yourself, I've got a spare key, I'll just pop in and sort it out for you').

He found Isla standing quietly in the kitchen, hands on the side of the sink, staring out at the little walled garden where the roses were blooming prettily.

'I wish she was here to see them,' she said, turning to him.

'Me too.' It was strange, but being in the cottage seemed to be making him feel more at peace. He could almost sense Ruth there with them, smiling with approval that he'd taken Isla along to help choose something for her to wear. When the funeral directors had asked if he had any thoughts about it, he'd looked blank. It hadn't occurred to him that they would want to change her clothes – but Ruth had always been well turned out. She wouldn't want to make her way to wherever she was going dressed in a nightie and a quilted dressing gown. The thought of it made him smile.

'What's funny?' Isla looked at him with her head to one side.

'Just imagining what she'd say if she was here. She'd be telling us to get a move on, and get the kettle on for a cup of tea, before she was too late to watch the lunchtime news.'

Ruth's cupboards were tidy and minimal – she hadn't been a believer in keeping hold of stuff she didn't need. Isla opened the wardrobe, and they chose something for Ruth to wear.

'Hang on.' Isla paused, looking down at the dressing table. There was a little black and white cameo photograph of Finn's grandfather sitting there. 'Do you think we should put this in with her?'

Finn picked it up, looking down at the picture. He hadn't noticed before just how much he looked like his grandad, who had died from a heart attack the year Finn was born. Ruth had been on her own from the age of forty-five, and never married again. He nodded, smiling at Isla. 'Yes, I think she'd like that.'

Isla looked up at the painting on the wall, done by Ruth as a young girl. It was a posy of wildflowers tied up with a ribbon, which her father – Finn remembered being told the story as a young boy – had framed for her as a surprise present. She'd kept it in her bedroom ever since.

'I'd like to do one more thing,' said Isla.

They left the house, and drove up through Kilmannan towards the funeral directors'. As they reached the park, Isla asked Finn if he'd pull over for a moment. She jumped out of the Land Rover.

'I'll just be a moment.'

He watched as she ran across the park to the far side, where the oak trees stood. A few moments later she came running back with something in her hand. As she drew closer, Finn realized with a smile what she was holding.

Isla climbed back into the car, cheeks flushed pink from running, her hair ruffled by the sea wind. In her hand was a posy of harebells, daisies, pink campion and the sweet peas that grew in a wild tangle, caught up in the hedge that edged the park.

'Wildflowers.'

Chapter Twenty-eight

It was a big funeral.

'They always are, here,' Kate, sitting at a table with a glass of sparkling water, explained to Isla – one island outsider to another. 'They do this sort of thing in style. Everyone knows everyone here, and they like to give them a good send-off.'

It was definitely true in Ruth's case. She'd been a much-loved member of the community, with friends of all ages who wanted to pay their respects.

Shona had arrived the day before the funeral. Finn, who had thrown himself into organizing everything – Isla suspected it was his method of avoiding the pain he was feeling – had everything under control. He'd collected Shona from the airport and offered her the spare room in his cottage, but Shona, who had Finn's blue eyes and the same smile, turned it down. Perhaps wisely, Isla reflected, she'd chosen to give Finn some space, opting to stay up on the hill in Murdo Gilfillan's hotel.

'She's lost her mum, remember,' Isla had said to Finn, quietly. It had taken a moment before he'd taken in what she said, and really understood it. He still had his – and a chance to rebuild the bridges. She hoped he would take the chance. Even after all this time, being around funerals reminded her of her own loss; made her think of how her dad had coped for all these years. She was so glad he'd met Estelle.

'That was a lovely ceremony. Ruth would have enjoyed it, do you no' think?'

Isla smiled to herself, overhearing two elderly ladies chatting as they washed their hands in the loos of the hotel.

'Aye. She would indeed.' The taller of the two women turned to Isla, who was brushing her hair. 'You'll need to look after that laddie of hers.'

'Aye, right enough,' said the other lady, reaching into her handbag to find a lipstick. 'Nice to see him settling down. I think we all thought Finn would be playing the field forever.'

Isla, who'd heard the same line several times already, just nodded vaguely and smiled.

'Oh, look at that,' said Kate, raising her eyebrows to direct Isla's gaze. Over beside the bar, Finn, who had been deep in conversation with Shona for over half an hour, embraced her with a smile.

He looked more peaceful than she'd seen him in weeks. Roddy returned from the bar with a tray of drinks, setting it down on the table beside Isla, who had somehow been installed with Finn's closest friends.

'Look, darling.' Kate put a hand on Roddy's knee.

'About time, too,' said Roddy, sounding exasperated. But his eyes were twinkling, and as he passed Isla a drink he toasted her, touching the edge of her glass and raising an eyebrow in complicity. 'That reunion's been a long time coming, hasn't it?'

'So, Isla –' Kate turned back to her – 'has Finn managed to persuade you that island life isn't completely awful yet?'

Isla couldn't help laughing. Roddy had told her how Kate had arrived in a whirlwind of chaos and fallen in love with the island, its people, the animals ('Quite a lot of its whisky, too,' Finn had said, laughing), and embraced the place completely. She, on the other hand, was still suffering major shopping withdrawal symptoms, but . . .

'He's done a reasonably good job. But Jessie's back now, so it's time for me to head back home to Edinburgh, really . . .' She heard her voice trail off. The truth was that whilst she was fairly sure Shannon could take over the reins if, as looked likely, Jessie decided to take at least part-retirement – and Jinny was delighted to have not one, but two jobs doing the thing she loved best – Isla herself had literally no idea what was going to happen next.

Her gardening leave was up, and all she had to show

on her CV for the last two months' work was a torn-out page from *Hello!* magazine.

'Oh, hello,' said Kate, straightening up in her chair. Finn was making his way across the room, Shona by his side.

She was fair, tanned from years in the Australian sun, and had picked up a slight accent. Finn made the introductions: 'This is Roddy, who you'll remember, and his wife Kate . . .' He turned to Isla, who stood up awkwardly, holding out a hand. 'And this is my –' Finn stumbled over his words. Isla felt her heart thud suddenly against her chest. Kate gave Roddy a very definite Look.

' – This is my friend Isla. She's been amazing, and Ma absolutely adored her.'

Isla, her hand still half-extended, was surprised when Shona leaned forward, embracing her in a warm hug.

'Isla, darling.' Shona took her arms, pushing her back for a moment to get a good look at her. 'Mum just *loved* you. She said you were a breath of fresh air.'

Isla smiled back at Shona, whose blue eyes, an exact match for Finn's, sparkled back brightly at her, tears beginning to spill over.

'She just loved you, and I have to hug you again,' Shona squeezed her tightly, 'for being there for her. Oh, I just wish she could have held on an extra few weeks until I was due to come over.'

Shona pulled up a stool beside Isla, Roddy handed

her a drink, and they sat chatting until Shona was called away to speak to another group of relatives.

It seemed to Isla that more people in the family were aware of the secret than Finn had at first let on. She'd heard several comments about rebuilding bridges and making the best of things, and it being what Ruth would have wanted.

'Well, you were a bit of a hit,' Finn teased her. 'Careful, or she'll be taking you back off to Australia in her suitcase.'

'She's lovely, isn't she?' Isla hadn't quite known what to expect – but she could almost hear Ruth laughing, that sing-song island voice saying, 'What would you expect of a daughter of mine?'

'I feel a bit of an idiot for making it all into such a big deal,' Finn admitted, shaking his head ruefully.

'It's done now, anyway.' Isla waved at a merry-looking Shannon and Jinny, who were hurrying past to the loos together, arm in arm. They both looked slightly unsteady on their feet, having taken advantage of the free drinks on offer. The guests were starting to drift off now, everyone having paid their respects. Shona had disappeared into a huddle of old school friends and had told Finn she'd catch up with him in the morning, blowing Isla a kiss across the room.

'Finn, Isla – we're going to head off now. Kate's knackered.'

Kate, who had blossomed and couldn't disguise the fact that she was pregnant any longer, was standing by the table, looking pale and worn out. 'Do you want to come back to the house?' She smiled, taking a sip from her water bottle. 'I'll be fine once I can get these clothes off and put on a pair of leggings and a T-shirt. Everything I wear is so blooming uncomfortable at the moment.'

Finn thanked her, but shook his head. 'You two get off. I think I'm going to take a walk down on the beach. Isla – d'you fancy it?'

It was a beautiful evening. They walked along the promenade and past Ruth's cottage. Her neighbour had just arrived home and was sitting outside in the warmth of the sun, still dressed in her black dress, feet in thick black tights slipped out of her fancy shoes and back in slippers.

'It's a shame that the person who'd most enjoy a funeral isn't there to take part, isn't it?'

Isla looked at Finn sideways.

'Ma would have loved today,' he continued. 'All her family, all her friends – everyone she loved all gathered together, *and* a nice buffet meal and a couple of glasses of sherry.'

Isla laughed. 'As long as we were finished in time for her to get back and watch *Emmerdale*.'

Finn raised an eyebrow, nodding. They walked on in silence for a while longer, following the road round where Isla normally ran in the evenings, the sea lapping peacefully against the shoreline, the air silent but for an outboard motor as a little fishing boat headed out for the evening.

They'd made it as far as Finn's place. They stopped by the water, climbing down over the rocks to the water's edge. Finn stood for a moment, looking thoughtful. He picked up a smooth, flat stone and skimmed it across the water. It jumped across several times, breaking the mirrored surface with quiet splashes, before disappearing out of sight.

He turned back to look at Isla, rubbing the stubble on his jawline, looking contemplative.

'Now, I'm going to warn you in advance – I don't have any Pot Noodles handy.' He smiled teasingly at her, his hair lit gold by the low evening sun. 'But I've got some whisky. D'you want a drink?'

He reached into his pocket, pulling out an engraved silver hip flask, turning it over in his hands for a moment before turning to face her. He looked up.

'Very funny.' Isla reached across, taking it from his hands. 'This is beautiful.'

'It was my great-grandfather's – he used to take it out shooting.'

She held it upright, and he unscrewed the lid.

'You go first.'

'Thanks.' Isla took a sip as he looked on. It felt like it was catching alight inside her, and with the still-warm sun on her skin, she felt as if she was glowing. The water whispered over the pebbles of the beach.

'I just wanted to say . . .' There was a catch in Finn's voice. 'I can't tell you how much you helped today. It made it bearable.'

Isla smiled, looking into his eyes, seeing the sadness there. Unthinking, she reached across, running a hand down his cheek. He caught it, turning it inwards, kissing her wrist.

'Sorry, I –' He closed his eyes for a moment.

'Don't be.' Isla felt herself leaning towards him. He was still holding onto her hand. He opened his eyes again, catching hers for a brief second. She breathed again – 'Don't be— ' and then he leaned towards her, drawing her in, wrapping his arms around her. She felt his heart thumping against his chest under his shirt and the heat of his skin, and she looked up into his eyes and they kissed for what felt like forever, sitting there on the rock in the sun of the evening, with the sound of the waves in the background and the birds wheeling over-head.

Not until the sun had slipped down beneath the mountains on the peninsula did they stop, and only then for long enough to head hand in hand across the road, pausing in the little archway that led to the stone steps, where Isla tangled her hands in his hair and he pushed her back against the cold flat stone of the wall and kissed her again, and again, until eventually they made their way inside.

Sunlight through the undrawn curtains fell across Finn's face, waking him. It was early, the sky still streaked pink. He heard a sound. On the other side of the room, Isla was pulling on her top, her movements stealthy. With a lurch in his stomach, Finn recognized the movements of a person trying to make an early-morning getaway. Knowing the sensation of guilt and regret, knowing how much she was dreading him waking up, and having to explain why last night was a bad idea, he closed his eyes and pretended to be asleep. He didn't open them again until he heard the click of the front door closing.

Isla, walking home along the coast road in yesterday's clothes, realized that this being the island, someone was bound to see her – even if it was five in the morning. All it would take would be one car passing, and word would be round the island in no time at all; and then she'd be another notch on the bedpost of Finn MacArthur. She'd woken that morning in his arms, and it had felt so deliciously right, and warm, and safe, that she'd immediately slipped out of them and into the bathroom, where she'd splashed her face with ice-cold water and looked at her reflection in the mirror.

Her eyes were glittering, almost black, her hair completely messed up. She ran a hand through it, raking fingers through the knots that had formed. Her chin was pink with stubble rash from hour upon hour of kissing, which had been . . . she felt her eyes widen. Anyway, the last thing she wanted to be was Finn's post-funeral one-night-stand. Every tale she'd ever heard about Finn and his behaviour – he'd even, he had admitted last night, had a fling with Kate while he and Roddy were supposedly on a break. Isla rolled her eyes. How many times had she heard *that* line?

Finn was an amazing person – kind, funny, thoughtful, sensitive – attributes she could appreciate in a friend, but couldn't quite trust in a lover. No, she wasn't going to risk anything. She had slipped back out of the bathroom, and made her escape.

It was Wednesday afternoon. With the salon closed, Jinny was heading off to Lily's place to do a Reiki training session with some of the retreat guests.

'She's getting more like blooming Lily by the day,' Shannon remarked, rolling her eyes, as Jinny, a long silk scarf dangling around her neck, hopped onto her moped.

'There's Rab.' Isla, who couldn't help wondering how safe it was to be riding a moped with all that stuff flapping around, looked up as she caught a glimpse of him out of the corner of her eye. Shannon slipped out of the door, waving, a bundle of hair magazines under her arm. Kate, who'd been delighted with her work at the wedding – and the way Shannon had somehow managed to charm the obstreperous Rose into cheerful compliance – had popped in that morning, asking if she could arrange a meeting with Isla, Shannon and Jessie to discuss how they could work together on a more permanent basis. Kate had admitted that despite planning to take some time off, they'd somehow ended up booking in more weddings over the next few months, as there was some major repair work needing doing to the central heating. 'Nobody tells you this stuff when you sign up to marry a laird,' Kate had said, laughing and pulling a face.

Isla was just locking up when her mobile rang.

'Isla Brown?'

'Speaking.'

Isla had looked at the unfamiliar number for a moment before answering, deciding it was probably a wrong number or a sales call. By the sounds of it, it was the latter.

'Hi, Isla, I'm Shirley Hepworth. I'm looking for a senior stylist for a salon I'm opening in Edinburgh, and you've come to me highly recommended. If you're still available, I'd love to have a chat with you.'

Isla leaned back against the door of the salon, stunned.

'Finn?' Shona's voice echoed through from Ruth's bedroom to the sitting room, where he was supposed to be sorting through the contents of her sideboard. He stood up, stretching the aching muscles in his back, and headed through. Since the day after the funeral he'd been working every hour he could, just to stop himself from thinking. He'd sent Isla a quick text, deciding that he couldn't bear losing her as a friend, just saying that he appreciated they'd made a bit of a mess of stuff and he hoped it wasn't going to be awkward.

Don't worry, funerals do weird things to people. Still friends?
X

Her reply had come back straight away, decisive and very clear. She didn't want anything more, and he had to get over it. In the old days, that would have meant heading out on the pull – but he had literally no desire to do that.

'Look at this.' Shona pulled open a drawer. It was neatly ordered, with the bare minimum of belongings. 'I think as soon as Doctor Lewis told Mum what was happening with her heart she decided to get herself organized.'

It certainly looked that way. The sideboard in the sitting room had nothing but a neat pile of books stacked on one side, and inside, every last drawer and cupboard had been sorted out. There wasn't a piece of rubbish or an old bill anywhere – and when Finn was growing up, Ruth had lived no more than an averagely tidy life. She certainly hadn't embraced minimalism to this extent.

He lifted up the lid of the jewellery box. Inside were the old familiar brooches, the string of pearls Ruth had been given as a wedding present . . . and in the section underneath, three envelopes, all addressed in her neat, spidery hand.

'Oh, Mum.' Shona looked down at them, her voice cracking.

Finn swallowed hard, holding back tears. He picked up the one with his name on the front, turning it over. There was one addressed to Shona, of course – and one for Isla. He'd have to see her. His heart thumped unsteadily at the thought.

'Do you want to –' Shona motioned to the letter. He shook his head. Somehow, he felt he wanted to wait and open it somewhere alone, take the time to have a last moment with his lovely Ma, breathe in her scent from the paper, trace his fingers along the words she'd written. He missed her with a raw ache in his chest that didn't leave, just subsided from time to time before soaring back, knocking him backwards with grief and regret.

They decided to leave sorting out the house until the next day.

Finn took the letter home. He sat it on the coffee table whilst he made himself a drink, putting it off, making himself wait. He made a coffee, and sat watching it go cold.

Shaking his head, he picked up the car keys, took the envelope, and headed out.

He drove the long way round the island, not noticing the view, ignoring everything he would normally drink in. He loved everything about this place, but right now he couldn't think past the envelope that sat beside him on the passenger seat.

Darling Finn,

I have to confess that the romantic in me has always rather wanted to write a letter that begins 'by the time you read this, I will be gone', but actually, now that I am sitting down to do it, I find it's not quite as much fun as I expected.

I'm so proud of the person you have grown into. You are a good man: one I know your grandfather would have loved to meet and – as I am sure you won't be surprised to hear me say – one I hope your mother will enjoy getting to know. I am so glad that when Shona comes over you'll be spending some time with her, and I hope I'll still be around to see it.

Now, there's another envelope in the dresser in the hall – something that, if by chance I don't make it, I had hoped to share with you and Shona. Have a sherry for me if I'm not there.

And Isla. It's not for me to say, but if you're reading this, you can't laugh and say 'well, why are you saying it, in that case,' so I'm going to tell you anyway. She's a treasure, and I think you know that the old matchmaker in me hopes that you two might get together one day, but . . . in the meantime, I'm leaving her a note, too. But before you give it to her, you need to talk about this with Shona and make sure she's happy. I'm certain she will be. As you already have your place, I'd like to let Isla have the use of my cottage for a while – a couple of years or so before you sell it, or whatever you and Shona choose to do with it. She needs somewhere to escape to if she's going back to city life, and that grotty little flat isn't going to tempt her back over to the island.

I'd write more, but I don't want to go on. You know how much I love you, my darling boy. I've had the honour of being both mother and grandmother to you, and every moment has been a delight.

All my love, always,
Your Ma

It was done. The last thing she'd ever say to him was there in his hand.

He stood by the rocks, watching the sea crashing against them, his heart aching almost unbearably, tears streaming down his face.

Chapter Twenty-nine

It was surprising how loud Edinburgh seemed after the quiet of Auchenmor. Isla had stepped out, unthinking, into a seemingly quiet road a couple of times, lost in her thoughts, forgetting until she heard the screaming of a car horn and saw a driver gesticulating wildly that she was back in the city, where noise and chaos ruled.

She smoothed down the grey dress she'd chosen. It was expensively cut, and the red heels she wore were the perfect pop of colour. She spread her fingers, looking at her nails, which matched beautifully. She closed the car door and pressed the button on the keys, hearing the locks slide into place.

Her mobile buzzed – who on earth would be ringing her this early in the morning? Her dad had already texted to wish her luck, and she'd spoken to Helen on the phone the previous night. She looked down at the screen, reeling back with surprise when she saw the name that was flashing up.

'Kat?' Isla tried to disguise the surprise in her voice. What the hell was she after, now?

'Isla. Just wanted to wish you luck.' She actually sounded like she meant it. 'I know you're seeing Shirley this morning, and I'm sure you'll walk it. To be honest, I don't think she's even seeing anyone else for the position.'

Isla saw her face reflected in the car window, confusion written across it. 'How did you –'

'I recommended you.' Kat sounded quite pleased with herself. 'Shirley was coming back north after her divorce, she's got a fantastic new salon opening – I have to admit, it's to die for – and you were a total shoo-in.'

'But the –' Isla wasn't quite sure if Kat had *forgotten* she'd sacked her, or what.

'You needed to get out and get some perspective. I've seen it so many times. You were making mistakes, and I could see you hitting burnout. That's why I let you go. And that's why I knew – after a bit of time away – you'd be hungry for this.'

Isla swallowed. The red shoes were already biting into her heels. It was going to be a long morning.

'Didn't take you long to dust yourself off, mind you,' Kat said, sounding pleased. 'I saw your picture in *Hello!* Good going. Trained you well.'

Isla shook her head, amazed. 'Kat, thank you *so* much. I'd better get going. Speak to you soon.'

'This is the one she was talking about.' Finn pulled a brown, A4 envelope out from the little wooden dresser in the hall. Looking to Shona for approval – she nodded, smiling – he opened it up, pulling out a sheaf of photographs. Each one was of a young Finn, and Shona. He picked one up, then another, studying them. Shona stood silently by his side. In every single one of these pictures, Shona was looking at him as he played, or was holding him as a baby, feeding him baby food as a toddler – the one thing linking every single image was the unmistakable maternal love that shone from her as she looked at him. He turned to look at her, still holding a handful of photographs in one hand. Shona had tears coursing down her cheeks.

'I did the best thing I could at the time, Finn –' she choked, trying to hold back a sob – 'I'm just so sorry that I couldn't –'

He reached out, pulling Shona – his mother – into his arms, and held her, and together they cried for the past they'd missed out on, and for Ruth, the mother they'd both lost.

Later – hours of talking later – they walked back from Ruth's house to town together.

'About Mum's letters.' Shona, her arm linked with Finn's, stopped, turning to look at him. 'Look, you know it goes without saying that if you wanted to join us in Australia, we'd love to have you, and there's always a place for you.'

Finn smiled back at her. Shona's husband, her two girls, and the life she'd built over there didn't need a hulking great thirty-five-year-old to come marching in and set up camp in the spare room, even if he'd wanted to.

'But I suspect your life is here. So I want you to know this – I've got some money put away for you. Mum says –' Shona looked stricken for a moment, correcting herself – 'said – you wanted time to focus on your art.'

Finn rubbed a hand over his eyes, thinking of all the times Ruth had told him to stop messing around, stop fearing failure, just get on with it. 'Yeah, well, she always could see right through me.' He laughed, sadly.

'Well, maybe it's time to give it a go.' Shona gave his arm an affectionate rub, and they carried on walking. 'And about the cottage. I think letting Isla have the use of it is a wonderful idea. She's a gorgeous girl.'

'I know.' Finn sighed. It was a bit late, really, for regrets. He hadn't heard from Isla in days. Time to start facing facts: he'd blown it this time, completely.

Chapter Thirty

Isla steered her car down the ramp and off the last boat. She'd only just made it, driving on with a smile of relief as the man on the ground waved her through. 'I'm only letting you on in the hope I can swap your wee car for my Ford Focus and drive off at the other side,' he'd teased, winking at her.

She'd only just made the shop in time, as well. With milk in one hand and a box of cereal for the morning in the other, she was juggling her purse and the car keys when she crashed – full on, ricocheting backwards – into Finn.

'I'd say fancy meeting you here,' he teased, 'but it's hardly downtown New York, is it?' He looked her up and down. 'You look amazing.'

Isla, still clad in her interview outfit, was seriously overdressed for Kilmannan. Over the last couple of months she'd eased off on her super-dressy work outfits, ending up spending most days in flats and slim black trousers. She'd been secretly quite relieved to lose the heels, and a day in them had just about killed her. Why on earth she hadn't packed something to change into was beyond her, but she'd been off the island on the first ferry that morning, and every bit of concentration had been used up on making sure she looked the part.

'Thanks.'

'I've been wondering where you were.' Finn rubbed at his neck as he spoke, clearly as uncomfortable as she felt. 'I was beginning to think you'd disappeared back to Edinburgh without saying goodbye.'

'I wouldn't do that.' Isla looked at him directly. With heels on, she was almost exactly his height. She took in the stubble, the shadows under his eyes, the hollows in his cheeks. He looked terrible.

'I'm glad.' He frowned for a moment. 'You don't fancy a quick drink? It's just – I've got something for you.'

'Let me take the car back. In fact, if you don't mind waiting, I might just change out of these shoes.' She smiled at him. 'They are absolutely *killing* me.'

Finn followed the little red convertible back to the street where Jessie's salon stood and waited outside in the Land Rover. Isla, surprisingly quickly, re-emerged in jeans and a pale cream shirt, a pair of Converse on her feet in place of the skyscraper heels.

'About that drink.' She opened the car door.

'Look . . .' The letter was burning a hole in his pocket. There was no way he could show it to her in the crowded pub in town. 'I think we need to go somewhere a bit less chaotic. You'll understand when I show you.'

'OK.'

He set out on the road that ran parallel to the sea, heading south to the tiny collection of houses that gathered around the pale red sand of the bay. There was a little country pub there where they could sit in quiet and he could show her Ruth's letter, letting her open it (or not – he remembered his own experience) in her own time.

'You're sure you just want a coffee?'

Isla nodded, reaching for the cup gratefully. 'It's been a seriously long day.'

Finn reached into the pocket of his shirt, pulling out a small cream envelope. 'I've been carrying this around every day since I found it, waiting for the right moment.'

'And then I crashed into you. Perfect timing.' Isla looked over her cup at him, laughing. He seemed nervous, not his usual self. It was probably grief – it affected everyone differently, and Finn had been so focused before Ruth's funeral on getting everything sorted that it wasn't surprising he was coming apart now.

'I'm going to give you a minute.' He handed it over. 'It's for you.'

Isla looked down at the letter for a second, and Finn slipped out of his seat. She watched him make his way across the empty pub to the bar, where he sat at the far end, looking out of the window and across to sea.

It was from Ruth. The fine, old-fashioned handwriting was instantly recognizable.

Darling Isla,

I can't tell you how happy I am that we met – kindred spirits – and spent time together. It's been an absolute delight spending time with you, watching you blossom. You've brought out the very best in those girls, and they adore you for it. And my Finn thinks you are wonderful – I can see it in his eyes. Now, I want you to know that I've spoken with Finn and with Shona already, and I'd like to offer you my little cottage as a place of your own. You've done your time in that flat, and I'd like to see you sitting by the sea, watching the boats go by, enjoying the sunshine – and the winter, of course – we get the most amazingly dramatic storms, and I just know you'd love them, too. So when you're back in Edinburgh doing your high-flying city job, you can escape here to our little island, take a stroll up to the park, look over Wildflower Bay for me and daydream. And don't forget to have fun. We've had a lot of fun together, you and I, and I am very grateful for it.

With all my love,
Ruth

There was a postscript, too, written on the other side of the paper, as if Ruth had saved the best part for last. Isla smiled at it, put the letter back inside the envelope and handed it back.

Oh, lovely Ruth. She looked across at Finn, who was glancing nervously in her direction. She smiled, beckoning him over.

'So.' He took a drink and looked at her. 'D'you think you'll make it over once in a while?'

Isla nodded. 'Once in a while, yes.'

Chapter Thirty-one

The skies were almost black, and at ten o'clock Finn still had the car lights on. Rain was thundering on the windscreen, and the wipers were struggling to keep up.

He'd been over to Duntarvie House early that morning, sharing a coffee with Kate and Roddy, talking about his plans. He'd decided that Ruth was right – he was taking a couple of years off, with the money Shona had insisted was his by right, and he was going to put everything he had into making something of his work. He'd stayed up late into the night, gathering a list of the galleries that he'd worked with before, researching potential new leads. It was time to get his work out there.

He looked up, waiting at the traffic light, seeing the ferry pulling into dock. At the front of the queue, dwarfed by trucks and hulking Range Rovers, Isla's car was a red exclamation mark. She was off again.

Kate had taken him aside that morning, whilst Roddy disappeared to take a call. In the quiet of their scruffy, comfortable sitting room, she'd beckoned for him to sit down.

'It's not a disease, you know.' She'd smiled at him, affectionately.

'What isn't?'

'Falling in love.' Kate raised an eyebrow. 'Happens to us all, Finn. Even you.'

'I'm not –' he began, hopelessly.

'Of course not.'

'Look, I fucked it up, Kate.' He ran a hand through his hair, groaning. 'It's too late now.'

'As you once pointed out to me, Casanova, it's never too late.' Kate had reached out a hand so he could pull her up from the sofa. 'Now get off your arse, and work out what you're going to do about it.'

Fine, thought Finn, *I'll show you.* As the light turned green, he turned the Land Rover right with a squeal of tyres on wet tarmac, and joined the ferry queue.

His was the last vehicle on the boat – the next one was cancelled, the ticket man informed him, so everyone had decided to cram on. He turned off the engine and headed upstairs to the cafe.

'All right, Finn, man, how you doing?' Rab, Shannon's boyfriend, raised a hand in greeting.

'Great, thanks, Rab.' Finn gave a nod, scanning the passengers who were sitting along the rows of benches. No sign of Isla's dark brown bobbed hair there. Maybe she was in the other lounge.

'Finn, darling!' Oh Christ, Sandra Gilfillan from the hotel. 'How are you, sweetie? Haven't seen you in ages . . .' Finn managed to give her a vague grimace of greeting, extracting his arm from her vice-like grip as he strode through the waiting area. No Isla there, either. He was beginning to wonder if he'd hallucinated her car. He spun round on his heel, checking the long coffee queue. No sign. More people trying to say hello. How the hell did he know so many people on one tiny boat?

'Kate.' Dark curls tied back in a ponytail, she was holding a paper cup of tea and an iced bun. 'What are you doing here?'

She put a hand to her bump, unthinkingly. 'Forgot I had a scan at the hospital. Mum turned up to pick me up in her car about five minutes after you left. I swear this pregnancy lark's doing something to my brain.'

'Right.' Finn looked over her head.

'What are *you* doing on here, anyway? Thought you were going back to sort out the workshop?' Kate's eyes lit up. 'Ahh.' She beamed at him. 'I think you'll find she's out on the deck.'

The rain had died down, but the wind was still whipping up spray. He opened the door to the outside deck, hauling it shut as a gust of wind tried to wrest it from his hands. The red metal seats were empty, soaked with rain.

Even the most dedicated smokers weren't outside in this weather. And there was no Isla. Unless . . .

He ran two at a time up the metal staircase to the viewing platform. She was holding on to the railing, her hair blowing madly in the wind, looking back at the island as the boat pulled away from the harbour.

Saying goodbye.

Chapter Thirty-two

Watching the island as the boat slipped away, Isla smiled despite the rain and the howling wind. She pushed her hair back, realizing it was completely soaked, but not caring. She never would have thought that she'd grow fond of such a funny little place: the weird people, the tattered little shops. Looking at it now as it grew ever more distant, each street familiar, she marvelled at how much had changed.

Hearing footsteps behind her, Isla turned.

'Finn?' He was soaked, with only a shirt on. It was already dark with sea spray and rain.

'Isla, I –' He stopped, a catch in his voice. 'It's bloody freezing.'

'I know.' She beamed at him, pushing another sopping wet strand of hair back from her face. 'It's lovely.'

'Are you mad?'

'Probably. It's all the time I spent on that place.' Isla motioned to the island, only just visible now as the boat gained speed.

'When does the new job start, then?'

'New job?' Isla couldn't help it – she was laughing at him.

'You went for the interview yesterday. I presume you got it – they'd be crazy not to take you, you're amazing.' He was completely drenched now, his shirt plastered to his chest.

'I got the job, yes.' She stepped forward and took his soaking wet hand in hers, lacing her fingers through his. She watched his blue eyes widen in surprise. 'Didn't take it, though.'

Shirley Hepworth had been stunned when Isla, with an apologetic smile, turned down the job in favour of staying on to help Jessie, who'd decided that she was absolutely certain about giving up working life. And Isla had decided, after staying up all night looking up her options online, that life was far too short not to do the things you loved. So she was off – on a whim, because she could – to spend a fortune in Glasgow on books, and get a head start on her part-time university access course.

But seeing Finn standing there in front of her, soaking wet, she realized that Ruth's final postscript had been right.

It's not for me to say, my lovely girl, but I've never seen Finn look at anyone the way he looks at you. And when you're together, you look like an old-fashioned love story. But it's not my story to tell, and I'm being the interfering old bag who . . .

Finn kept looking into her eyes as he reached into his pocket with one hand – the other still clasped in hers – and shook the letter out, raindrops splashing onto the page. He flipped it over to the reverse side where a post-script had been written, and quoted: 'She might have been "an interfering old bag who read too many romance novels" . . .' He folded the letter up, and tucked it back into his pocket. 'But I think she knew what she was talking about, don't you?'

Acknowledgements

A book is a team effort, so I have lots of people to thank for getting this from a heap of scribbled Post-it notes to where we are now, which is basically the I-pretend-I've-won-an-Oscar bit where I say thank you.

Thanks to Shirley Hepworth, winning bidder in the Authors for Nepal auction, and to Kat Black, who was the highest bidder in the Clic Sargent Get in Character auction, both of whom are featured in this novel as a result. It's an honour to be able to support both of these causes in this way.

My gorgeous Book Camp girls Cesca Major, Emily Kerr, Helen Redfern, Holly Martin, Kat Black and Katy Colins and Basia, with her delicious food and calming presence. Thank you for reminding me why I love this job, and for making me cry with laughter on a regular basis. If I'm going to be electrocuted in a hot tub in a haunted house, there's nobody else I'd rather have by my side. (Next time, we're bringing spare candles . . .)

349

To my friend Jax, I send inarticulate expressions of tremendous affection (in a silent, side-by-side manner) and huge thanks for always being there, ready to read bits of half-formed book, and listening to my wailings.

To Miranda Dickinson, my beloved spooky writing twin, for moral support and general loveliness. And to Cathy Bramley, because I adore her. And to my dearest chum, Melanie Clegg, because she is splendid (and because hopefully this makes up for punching Courtney Love in the face). To Dawn Walton for friendship, inspiration, and for helping me see what was already there.

Thanks to the Prime Writers, for being the best support network (and procrastination partners) I could hope for.

To my North West writing gang Carys Bray, Keris Stainton, and Caroline Smailes for coffee, cake and the other thing.

Huge thanks as always to my amazing agent, Amanda Preston, who is a complete star and all round wonder-being. Your belief in me makes all the difference.

Thanks as always to everyone at Pan Mac for all the fab things they do so well, especially editors Victoria Hughes-Williams and Caroline Hogg.

ACKNOWLEDGEMENTS

I'd like to thank Munro's B&B on the Isle of Bute for providing me with a beautiful space to write, and Karen at Print Point bookshop in Rothesay, who does such a brilliant job of sharing my island books up there.

Readers who know the Isle of Bute well might recognize the retreat setting – I took the liberty of borrowing the story of Edmund Kean and Woodend House, and altering it for my own ends. I'm grateful, too, to the Mount Stuart Estate – my time living there many years ago provided inspiration for both *Sealed with a Kiss* and *Wildflower Bay*. I'd also like to note that Isla might start off grumbling about being stuck there, but by the end of the novel she's fallen in love with the fictional Auchenmor, which of course bears quite a lot of resemblance to Beautiful Bute.

Huge thanks to Nina Pottell for her help and advice on salon life – I should add that any howling errors are mine, not hers!

I'd also like to thank Gladstone's Library for the space, quiet, and cake on my regular writing escapes.

Huge thanks go – of course – to the Facebook/Twitter/Instagram gang who cheer me on when I'm stuck, and to the amazing, hard-working book blogging community who do so much. I am enormously grateful for all the work you do.

ACKNOWLEDGEMENTS

This book was written during a difficult year, but one we filled with family, love, and laughter. Being sprung from a silent library and taken for cake and gossip by my Aunty June, all the way from Tasmania, is one of my favourite memories. To Mum, Chris, Zoe and Mae – thanks for making me smile, and for holding my hand.

To Ross, who drops everything to read chapters sent by text message whilst doing the school run, juggles writing and children when I disappear off on writing retreats, and copes with my, er, creative temperament – and who makes me laugh every day – thank you, darling.

To Verity, Archie, Jude and Rory – I love seeing you grow into such funny, interesting people. You are amazing. (Have you tidied your rooms yet?)

Lastly, this book is written in memory of my Uncle Stewart, the kindest, funniest, most thoughtful man. You have left an enormous hole in our family, but we will try – as you would want us to – to fill it with love.

Sealed with a Kiss

By Rachael Lucas

Kate is dumped on her best friend's wedding day by the world's most boring boyfriend, Ian. She's mostly cross because he got in first – until she remembers she's now homeless as well as jobless. Rather than move back home to her ultra-bossy mother, Kate takes a job on the remote Scottish island of Auchenmor as an all-round Girl Friday. Her first day is pretty much a disaster: she falls over, smack bang at the feet of her grouchy new boss, Roddy, Laird of the Island. Unimpressed with her townie ways, he makes it clear she's got a lot to prove.

Island life has no room for secrets, but prickly Roddy's keeping something to himself. When his demanding ex-girlfriend appears back on the island, Kate's budding friendship with her new boss comes to an abrupt end. What is Fiona planning – and can she be stopped before it's too late?

'Wonderful escapism with a gloriously romantic setting'
Katie Fforde

'A wonderfully feel-good read'
Julia Williams

Sealed with a Christmas Kiss

By Rachael Lucas

*Escape the stresses of the Christmas season
with this warm, funny and truly inspiring novella
from bestselling author Rachael Lucas*

Kate has taken to life on the remote Scottish island of Auchenmor like a seal to water: she's given a new lease of life to the Laird's estate in her day job; she's befriended the once-nosy locals; and even young Laird Roddy is not quite so grumpy these days.

Better still, Kate has just had her best idea yet: they'll turn the castle into the most gorgeous wedding venue in Scotland. The pressure's on as the first wedding is booked in for Christmas Eve – just weeks away. But with a mismatched bride and groom, a hysterical PR on her case, her own relationship woes and a huge storm blowing in, can Kate pull it off in time?

Coming Up Roses

By Rachael Lucas

Country air, cowslips and a charismatic rogue . . .

Would-be gardener Daisy can't believe her luck when her parents announce they're off on a midlife-crisis gap year, leaving her in charge of their gorgeous garden. After a turbulent few months, a spell of quiet in the countryside is just what she needs.

A shoulder to cry on wouldn't go amiss either – so when Daisy comes across Elaine and Jo, she breathes a sigh of relief. But her new friends are dealing with dramas of their own . . .

As Daisy wrestles the garden into something resembling order, her feelings for handsome Irishman George begin to take root. But Daisy's heart's desire – her parent's garden – is under threat, and she is forced to confront nosey neighbours and fight greedy developers. Village life is turning out to be far from peaceful.

It's time to relax with your next good book

THEWINDOWSEAT.CO.UK

If you've enjoyed this book, but don't know what to read next, then we can help. The Window Seat is a site that's all about making it easier to discover your next good book. We feature recommendations, behind-the-scenes tales from the world of publishing, creative writing tips, competitions, and, if we're honest, quite a lot of lists based on our favourite reads.

You'll find stories and features by authors including Lucinda Riley, Karen Swan, Diane Chamberlain, Jane Green, Lucy Diamond and many more. We showcase brand-new talent as well as classic favourites, so you'll never be stuck for what to read again.

We'd love to know what you think of the site, our books, and what you'd like us to feature, so do let us know.

 @panmacmillan

 facebook.com/TheWindowSeat

WWW.THEWINDOWSEAT.CO.UK

extracts reading groups
competitions books new
discounts extracts extracts
competitions reading groups
books new discounts
reading groups events
new events books
extracts new titles reading groups
interviews
events extracts
discounts
new books events
events new
discounts extracts discounts

www.panmacmillan.com

extracts events reading groups
competitions books extracts new books